Based on a Screenplay written
by Diane Thomas

ROMANCING The STONE

Catherine Lanigan writing as
JOAN WILDER

G.K.HALL & CO.
Boston, Massachusetts
1985

Published in Large Print by arrangement with Avon Books, courtesy of Twentieth Century-Fox Film Corporation.

G. K. Hall Large Print Book Series.

Set in 16 pt Times Roman.

Library of Congress Cataloging in Publication Data
Main entry under title:

Romancing the stone, Catherine Lanigan writing as
Joan Wilder.

(G. K. Hall large print book series)
1. Large type books. I. Thomas, Diane, 1946–
[PS3550.R66 1985] 813′.54 85-7669
ISBN 0-8161-3886-9 (lg. print)

For all the romantics,
especially my parents.

Chapter One

INSIDE THE MOUNTAIN cabin Angelina stirred a pot of rabbit stew. She brushed a long lock of auburn hair away from a creamy cheek and jerked once again to swat at an annoying fly. Tanned hides hung from the beams above and a bear skin lay in front of the fireplace. The walls were made of rough-hewn timbers fused together with a mixture of mud, sand, and grass, which kept the coldest winter blasts at bay. One small window had been fitted with glass panes and because they were a luxury, she kept them sparkling clean.

The primitive abode was a drastic change from the enormous ranch house she had grown up in. There were no more parties or barbecues to excuse the purchase of a new silk dress.

Gone were the days when she and her sister, Yolanda, would spend hours bathing in copper tubs filled with luxurious, hot, rose-scented water, and Conchita, the housemaid, would curl their hair with irons. How they used to tease each other and pretend to fight over hair ribbons and petticoats!

How proud Papa had been that both his daughters were not only the prettiest girls in Texas but the best shots, and next to Rex, the foreman, the best horseback riders in the county. Papa had taught them everything he knew about breeding and raising cattle, and given them the managerial skills to do so successfully.

He often joked about the kind of man it would take to tame one of his daughters. Not only were they smart and pretty, but they were every inch—a woman.

How well Angelina knew that! As her body had blossomed into the soft, rounded curves of a woman, her desires had grown with them. Many times she had been forced to walk in the cool evening air to chill the fires that burned within her.

Now it seemed that everything inside her was dead, and it was useless to dwell on the past and the way things used to be—the way she used to be.

She liked this time of afternoon when only the sound of the tumbling waters broke the stillness. She took care not to splash her doeskin skirt or the lace camisole she wore, for they were all she had.

Suddenly the bolted door was ripped from its hinges as a gigantic boot kicked through the wooden planks. Angelina whirled from the old stove and gaped at the dark hulk of a man filling the doorway.

A lit cigarette dangled from his parched lips as he cocked his shotgun and aimed it at her.

"What's it gonna be, Angelina?"

She stood frozen, thinking it impossible that Grogan had found her. She had been so naively certain that she had lost him at the river during the winter of 1874. Would his pursuit of her never end?

Grogan moved closer, pointing the shotgun at her half-exposed breasts. Surreptitiously, she began to slide a dagger from her boot.

"You can die two ways, Angel. Quick like the tongue of the snake, or slower than the molasses in January."

Angelina's emerald eyes blazed hatred at him, but it only spurred him on.

"I'd kill ya if it was the goddam Fourth of July. Where is it?"

She watched as his eyes darted about the room and then locked onto the saddlebags that hung over the post on the bunk. Momentarily, he forgot about her, intent on the saddlebags and their contents.

With one graceful movement, Angelina grabbed the dagger's tip and flipped it underhand. A silver flash streaked through the air and sank into Grogan's back; with a heavy thud he fell through the doorway, his dead eyes staring up at his assailant.

With trembling hands Angelina threw on a doeskin poncho and clutched the precious saddlebags to her chest. That was the end of Grogan, she thought, the man who had killed her father, raped and murdered her sister, burned her ranch, shot her dog . . . and stole her Bible.

She didn't feel the first pang of guilt over the murder she had just committed or the shotgun she pilfered off his carcass. Carefully she stepped out into the blazing afternoon sun. She cocked the gun and scanned the area, on guard for any inexplicable movements. She bolted for her horse, which was tethered near Grogan's mount. She held the reins steady and gripped the sides of the horse with her thighs. Grogan had come alone, she knew, but if there was one law in the west . . . bastards had brothers.

Galloping over the badlands, Angelina suddenly reined in her horse as she approached the end of a gulch. There in front of her were four matching stallions thundering down the gorge. The riders wore identical ankle-length dusters, dark hats, and bandannas to shield them from the blowing sand and dirt. Simultaneously they pulled up short and squinted into the sun behind her.

Angelina glanced over her shoulder, focusing on the high ridge. The silhouette of a tall man cast a menacing shadow on those below him. From the erect manner he sat the horse and the particular tilt to the brim of his hat, Angelina knew in a flash it was Jesse.

Jesse McCoy was her man, for she had claimed him two years ago when she had willingly given herself to him. It had been on the night of one of her father's infamous barbecues at the end of the roundup season.

All day long the cooks had roasted and basted two whole steers over open pits. There were mountains of corn on the cob, fresh green beans, and cooked okra; pots of beans and chili; and baskets of cornbread. Homemade pecan pies and strawberry ice cream were made especially for the festivities.

The Mexican tiled patio with its huge oak in the center was decorated with colorful lanterns and round clay pots filled with red geraniums, Angelina's favorite. A five-piece band played music while the guests danced beneath the wisteria arbor overhead.

Angelina had spent over a month with Conchita making her dress, which was a copy of a Worth original of Paris. Angelina had ordered the emerald silk satin from New York along with the wide lace she used for the sleeves. The dress was cut square across the breasts, with a tight-fitting waist. The skirt gathered in folds over the bustle in back, which gracefully fell into a train. The short puff sleeves she lined in the lace as well as the back of the train, using two layers of lace along the hem in front. When the dress was finished, she stood in front of the cheval mirror appraising herself.

Something was not quite right, though Conchita, proud of her needlework, disagreed with her. It didn't take Angelina long to realize what was wrong with the dress. Two nights before the party, Angelina secreted herself away in her room and did not emerge until morning, when she had successfully lowered the neck by a full three inches. Now when she wore the dress, everyone would know that Angelina had indeed grown up.

Never had she felt so womanly, so sensual. She spent hours on her toilette, creaming her skin with rosewater and lotion. She wore emerald studs in her ears, a gift from her father last year on her sixteenth birthday. Around her neck she wore an emerald satin ribbon with her mother's cameo. Her auburn hair glistened with coppery highlights. As Angelina stared at herself in the mirror, she wondered if it was the dress or had her eyes altered somehow in the last few days, for they had acquired a sparkle she'd never seen before.

Yolanda stood aghast in the doorway, a vision in pink and burgundy satin. "What *have* you done to your dress? Papa will murder you flat on the spot!" she exclaimed, wide-eyed.

Angelina's chest swelled in pride and the strain nearly split the satin. "If I am to die, then I shall live life to the fullest tonight! What do you say to that, little sister?"

Yolanda shook her head, her blond curls dancing merrily over her creamy shoulders. "It's your life!" she said, and giggled mischievously.

"You go downstairs first. I want to make an entrance."

"I almost forgot what I came up here to tell you! You know that man Papa was talking about? Jesse McCoy—who snatched up the old Peterson ranch when they went bankrupt last spring?"

"Yes, yes," Angelina said, exasperated with her sister's sense of the dramatic.

"Well, he's here! Right in our very own parlor! Can you imagine the nerve he has showing up here when he knows every rancher in the territory hates him for forcing the Petersons out in the cold."

"Really, Yolanda. I hardly think he did that. Mr.

Peterson lost his ranch all by himself. It wasn't Mr. McCoy's fault at all. Still," she said pertly, "it takes a lot of guts to be here!"

"Angelina! Your language has a lot to be desired and it's not fitting of a young lady to talk the way you do. But don't worry. I won't tell Papa. You're gonna have your hands full explainin' that dress."

Angelina picked up her lacy fan, checked herself one last time in the mirror and started toward the door. "I can handle Papa, and as for some old man who bought the Peterson ranch—"

"That's just it! He isn't old at all. I'm not quite sure if he is thirty yet. 'Course, you're a better judge of that than I am," Yolanda said, deferring to the year in age between them.

"Yolanda! I'm surprised at you. You sound as if you were taken with this man, despite your view of his jaded character."

Yolanda flashed an amused smile at her sister. "You'll see," she said, and swished her skirts as she turned and went downstairs.

Angelina adored her sister but believed she had a great deal of maturing ahead of her. As Angelina reached the landing she marveled at the decorations Conchita had made.

The banister of the curved staircase was draped with garlands of woven vines and wild flowers. Below her in the parqueted reception area were blue and white porcelain crockery filled with pink begonias, and baskets of pink geraniums hung from the beamed ceiling above. Black wrought-iron floor candelabra held fat white candles that cast a romantic glow about the spacious main rooms of the ranch house.

Angelina started down the stairs, noting the familiar faces of their neighbors and friends. At the base of the staircase, her father was talking to a man she had never seen before.

His wavy hair was as black as a raven's wing and it glistened in the candlelight. He was tall with broad shoulders and a torso that narrowed into muscular flanks. He wore a black suit, white ruffled shirt, and string tie. Never had she seen a man's trousers fit that snugly!

When her father glanced up the stairs and saw her, his jaw dropped in astonishment. The stranger, noting his reaction, followed his gaze. It was then that Angelina's green eyes locked with the stranger's.

They were the color of bluebonnets in the spring, a blue so vivid they mesmerized her. His mustache was dark and beneath it his sensual lips parted in an approving smile. She watched how his eyes assessed every inch of her, lingering a bit too long and too leeringly at her bosom. She felt her heart pound and her nipples harden against the thin silk of her gown. An unfamiliar excitement stirred within her and she found herself smiling back at him. Boldly, she continued to stare into his eyes.

Her father walked up and took her hand, and, though he kept smiling, she knew he was none too pleased with her wanton display of "her charms." Angelina, still watching the stranger, thought it the best decision she'd ever made in her life.

"Aren't you going to introduce me to our new guest?" she asked her father sweetly, ignoring his sideways glances.

"Of course" was all he could say. "Angelina, meet Jesse McCoy."

From the moment Jesse took Angelina's hand and kissed it, she knew she would be his. At her suggestion they walked out to the patio. They conversed about his ranch, the weather, and she introduced him to several of her guests. When the band played a particularly romantic song, he asked her to dance.

Angelina was convinced there had to be something special about a man who could elicit such strong emotions in her. As he held her in his arms, one moment she felt as if she would break out in a sweat and the next moment goose bumps covered her skin.

When supper was served, Jesse disappeared for seemingly endless moments and when she saw him again, he was seated at a round table near the edge of the patio conversing with Yolanda! Angelina's temper raged.

Quickly she grabbed the arm of Josh Logan and asked him to share barbecue with her. Josh had long been infatuated with Angelina and his constant mooning over her usually bored her to tears. Tonight she intended to put him to good use. All through supper, Angelina ignored her food, keeping one eye on Yolanda and the other on Jesse McCoy. Not once did Jesse look her way, so intense was his absorption with her little sister.

When the dancing resumed once again, Angelina found herself dancing with every male at the party except Jesse McCoy. By midnight, her father and some of the older ranchers were discussing local politics over brandy in the salon, and Angelina had decided that she hated Jesse McCoy for spoiling her party.

She excused herself from her last dance partner and decided to go for a walk to cool her anger. As she walked through the cool pines and listened to the wind rustle through the trees, she chided herself for being foolish. Jesse McCoy was just a man, after all, and she could have any man she wanted. Damn him! she thought as she kicked a small limb with her foot. A sharp pain shot up her foot. "I should have remembered I was wearing dancing slippers and not my boots!" She leaned against a tree and massaged her stubbed toe.

When she looked up, she saw a tiny red glow coming toward her. A cloud passed across the face of the full moon closing off its light so that she could not see what it was.

"Isn't it a bit dangerous for you to be out here all alone?" a voice said.

Just then, a ray of moonglow illuminated his face and she saw it was Jesse McCoy smoking a cheroot.

"I don't think so. It's my property," she answered with crisp authority.

He flicked his cigarette to the ground and crushed it out with the heel of his boot. "And who will protect you from me?" he said, his face drawing nearer to hers. He placed an outstretched arm on the tree trunk and leaned his body very close to hers.

"I think I should see to my guests."

"I'm one of your guests, Angelina," he said in low breathy tones. He placed one hand on her waist and another on her neck. Angelina held her breath as she listened to the thundering of her heart.

When his lips met hers, it was a gentle touch as if he were exploring the territory for gold and was unsure if he had found it. Then more hungrily, his lips pressed against hers. Angelina's eyelids closed and behind them she saw white and blue streaks of lightning. His lips parted hers and his tongue probed the interior of her mouth, tasting her tongue and lips and teeth.

His hand held her neck and toyed with her auburn curls. He held her in such a way that she could not have moved away if she had wanted to. Angelina did not want to. "This must be lust," she said to herself, for surely desires this exciting and wonderful could not be anything but evil.

He lowered his head and kissed her ear, tracing the outline of its shell-pink lobe. He branded her neck and bosom with searing kisses. Angelina's breasts and nipples ached for the touch of his lips and the soft brush of his mustache. It was she who wantonly moved her hands to her breasts and lowered her bodice. She heard his sharp intake of breath when he saw her creamy breasts glisten pearllike in the moonglow.

"My God, you are beautiful. And every inch a woman," he breathed as he filled his hand with one voluptuous breast. He rubbed and pulled at her nipple until it was hard and she thought she would scream aloud with the pleasure it brought.

Somehow he had unfastened the back of her gown and it fell into a heap on the ground. He took off his jacket and laid her upon it. His blue eyes gleamed with the heat of passion as he lay down next to her nude body.

With his tongue and lips he blazed a trail from the tips of her fingers, down her arms, and onto her breasts. He massaged and caressed her, memorizing every inch of his claim. Down across the valley of her abdomen, around the hills of her hips and thighs he traveled. His head came to rest at the oasis between her legs, where he tasted her sweet juices.

Angelina's pleasure was pitched to a fever-frenzy. She twitched and twisted as she clutched his head with her hands, his black curls winding around her fingers. She wanted to scream, but managed to muffle her cries to soft moans. She could feel him growing hard as he moved against her leg. Slowly he raised himself up on his elbow and hovered over her.

Angelina knew this was the moment that was supposed to cause pain, but when he entered her so effortlessly, she wondered if perhaps she weren't a true virgin. Angelina felt nothing but pleasure. As he stroked her with his hard shaft, she knew then there could be nothing evil about their lovemaking. Not ever.

Slowly and expertly he delved deeper and deeper. He teased her unmercifully, withdrawing, dancing around just outside her and then plummeting himself into her again.

Angelina's head was pressed into the ground, her hips thrust up to meet him. She felt herself being carried away into the heavens. She was certain stars and meteors were exploding around her. Surely it was the end of the world. When he shuddered inside her, he muffled her climactic cries with his mouth as he continued stroking her until she lay utterly fulfilled and exhausted.

His hair was matted with sweat as he gathered her into his arms. He pressed his furry chest against her bare breasts and held her tighter still.

"You are mine now, Angelina. No man will ever take you except me. Do you understand?"

Angelina said nothing. Somehow his words left her feeling empty, when only moments before she had been so full. "No! I do not understand!" she said, jerking away from him and sitting upright.

Jesse yanked her arm and pulled her down on top of him. His blue eyes were intent and serious when she looked at him.

"I love you, Angelina. Is that what you wanted to hear? I promise you that from this day, nothing will keep us apart. I will always take care of you and be there when you need me. I always keep my promises."

Angelina smiled. "We shall see about that."

Theirs had been a tempest-tossed love affair over

the years. Misunderstandings, distance, tragedy, and natural disasters had kept them apart. But Jesse had been right. When Grogan had laid waste to everything that was precious in life to Angelina, Jesse had promised he would stop Grogan and his brothers.

As Angelina sat on her horse looking at him on the ridge above her, she knew in her heart that Jesse always kept his promises.

As his horse bolted down the slope, Angelina heard Grogan's brothers draw their guns. Galloping past her, he whipped out a lever-action Winchester and began firing with shots that were quick and sure. The first of his bullets spun a revolver high into the air and the second blew off the hat of the man at the end of the line. Jesse's third shot snapped a saddle cinch, which resulted in dumping the rider. Jesse fired at the man in the middle and the bullet hit the barrel of his rifle, which exploded in the man's face. The man's screams echoed through the gulch.

Jesse gave chase after the brothers as Angelina spurred her steed on with her legs. She was a rider in the whirlwind, as she roared away into the twees . . .

Joan Wilder stared at the typewritten page in front of her. Her self-correcting IBM Selectric backtracked and lifted the *w* off the page. *Trees*.

Joan snapped off the IBM and stretched her arms over her head, her stiff elbows cracking. She rolled her head and shoulders and massaged her aching neck. Angelina was certainly her antithesis, she thought, knowing *her* heroine would not be physically undone by a day at the typewriter. She reached over and found that her "I Love New York" mug was empty. With customary resignation she had turned back to her work when the doorbell buzzed. She hesitated for a moment, then checked her calendar. Odd, she thought. She had no appointments for that day. The bell buzzed again.

She stood and tied the self-belt of her terrycloth robe around her waist. As she moved toward the intercom, she passed her Exercycle, promising herself she *would* use it tomorrow. On the wall next to the buzzer hung the framed covers of her novels: *The Ravagers* and *The Return of Angelina*.

When the buzzer sounded twice more in quick succession, she depressed the speaker button.

"Hello?"

"Joan Wilder?" the voice asked in a heavy accent.

"Yes?"

This time, a hacking cough, like that of an elderly man, answered her.

"Hello?" she said. "Hello?" At first the continued silence was unsettling, but as she continued to speak to someone who obviously was not there anymore, an eerie sensation gripped her. She folded her arms across her chest and rubbed her hands up and down her arms, trying to still her nerves. She was always such a ninny when things like this happened. Self-confidence was not one of her strong points and she no longer tried to buck it, either.

Joan crossed to the window and peered three stories down into the street. She failed to notice the ominous-looking man in a dark overcoat and aviator sunglasses climb into a waiting taxi. Joan's eyes were intent on the young couple who strolled hand in hand along the sidewalk. They stopped under an oak tree that was frosted with last night's snowfall and kissed. She watched as the man took off his neckscarf and tied it around the woman's face to cut the blistery cold.

They were very much in love, Joan thought, and wondered what it would be like to have a man care for her and want to protect her from the New York winter. As she drew back from the window, she knew there would never be any chance of that happening to her. Joan Wilder was a spectator. She lived amid her books and maps, an antique globe, and stacks of *National Geographic,* observing life but never living it.

She was intelligent. That was why she knew that no worth-having man would take a second look at her. She possessed a great deal of control, and if her body and instincts were at war within herself, she successfully crushed them and claimed her mind as the conqueror. Joan chose not to remember the painful moments in her life, priding herself on the stability and security of her life-style, never realizing that her only victory lay in the fact that she seldom met any challenges head on.

Joan let the curtain fall. On the table next to her

was a photograph of herself and her older sister, Elaine. Elaine stood in the foreground, a radiant smile on her lovely face, while Joan cowered behind her as if afraid the camera would steal some of her essence.

Joan and Elaine's childhood in Akron, Ohio, had been a normal and happy one. Joan's father had been a vice-president at the First National Bank of Akron, and other than his weekly golf game he spent all his free time with his family. Every year they used John Wilder's two-week paid vacation to tour America by car, so that by the time Joan was eighteen she had visited all forty-eight continental states. The year that the family was planning to fly to Hawaii, Joan's first plane flight, John and Eileen Wilder were killed in an auto accident coming home from an Ohio State football game.

Elaine was two years older than Joan and was enrolled at NYU. Elaine, "the manager," as their mother had nicknamed her, took financial matters into her own hands. She spoke with the family lawyer, arranged for the house to be put up for sale and insisted that Joan move to New York and live with her. Together, she said, they could both continue their education, split expenses and invest their inheritance as wisely as possible. Elaine changed her major from fine arts to business, and Joan enrolled as a history and English major. Joan always marveled at Elaine's quick, realistic decisions despite her young age.

Elaine had always been the more popular of the two Wilder sisters and in high school she had been chosen both Prom Queen and Homecoming Queen. Joan had failed to be elected even as a representative to Student Council. Joan knew that luck had nothing to do with her sister's successes, for Elaine just simply never knew when to stop trying. The few times that Joan had tried to be more outgoing, she had always met dismal results.

High school had been a fairly harmless time in Joan's life. Her parents were still alive and during her junior and senior years, Elaine had been off at college. Joan and her small clique of four girl friends did most of the things that come naturally to teenagers. They stole cigarettes from their parents and smoked them on the sly, went to slumber parties and drank too much beer, and went to every home football and basketball game. There were class parties and outings and beach parties in the summer. And one by one they all discovered the world of dating.

It was the summer between Joan's junior and senior years that, on a lark, her girl friends dared her to buy her first bikini. Emily Mills's father had just installed a new swimming pool and Emily was bound and determined that her first party was going to be a smash.

Emily, who tended toward the plump side, had purchased a two-piece, blue and white, gingham bathing suit. When Joan walked out of the dressing room at Lazarus's, wearing a one-piece black suit, she was immediately hissed and booed back into the dressing room. Emily handed her a scandalously small red bikini. Joan pretended indignation at the idea of the two skimpy pieces of cloth, but was secretly pleased with the shapely form her body had acquired since last summer. Suddenly she had breasts, rounded hips, a flat stomach, and fabulously long slender legs. Rather than show her friends, she stepped out of the suit and told the saleswoman she would buy it. Her friends were startled at her daring, but pleased they had finished their shopping and could now stop at Baskin Robbins for ice cream.

The night of the pool party was warm with a star-filled sky and soft, silky breezes that only those who grow up in Ohio can appreciate.

Mr. and Mrs. Mills had "gone all out" for Emily's party. Picnic tables were draped with Hawaiian print cloths and centered with pots of summer blooms. Two carved watermelons were filled with fruit compote and there were barbecued ribs, hamburgers, and chicken. Washtubs full of ice and sodas sat next to the stereo that blasted the latest rock-and-roll hits. The pool deck was crowded with over seventy-five of Emily's and Joan's classmates.

Sixteen-year-old boys have been known on occasion to be insensitive to others and overly sensitive about themselves.

When Joan arrived at the party wearing a white eyelet cover-up, not much was said about her attire. Two hours after the party had begun and every other girl had been tossed into the pool by one or more boys, she was conspicuous by the fact of her dry clothes. For a long while no one seemed to pay much attention, but then out of the corner of her eye, Joan noticed a group of three members of the football team whispering to each other and pointing to her.

It was Emily who warned Joan that they were plotting against her and were fully intent upon tossing her into the pool with the rest of the girls.

Joan watched as they broke up and began circling the pool, each taking a different position, so that no matter which direction she went, she would run into one of them.

Slowly Joan unbuttoned her cover-up and placed it over a lawn chair. Watching them carefully, she turned and walked toward the diving board. By the time she reached the end of the pool she noticed that not one of them was making a move toward her and that everyone in the pool and on the "dancefloor" was watching her. Now she really felt as if they were plotting against her. She stepped onto the diving board, walked out to the end, tested its spring, and walked back to the edge again. Still no one moved toward her. She took a running walk, jumped on the edge of the board, sprung up into the air, and did a perfect jackknife into the pool.

She surfaced, swam to the edge and climbed out of the pool. Her girl friends were staring at her with gaping mouths. Joan couldn't for the life of her understand what she had done wrong.

At that moment, Alan Jennings burst into raucous laughter. "What a show-off!" he yelled across the pool. "Aren't we Miss Hot Shot. Who are you trying to impress?" The rest of the boys pointed at her and laughed, "Miss Hot Shot."

Joan grabbed her towel and cover-up, and raced inside the house before anyone could distinguish between the pool water on her face and tears.

What Joan did not realize at the time was that her body clad in the red bikini, coupled with the precision of her dive, made every single person present feel inferior to her. It was an incident she never forgot. Often when she wanted to buy something sensual and feminine, she would decline, remembering the party and how she had felt wretched for weeks thereafter.

During her senior year she often thought it odd that none of the boys from her own class asked her out to the movies, but the boys from the nearby schools did.

It was not until her sophomore year at NYU that Joan found herself in love for the first time. Early September that year had been blazingly hot. Joan had been pleased with most of her classes, except Eighteenth-Century Literature. Not only did she not like the period, but the professor was new to NYU and no one knew anything about M. Stevens.

As usual, Joan sat in the front row, so she could concentrate and pretend she was alone in the classroom and not have to look out over a sea of heads. When M. Stevens walked into the room, Joan blessed her proclivity for front row seats. Standing in front of her was probably the most gorgeous male to hit a school room since James Franciscus.

M. Stevens was tall, blond, and green-eyed, with a little-boy grin that she could tell he'd used often and well to melt female hearts. That day he was dressed in summer white, and before the class was over he had discarded his jacket and blue silk tie. Within three hours after class, Joan had put her investigative powers to work and discovered that M. (for Michael) Stevens was from a wealthy background, his family hailed from Newport, Rhode Island; he had attended Harvard and was currently working on a novel, which had been sold to a publisher from four chapters of the manuscript and a short summary. He taught only this one class at NYU, out of love for the period and its writers.

Joan decided that day she possessed a disdain for anything that was not born of the eighteenth century. After her third day in M. Stevens's class, Joan found she was having excruciating difficulty understanding the period and its particular word usages and style. She simply *had* to plead her cause to M. Stevens.

Before she did, she went to the optometrist and was fitted with contact lenses. She bought a clinging silk print copy of a Geoffrey Beane original, a new pair of Charles Jourdan shoes, and had a makeup demonstration at the Estee Lauder counter at Macy's. She bought a Clairol highlighting kit and persuaded Elaine to spend her Saturday night fishing tiny strands of her hair through a plastic cap.

One week to the day after she had first seen him, she sat across the table in a small Italian restaurant from M. Stevens who was more than passingly interested in her plight. They agreed it would take much out-of-class work for her to understand the eighteenth century.

Joan met him in Central Park on Saturdays, at Maxwell's Plum on Thursday nights, and at the Metropolitan Museum of Art on Monday afternoons. Joan thought she could listen to him for hours, no matter how dull the eighteenth century sounded to her, M. Stevens loved it.

They had been meeting for over a month when, one Saturday afternoon, he suggested they take a room at the Plaza. Even though she was only nineteen years old, it had never occurred to him that she was still a virgin and he told her so. Joan suddenly felt as if she had leprosy, but wonderfully, he didn't laugh at her. Instead, he took her in his arms and kissed her. It was then she knew this was no ordinary love affair and he was no ordinary man.

Their room was beautiful with a black marble antique fireplace which the room steward lit for them. The draperies were a lovely shade of gold damask that blended with the soft blue in the wallpaper and carpeting. The king-sized bed was turned down, displaying fine Irish linen sheets and lace-edged pillow shams.

Joan was surprised at the knock on their door, but M. Stevens was not. He had ordered wine, shrimp cocktail, crisp green salad, and Red Snapper Ponchartrain from the Oak Room downstairs.

Joan found it difficult not to succumb to the romance of it all. After their meal, they sat in brocade fauteuil chairs in front of the fire, sipping Courvoisier from enormous brandy balloons.

When he took the glass from her hand, placed it on the glass coffee table, and kissed her, Joan thought that her life had begun with the touch of his lips.

He carried her to the bed and gently laid her down, his lips never leaving hers. He peeled off his clothing and sensuously discarded hers. They lay naked next to each other, only their fingertips touching. He kissed her once, long and forcefully, and then moved over her. With no other preparation he entered her.

It was painful for Joan, even though a sticky wetness inside her relieved the chafing she felt with every one of his strokes. She felt as if she were being hammered. He whispered lewd words in her ear, which caused her to turn her head away. He pushed his hands under her hips and brought her up to him for his last penetration before he came. He collapsed in a heap on top of her.

Joan looked over at the tiny quartz clock on the nightstand and realized with a shock that making love took less than ten minutes.

While M. Stevens napped in the king-sized bed, Joan went to the white-tiled bathroom and washed the blood off her leg. She returned to the table, and finished the red snapper she had been too excited to eat. She drained the rest of the wine and searched in his pockets for a cigarette.

She was just pulling her pink slip over her head when M. Stevens awoke. He pulled her down onto the bed beside him.

"You were wonderful. I had no idea what a luscious body you had hidden beneath your skirts."

Joan tried to tell herself for weeks afterward that everything was still the same, but she knew it wasn't.

One day while she was sitting in the coffeeshop near campus, Melanie Hoffman, the girl who sat next to her in M. Stevens's class, spied her and sat down next to her.

"What's the matter, Melanie? You look really depressed," Joan said.

"I am. It's the worst thing ever!"

"Is there anything I can do?"

"No. I wish there were."

"Well, if it's too personal . . ."

Melanie hesitated. "I haven't told many people, but I suppose it is all right to tell you. I've had this awful crush on Mr. Stevens ever since the first day in class. I know what you're thinking, I've told myself all those things too, but they didn't help. He's just so good-looking."

Joan was growing impatient and feeling a bit guilty. "I don't see—"

"Today I found out that Mr. Stevens, the man of my dreams, is married! I was devastated!"

Joan couldn't believe her ears. "How do you know that?"

"Why, his wife came by his office while I was there picking up my term paper. You know, the one I flunked."

"That . . . that is bad news . . ." Joan wanted to die, but first she ran to the bathroom to throw up. Melanie chased in after her, all the while scolding her for ordering a hamburger at nine o'clock in the morning.

Fools, Joan decided, deserved what they got, and she was determined never to be a fool again.

When Joan graduated from college she had no plans for her future, unlike Elaine, who was immediately hired as an assistant to the director of financial planning at Hewitt Corporation. Everything she thought of doing gave her an instant case of hives. It was during one of her worst attacks of nerves that she began writing *The Ravagers*. When Joan finished the novel, it was Elaine who submitted the manuscript to a friend of a friend who was a literary agent. In less than three months, the novel was sold to Avon books, and the editor wanted to know when her next novel would be finished.

To Joan, her newfound writing talent was a godsend. She no longer had to subject herself to ulcer-inducing interviews for jobs she didn't want in the first place. Elaine no longer badgered her about the way she dressed (not enough tight-fitting slacks and sexy dresses) nor scolded her for looking down at the floor rather than into people's eyes. Since she now had deadlines to meet, research to compile, and storylines to complete, she no longer had to search for excuses when Elaine tried to bully her into going out on the weekends.

Just over a year ago, Elaine had met a handsome and likable man who swept her off her feet. In four months time Elaine had called Joan at two o'clock in the morning from Las Vegas, Nevada, to inform her that she had just eloped. Joan was thrilled for her sister, thinking it about time the American male public did something about this wonderful, gorgeous sister of hers.

Joan now had the apartment to herself. She could come and go as she pleased, write all night long and sleep all day without disturbing anyone. She tried not to pay attention to the voice inside her that kept telling her she was lonely.

Joan stole a last peek at the lovers on the street before she returned to her typewriter. With renewed determination her fingers raced across the keyboard:

> Angelina and her mount melded into one as they raced into the trees. Angelina's eyes darted over her shoulder.
>
> "I knew then that Jesse would never disappoint me. He was the man I loved, the one man I could trust. And we would spend the rest of our lives . . . together."

Once again Joan backtracked the typewriter and underscored the word *together.* With a satisfied smile she leaned back in her chair. "Right!"

The following morning, Joan was in a rush. Her alarm did not go off, and rather than admit she had forgotten to set it, she reminded herself to stop by Macy's and purchase a new, more dependable machine.

On the way to the elevator she stole a glance at herself in the hallway mirror. She wore her straight brown hair parted down the middle and pulled back behind her ears with a tortoiseshell barrette to hold it in place at the back of her neck. She was dressed, as always, in a conservative straight skirt whose perfectly aligned hem had caused her hours of frustration. She wore a matching cashmere camel and dark brown V-neck sweater over a rust blouse and a pair of Italian brown pumps, her only concession to couture. She was "spic and span" neat, as her mother used to say, and she looked nothing like any of the heroines in her romance novels.

When the elevator arrived she pressed the lobby button and watched as the doors closed. Almost. Astonished, Joan watched as a hand thrust itself between the doors and forcefully yanked them apart. Joan's hand flew to her breast, her imaginative mind running wild. Was it a burglar being pursued by the police? A rapist in search of another victim?

No, it was Andrew, the stock broker. He wore a blue-gray Brooks Brothers' three-piece suit, white shirt, and striped tie. From his expertly cut hair to his meticulously manicured nails, he was a man who coveted his own essence. As Joan looked down at the floor, she wondered if he starched his underwear.

"Ah . . ."

"It's okay," she said, knowing this chance meeting was awkward for him, too.

"Joan, ah, look . . ."

"It's really okay."

"I'm sorry."

"No, really."

"I should have called. I, ah, my boss shanghaied me into a . . . a . . ."

When she finally raised the nerve to turn and face him, her voice was almost apologetic. "It's okay, really, better things come up. I mean, God!"

Fortunately the door opened and rescued her from any further embarrassment. "Forget it, really. *I* have," she lied.

Joan walked so fast she was tripping over her own feet. Damn! What was the matter with her that she would allow a jerk like that to so much as ruffle her feathers? She stepped onto the curb and tried to hail a cab, but it passed her up and stopped not ten feet farther up the street where a ravishing blond was standing. Joan frowned. As she looked further up the block, she noticed a group of five very tough-looking punks smoking a joint around a lamppost. Rather than invite trouble, she crossed the street and proceeded on her way.

After two more failures, Joan succeeded in procuring a cab. When she pulled up in front of the book store, she noticed the full-color posters announcing her newest book, *The Return of Angelina*. Taped across the top of the poster was a wide banner proclaiming: "Joan Wilder, Here Today."

Two people from Avon stood just outside the door of the bookstore. Her dark-haired editor Richard was pacing back and forth; his pretty junior editor Carolyn stood impatiently, hands shoved into the pockets of her white wool coat. Carolyn was none too pleased with Joan's tardiness. She rushed up to the cab and held the door for Joan.

"Joan, come on, you're late. People are waiting!"

"Carolyn, please, I'm nervous enough. You know how I hate these things. I'm not going to have to speak, am I?"

"You *don't* have to speak," she answered exasperatedly. "It's a simple book-signing session." Carolyn's heavily mascaraed blue eyes rolled. She grabbed Joan's arm and nearly dragged her to the door. "We've been over this a million times. Just charm them."

Joan's natural instinct was to resist, and this one time she gave in. She pulled back abruptly, causing Carolyn to stumble, but her rubber-soled calfskin boots adhered to the icy pavement.

"You know I have nothing to say," Joan stated emphatically.

"Joan, this crowd is interested in Angelina, not in you."

Joan's eyes darted furtively to the bookstore window. "Crowd? What crowd? You said it was a simple book-signing session."

"For God's sake, Joan! It's ten o'clock on a weekday morning. How many people can there be?"

Carolyn, determined that her reluctant novelist would not undo all that she had worked so diligently for, shoved Joan through the bookstore door before she had a chance to protest further.

Joan felt her stomach land somewhere on the

floor between her legs. A quick count told her that roughly eight billion housewives had somehow crammed themselves into the store.

This was how Normandy must have looked after the Allies landed, Joan thought, as she surveyed the littered aisles at the end of the day. Was it possible that simply signing one's name to a book could deplete a normal healthy young woman of all her energies? Her stomach growled from not eating all day. It would take an entire bottle of Vivarin to give her the strength to consume even a cup of soup. Tomato soup, she thought, then I won't have to chew.

One lone customer remained and she had an iron grip on Joan's arm that was worthy of Arnold Schwartzenegger.

"You're my very favorite romance novelist. I mean it! Angelina is my favorite character. I just *love* her! Your books have *saved my life!*"

"Uh, well. I'm very happy that—they have?"

"Oh, you don't know—you simply do not know."

With renewed interest in what the woman was saying, Joan searched deeply into the woman's eyes, trying to find what it was that the woman knew and she did not. Quite suddenly the woman rushed off without another word.

Joan walked over toward Richard, who was meticulously packing his briefcase. He smiled at her. "I think you charmed them."

She made a face. "By stammering a lot and staring at my toes?"

"People expect great writers to be eccentric, my dear."

"Oh, Richard. If *Return of Angelina* is great writing, the world's in a lot of trouble."

"Half a million copies in advance sales do *not* lie. And you always say things like that when you finish a new book—especially when it's late."

Joan smiled wanly. "Look, Richard, I think I'm running out of steam. Maybe we could talk about it at dinner tonight?"

She didn't have to hear his words to know what he was about to say. His guilt-ridden face could be read from across the store. "Oh, Joan, I'm sorry. I forgot an appointment I made and—"

"No, no, sure, don't worry. I don't mind."

"Next week. For sure." He latched his case securely. "Anyway, have a nice evening."

"Thanks, Richard, but I've made other plans." She watched him walk away, striding purposefully toward the door. She surveyed the rubble in which he'd left her and then noticed Carolyn making her way toward her, obviously searching for two clean cups in the mess that surrounded them.

Brushing past the debris, Carolyn at last located two cups. "Joan, why do you subject yourself to types like him? You could do so much better."

"Yeah? In what other life?" She paused for a moment. "A woman just said my books saved her life," Joan said, still incredulous at the statement.

"Well, where else will men keep their word, women hold their own, and love burn through to the end? We all need our fantasies, right?" Carolyn handed Joan a cup which she accepted. "And our vodka."

Joan ignored the joke, a grim look on her face.

Carolyn instantly regretted her offhanded humor. Her voice was concerned when she said, "I know what bad timing this was. Your sister due in . . ." She paused as if hesitant to finish. "Did they find her husband's body yet?"

"No. Only the . . . the one piece."

"My God." Carolyn shook her head. "Is she holding up?"

"Elaine . . . she's always been the tough one in the family. Elaine always manages," Joan said, thinking how she would not manage well at all in the situation.

Chapter Two

TURQUOISE BLUE WATERS waved white gloved hands as they rolled onto the sands of Colombia's coastline. Voluminous clouds frolicked across the sky and headed toward the mountains, and masses of verdant plants swayed in the soft breezes. It was a picture-postcard day that she slammed white-painted shutters against. Her long slender legs quickly stepped into a pair of tight-fitting designer jeans. She pulled on a red silk, long-sleeved blouse and continued buttoning it while she went about her packing. She jammed her things into the suitcase, then sat on the lid trying to close it. Her nervous fingers fumbled with the latch and finally it held. Though the suitcase was filled to overflowing and some clothes were hanging out, there was no time for neatness.

When she grabbed the suitcase on her way out of the room, the latch came undone and the contents spilled across the wood-planked floor. A photograph of two young women, one smiling and the other, behind her, timid and reluctant, landed atop the pile of clothing.

Elaine retrieved the picture, wondered momentarily if she would ever be able to smile that way again, and shoved the picture back into the case. She hurried to the mirror, tied a black chiffon scarf around her hair, and tucked the ends into the collar of her blouse. Her eyes were red and swollen from crying. She scrambled through her purse and found her sunglasses. They still were not able to mask the desperation that creased her brow and caused the tight set of her mouth.

Without a backward glance she left the room and headed for the garage.

Luckily she had left the keys to the Cobra inside the car, so she wasted no time in backing out of the garage. As she drove down the hilly curving path to the gates, she glanced back only once in the rear-view mirror. The villa sat majestically on top of the hill. In front, the lawns were clipped and bordered with brightly leafed crotons and other tropical plants in reds, yellows, and greens. Bird of paradise blooms filled the planters near the brick wall that circled the pool area. Behind the white-bricked mansion with its open verandas and canopied terraces, loomed the mountainous, primitive jungle.

Elaine pulled the Cobra to a sudden stop, jumped out, and left the car door open while she closed the heavy iron gates. Just outside the gates she noticed some children playing near the edge of the street. A frail young boy with black hair and wide, sad, black eyes was practicing with a bola near a fountain across the way. A group of smaller children were playing the Columbian equivalent of jacks.

As Elaine locked the gate with her key, she stole nervous glances over her shoulder. She rushed back to the waiting Cobra. Just as she placed one foot inside the car, the boy by the fountain slung his bola.

The bola wrapped around Elaine's neck and one of the balls struck her on the side of her head. She fell unconscious into the car.

Racing across the street, the boy shoved Elaine across the seat onto the passenger's side while he slid behind the wheel. He shoved the car into gear and raced away, unnoticed by the other children, who saw nothing extraordinary in the happenings in their neighborhood.

The red Cobra raced through the narrow city streets of Cartagena, dodging vegetable vendors and peddler carts, and on past the open-air markets with their flowers, crates of live chickens and exotic birds. Gravel and sand spewed from beneath the Cobra's tires as the boy whipped around turn after turn. Down steep inclines the car manuevered expertly, around a stalled 1953 Ford pickup truck and past a battered taxi. With the snowcapped Sierra Nevada mountains in the background, the Cobra roared down the ocean drive beneath rows of towering palm trees. Taking a corner at breakneck speed, the Cobra sped up the avenue toward the harbor.

Yachts sat next to maelstrom-demolished fishing vessels and sleek six-passenger sailboats. Row upon row of unlikely sailing neighbors bobbed up and down in the harbor as the waves lapped against the sides of their hulls.

An old fort with rickety battlements sat at the end of the harbor where river and sea met. A barnacle-encrusted, dilapidated freighter sat next to the fort, its crew members leaning over the rusty railing, intent on the approaching Cobra.

They were a menacing-looking lot with unkempt hair, yellow cavity-filled teeth, and eyes that had seen too much. When the Cobra pulled to a stop, Elaine was still unconscious.

"The kid's here with the broad," Ralph said to his cousin Ira.

Ira, indifferent to the Cobra or the unconscious woman inside, was busily pitching chicken entrails over a wall and into a bog swamp below him. The swamp was infested with large crocodiles that looked as if they would rather eat the arm that fed them than the meager entrails it tossed.

"Look at those snappers, will ya?" Ira said, fascinated by the large jaws and the dexterity with which such huge beasts could move.

Ralph rolled his eyes in exasperation and walked over to Ira. Ralph had always been the most put-upon person in his neighborhood. He was squeamish about a lot of things and to him, crocodiles and unconscious women meant nothing but bad news.

"Ira, I'm real nervous about this whole thing. I'm not kidding. It's nothing but trouble. It's a piss-poor idea."

"Whoo! D'ya see that? Look-it, Ralph, that ugly,

striped sonuvabitch down there. Y'see him?"

Ira finally exhausted his supply of entrails, wiped his hands on his matty trousers and began heading toward the freighter. As always, Ralph trailed him with his little skip-hop walk, looking like a lost puppy in search of a master.

"Let's eat this one, Ira," Ralph said. "Whaddya say? We'll take the loss on this one."

Ira pretended he didn't hear a single word. "Geez, those crocs are nasty buggers, I tell ya."

When Elaine finally awoke, there was a large bump on the side of her temple and her head ached with sharp, dagger-like pains. It took her seemingly endless moments to focus her eyes. She was sitting in a huge tufted leather chair in the middle of a plush stateroom. Behind a rococo, black lacquer and gilt desk stood a lighted glass case filled with expensive and unusual Columbian art and sculpture. Wide banquettes upholstered in a maroon raw silk with bronze and teal throw pillows filled the corner of the room opposite her. Buffed bronze cornices marked the ceiling in whose center hung a crystal chandelier.

Though still groggy, she heard the sound of something ripping. A short man in baggy unpressed trousers and a soiled, short-sleeved knit shirt was cutting her valise to shreds. She watched as he picked up a Pucci silk slip and an apricot chiffon negligee and inspected them with leering eyes. He withdrew her creme brocade jewelry packet and fondled the contents with his stubby fingers. Just watching him made her stomach lurch. Frightened and confused, she watched as he pocketed a small wad of Colombian currency.

"What're you—what're you doing?" she asked as a new pain shot through her temple.

Ira circled the chair and stood in front of her. Ralph, now finished with his inspection of her belongings, looked at Ira.

"It's not here."

"What? What are you looking for?" Elaine asked.

Ira leaned over, his forehead nearly touching hers. She smelled the stench of garlic on his breath. She winced.

"I realize this is a difficult time for you, but I'd just love it if you gave me the map without any discussion."

"What map?"

"The map your husband acquired before his untimely demise. If you think I'm gonna be squeezed out by the widow of a two-bit antique dealer—"

"My husband was just a bookseller," she said defensively and then gasped as she realized her inquisitor was losing patience. His round eyes seemed to bulge out of his head as he glared at her. The man who had been fondling her underwear let out an audible sigh.

Ira's hands were clenched in fists and Elaine knew he would just as soon let loose with a few punches to her face as anything.

"Hate to break it to you, sweetheart, but your husband was a smuggler—rest in peace. And I ran his stuff outta the country for him.

"Which makes *us* the inheritors of his estate—not you. Y'understand?"

"You killed him?"

"No, I didn't, although I had plenty of reason to. You don't know who I am and that's very good. You didn't even know who your husband was and that's why we're havin' this conversation."

Elaine looked at him in disbelief. She was brought back to reality by the cry of pain from the man who was tearing apart the linings of her suitcase. He had apparently stabbed himself with the scissors. She looked back at the scruffy man who hovered over her. "Eduardo was a respected archeologist," she said with what small defiance she could muster. It was so hard for her to believe that any of this was actually happening.

At the word *archeologist,* her captors laughed and sputtered.

"The way your Eduardo was used to livin'? He was a smuggler—okay?—until one day he lucked onto a certain document—a map. He held it in his hand for about five minutes before someone diced him up."

"And you think *I* have it?"

"No, *he* thinks you have it. But I know what happened. Eduardo sent it out of the country. And he stupidly told a third party where he sent it. That's why he's a memory. He's dog food. Now all you gotta do is tell me where he sent it. Ain't that right, Ralph?"

As Elaine tried to make sense of what he was

saying, the man who was leaning over her suddenly reached toward the one called Ralph and snatched the scissors out of his hand. With his next movement, he grabbed a lock of Elaine's hair and threatened it with the scissors.

She jerked away from him, totally unnerved by his gesture. "Please, please—don't . . ."

Ralph gestured toward his companion's bald pate.

"What's the matter? Don't you want to look like Ira?"

Ira hovered over her again. "Now all you gotta do is tell us where you mailed it, pretty lady, so I can get to it first. Please tell us. That way no one else ends up on a meathook."

As he tugged at her hair again, Elaine's resolve melted. "I know that he mailed some things to my sister."

He dropped his hold on her hair. "You hear that, Ralph? Her sister!"

"What's her number?"

Hating herself, Elaine recited Joan's number.

Chapter Three

THE WIND WAS howling outside Joan's apartment when she decided to take a break from Angelina's exploits and build a roaring fire in the fireplace. Since she had forgotten to open the flue, it took her an hour and a half to rid the apartment of the smoke. She placed a romantic duet on the stereo and hummed along as the opera music drifted through the room.

She arranged her small oak table with an artistic eye. She placed a still-blooming poinsettia, a Christmas present from her editor, in the center of the table and flanked it with crystal candlesticks and tall white tapers. Atop her mother's antique, lace place mats she placed nonmatching Bavarian china in cobalt blue with gold rims. A Baccarat goblet and Belgian linen white napkin completed the picture. She smiled as she critiqued her arrangement, complimenting herself on its sensitivity.

She went to the kitchen and returned with her meal. In the center of the antique plate she placed a now-cold Big Mac. She was just emptying the french fries, a large order, when the telephone rang. Momentarily she looked embarrassed, knowing the phone had caught her at being too natural.

She turned the stereo down and answered. "Hello?"

"Joan? Joannie?" Elaine's voice was distant.

"Elaine! Honey, are you all right?"

"Joan, listen to me."

"What is it, Elaine? What can I do to help?"

This time when Elaine spoke it was in cool, measured tones.

"Joan, listen to me, *please*. Has any mail been forwarded to you—anything for me, for Eduardo?"

Joan opened the drawer and withdrew the stack of mail she had neatly kept together with a rubber band. "Ah, yes. There are some things. I have them right here."

"Is there—I don't know—an envelope that stands out—a big envelope?"

"Uh, yes."

"Open it," Elaine said.

Joan used a letter opener to slit the side of the envelope. "Elaine, what's wrong?"

"Open it, Joan. Is there a map in there?"

Joan withdrew a clear plastic envelope, which contained two old crumbling pieces of a map that had been taped together. It was an odd-looking map, she thought, with drawings and scribbled lines on it.

"Yes, Elaine. It says, 'El . . . Corazón'?"

Elaine's voice sounded relieved at the news.

Joan was more puzzled than ever.

"Now, Joan, listen to me. You must bring it to me. You have to bring the map to Colombia."

"Elaine! For God's sake—"

"Yes. There are some people here who want the map. If you don't do it, they're going to kill me. Joannie, do you understand?"

"Elaine, my God!"

"You can't tell the police, you can't tell anyone. You have to come here, Joan, with the map, and everything will be all right."

Joan was crying, her hands shaking so much she could barely hold the phone to her ear. "Elaine, *please*."

"You have a room waiting at the Hotel Emporio in Cartagena. Write it down, Joan. Hotel Emporio. When you get there, they'll give you this number: 64 58 24. Are you writing this down?"

Joan was fumbling in her drawer for a pen—a writer with no pen! She tossed out ribbon cartridges and correct tapes and found no pen or pencil. She was frantic. Finally, at the back of the drawer under some stamps she found a pencil. She scribbled the name of the hotel and the number on the title page of her new book.

"You have a passport don't you?"

"But I've never used my passport, Elaine. You know I can't do this. I can't go to Colombia by myself. You know how I hate to fly!"

"You know I wouldn't ask. You know I never have . . ." Elaine's voice cracked and Joan could barely hear her through her sobs. "They'll hurt me,

Joan. They'll hurt me."

"I'll get there, Elaine" Joan said. But the line was dead.

Joan was numb when she hung up the phone. This was all some dream! It couldn't be really happening to her—to Elaine. Her movements were slow and mechanical as she went into her bedroom to pack. She threw things at random into her Pierre Cardin suitcase she'd bought through a flyer in the mail. Ordinarily she would have spent days planning, laundering, ironing, and meticulously packing, but this was no ordinary trip. She was on a rescue mission. She was the only chance her sister had to escape alive. Elaine was depending on Joan . . . and the map.

The deadbolt to Joan's apartment softly clicked and then the doorknob turned slowly to the right. A black, gloved hand reached in and with a pair of wire snips cut the chain lock. As the door eased open, the black, gloved hand flicked open a stiletto which flashed silver in the moonlight. A tall man slipped in the door and stifled a rasping cough.

His aviator sunglasses concealed the forty-plus years of wrinkles around his eyes. His thin lips were cruel and ruthless. He had an angular face with cheekbones so high and sharp they looked as if they would slit through the skin. With panther-like moves he stole down the dark hallway.

Noiselessly he opened the bedroom door. The light from the window revealed an empty bed. The man retracted his stiletto, placed it in the pocket of his dark overcoat, and flipped on the light. He crossed to the cherry, Tudor-style bureau and ransacked the drawers. When he opened the closet there were obvious articles of clothing missing.

On the closet floor he noted a carton filled with books, all with Joan Wilder's picture on the cover. On the other nightstand he spotted a telephone and phone pad.

He picked up the phone pad and read: Cartagena, Pan Am flight #82, departure—9:45.

The cabin lights had been dimmed, since most of the passengers were asleep. Joan Wilder was not. On the tray in front of her were five tiny liquor bottles—two whiskey and three rum. With each drink she had nervously shredded the cocktail napkins. She toyed with the peanuts in front of her, wondering if they would help her queazy stomach. Instead, she opened her air sickness bag in case she would need it. To occupy her mind, she memorized the exits listed on the flight safety card.

The intercom from the cockpit turned on and the captain spoke to the passengers.

"Ladies and gentlemen, we've just been informed that Cartegena airport is temporarily closed. We'll be making an alternate landing at Barranquilla. Complimentary ground transportation will be provided for passengers bound for Cartagena. We apologize for the inconvenience."

Joan had not recovered from this bad news when a stewardess leaned over the seat and startled her.

"Feeling better? Can I get you another dramamine?"

"No, no thank you. What about this airport . . ."

"It's Colombia. Happens all the time."

When the stewardess left, Joan felt like calling her back and asking for a dose of her nonchalance.

The stewardess walked to the rear of the 747 and passed the only other passenger who was not asleep. As he smoked a cigarillo, common to Colombia, the smoke drifted up into the ray of his pinpoint reading light. He was watching Joan Wilder with keen interest.

Joan was fumbling in her purse for some breath mints, anything to soothe her nervous stomach, and withdrew the map to make room for her overstuffed wallet. She freshened her lipstick and checked herself in her flowered compact mirror. Every bit of her makeup had been erased. She snapped the compact shut and replaced it in her purse. She started to put the map away when suddenly her interest piqued. She opened it and studied it.

Joan did not know that the man four aisles back on the opposite side smoking a cigarillo was watching her. Nor did she see him lower his aviator sunglasses.

Chapter Four

THE BARRANQUILLA BUS terminal was an inferno of noise and confusion. After spending two hours waiting in line in the middle of the night for the customs inspector to clear her and her luggage, all Joan wanted was a hot bath and comfortable bed. Instead, she was caught in a crosscurrent of Indians carrying poultry, screaming babies, and masses of makeshift luggage and bundles. Joan was swept up by the crowd as they swarmed like flies outside the concourse.

Joan did not notice the tall Colombian with aviator sunglasses following her. He paused by an armed soldier and flipped out a badge. The soldier stiffened and saluted his superior officer.

"*Pardon,* Zolo," the soldier said.

Zolo confiscated the man's pistol and continued after Joan, who was making her way as best she could through the crowd.

A string of paint-chipped old buses of questionable mechanical durability awaited the passengers at the end of the walkway. Joan saw no markings to signify the Cartagena bus, so she stopped an approaching official.

"Excuse—"

He walked past without so much as looking at her. Presently a man assigned to load all the luggage grabbed Joan's suitcase and handed it to another man atop the bus she was standing nearest.

"Wait a minute—momento. Cartagena?"

The man was too hurried to listen to her. *"Vámonos, vámonos."*

"Is this the bus to Carta—"

Just then a tall, Colombian man helped the loader with her suitcase.

"Si, Cartagena," Zolo said.

At the far end of the concourse, a battered old Renault convertible bounced up onto the curb. The door opened and Ralph jumped out, searched the crowd for a moment, and then grabbed an official by the arm.

"The flight from New York to Cartagena—the flight that was diverted here—has it arrived already?"

Before the official could answer him, Ralph spotted Joan disappearing inside the bus. He glanced down at the photograph of her on the cover of the book he was clutching. He let go of the airport official and began fighting his way toward the bus.

Joan selected a window seat, thinking she could avoid the stench by hanging her head out the window. She kept her shoulder bag strapped close against her body and while a fat Indian man squeezed in beside her, she looked around the bus at the Indian children and squawking chickens. She was tired and disoriented and her eyes focused only long enough to notice the tall Colombian who had helped with her luggage sitting in the back of the bus calmly smoking a cigarillo.

The gears ground loudly as the bus lurched forward, launching several passengers out of their seats.

The unpaved roads were filled with potholes and uneven areas that caused the bus to pitch and sway. But even the cackling chickens could not keep Joan awake any longer, not having slept all night. She had been asleep approximately fifteen minutes when the bus came to a crossroads. The bus downshifted and turned off the main road in a direction contrary to the arrow on the Cartagena road sign.

Only minutes later a Renault convertible approached the crossroads and it too made the same turn as the bus. Though Ralph pressed the accelerator to the floor, his Renault was losing ground. He tried rocking his body to make the car pick up speed, but nothing worked. He watched as the bus's tail lights grew smaller and then vanished in the darkness.

Dawn's red-gold rays slithered down the slopes of Colombia's spectacular mountains, burnishing the virgin wilderness with warmth and light. Exotic, colorful birds began their ritualistic cacophony to the new day. Flamboyant blossoms opened, creating a natural sideshow for the passengers on the bus as it twisted through the narrow mountain passages.

When Joan awoke, she found the bus had stopped and many of the passengers were disembarking. Joan looked out the dusty window, then struggled with the rusty levers and lowered it. The panorama of the rain forest and jungle was breathtaking. But where was she?

"*Excusa*—uh—Cartagena?" She nudged the Indian beside her. He was still groggy from the bad night's sleep. She pointed out the window to the wilderness beyond. *"Donde está?"*

"Cartagena?"

"*Si,* Cartagena," Joan said, assuming he was verifying her question, and turned away from him. She didn't see him shrug his shoulders, not understanding what she wanted.

The bus doors closed, the gears made their familiar grinding noise, and they were on their way again. The road ahead was nearly straight uphill and the motor strained with the task. Finally they reached the top of the hill, and with their descent the bus picked up speed.

Still unsure about their location, Joan decided to question the one person of authority on board, the driver. With difficulty she picked her way up the aisle, stepping over sleeping children and bundles. With their downhill descent and the bumpy terrain, she clutched a pole to remain standing.

"I'm sorry to bother you," she said to the driver, still holding on to a pole behind his seat.

He glanced over his shoulder at her, but she could tell his concentration was needed to maneuver them safely over the tricky road ahead.

"*Qué?*" he asked.

"What time do we arrive in Cartegena? Uh—*qué hora*—"

"Cartagena?"

"Yes, *si*— Am I on the right bus?" she asked as they came to a blind turn which they took a bit too fast to suit her, just missing the narrow cliff's edge on the right.

"Cartagena *no es*—" The driver began when he glanced forward once again.

Joan screamed. "Holy shit!"

Parked squarely in the middle of the road was a Land Rover! The driver slammed on the brakes but there was no avoiding a collision. The brakes screeched and luggage from the overhead racks came tumbling down on top of the passengers. When the bus and Land Rover made impact, a horrible crashing sound filled the jungle around them.

From the center of the rubble, flocks of fabulous multicolored birds soared into the air, leaving a cloud of churning dust below them.

Joan was lying in the aisle when the bus crashed. One lone last bag fell from overhead and crashed onto the floor, narrowly missing her head. Carefully Joan pulled herself up, mentally checking for broken bones. There were none. She looked out the front windshield at the chaos in front of her.

Startled and shaken, the passengers and driver filed out of the bus. The driver walked to the front of the bus and surveyed the wreckage. The entire front end was caved in, the engine was smoking and three of his four tires were flat. He threw up his hands helplessly.

The driver walked around the Land Rover and the Indians followed him. They looked up into the surrounding hills, wondering where the owner had gone.

Joan held her hand over her eyes as she scanned the terrain and the road in front of them. The owner obviously had had a breakdown of his own and had abandoned the Land Rover. Suddenly the radiator on the bus blew up, emitting a cloud of steam.

The driver walked over and kicked the bus. *"Terminar! Terminar!"* he yelled in frustration and anger.

Joan brushed the dust off her gray suit she had purchased only a month ago at Bergdorf Goodman. Her trip was really going well.

The Indians picked up their belongings, chickens, and children, and began trudging back down the road, the way they had just come. It was clear to Joan that this was a normal occurrence for them. Resolutely, she went to the bus to retrieve her suitcase and join the others.

"You don't have to walk. Another bus will come along," Zolo said.

Joan turned around and stared at him. He was calmly smoking a cigarillo and seemed unperturbed by the incident or their being stranded in the middle of the jungle.

"They know nothing. They are peasants," he

said, indicating the others with a slight tilt of his head.

"Another bus? Really?"

"Of course. There are schedules to be maintained. Even in Colombia." He smiled at her and she thought she had never seen such a slimy grin on a human.

Joan looked down the road and watched as the rest of the passengers marched away. She placed her suitcase on the ground and sat on top of it. She leaned over and placed her chin in her hands, hoping it wouldn't be too long a wait.

Zolo patiently watched her, smoking his cigarillo.

Joan glanced up after a while to see the last Indian go around the bend, pulling a lingering child with her. It was suddenly very quiet in the jungle. Deathly quiet, she thought.

She heard a rasping cough and looked up—into the barrel of Zolo's gun! Slowly she stood, cautiously backing away from him.

"What're you . . ." she began.

He advanced toward her, motioning with his unarmed hand.

"The purse."

Over his shoulder and to the right, Joan thought she saw something move.

Zolo turned to see what she was staring at.

There, outlined against the morning sun, stood a man. Joan noted the particular manner in which he wore his hat. *Jesse?* she wondered. No, she admonished herself, that was one of her stories, a fantasy. She blinked her eyes twice, but he was still there, advancing toward her. She noticed he carried a water bag. She blinked again. He *was* real.

Zolo spun on his heel and fired his pistol. His shot exploded the water bag, but it missed the man. In a lightning-quick move, the stranger whipped a Winchester 12 gauge rifle from his shoulder and began firing.

In a reflex action, Joan dived toward the bus and rolled beneath. Zolo jumped inside the bus and continued firing his pistol at the stranger.

Joan could hear the Colombian's steps as he moved to the back of the bus. In front of her, the stranger moved closer, pumping off one shot after another at the bus windows. The shots echoed through the mountains sounding like Armageddon. Joan covered her ears and prayed.

Shattering glass rained down on the ground around her. Joan cringed and then curled into a ball closer. The bus was moving back and forth, and she was afraid it would somehow fall down and crush her. She heard Zolo smashing the back door down. Finally the doors flew open and Zolo landed in a roll. He scrambled to his feet and took off running as the stranger continued pumping off more shots.

Joan didn't breathe for long moments as she watched the boots of her savior walk the length of the bus and over to the jeep. Then the boots came walking back toward her. When they stopped in front of her eyes, she scrambled through her purse for her Spanish-American dictionary.

He crouched down and peered at her.

"Por favor . . . por favor . . ." She stumbled over her words, her tongue a knotted mass in her mouth.

He snatched the dictionary out of her hands and glared at her with angry blue eyes.

"Where are my birds?"

Chapter Five

THE RENAULT CONVERTIBLE wheezed its way up the mountain road, passing a string of Indians carrying beaten-up suitcases and bundles. Ralph was observing them with mild curiosity when suddenly a tall Colombian man jumped into the road and began waving his arms over his head. Ralph didn't know whether to clutch his pounding heart or hit the brake. He chose the latter.

Zolo flashed his badge at Ralph. Seeing the lawman's silver badge made Ralph feel faint. Zolo got in the Renault just as Ralph spun the car around. The passenger door flew open and then shut, nearly ejecting Zolo. Ralph gunned the car and they sped down the mountain road, overtaking the stranded Indians.

Ralph was totally unnerved riding with a policeman. He pulled his straw hat further down over his eyes and with stolen glances he saw Zolo inspecting him with appraising eyes.

Zolo spoke in Spanish. "Don't I know you?"

Had Ralph's hands not been clutching the steering wheel to steady himself, he would have freaked. *"No comprendo."*

"You are American?"

"American! Pah!" Ralph spat the words out. "I hate American. I spit on American!"

"You must be French."

Ralph thought he would vomit.

Joan watched as her "savior" rummaged through the wreckage that had once been his Land Rover. He pulled the door and it came off in his hands. The driver's seat was smashed into the steering wheel and there were pieces of broken crates everywhere.

Carefully he withdrew a picture that was inside a cracked frame. He picked off the broken glass and lovingly removed a picture of a boat. It was a sleek luxury boat with wooden decking and hand-carved rails, and it was Jack Colton's biggest dream. He folded the picture, crouched down and placed it safely in his backpack. He didn't notice Joan standing before him.

"Uh, excuse me. Sorry."

She had dusted off her three-piece suit, retied the bow of her Bergdorf blouse, combed her hair, and applied fresh lipstick. He noticed she wore two-inch heels and sunglasses. Being neat must have been her way of coping with the situation and he thought her weird as hell.

"Do you know where I might find a phone?"

He looked at her incredulously. "Lady, I have no idea."

"It's very important that I—"

Jack returned to his job of salvaging his belongings from the wreckage. "Well, we all got our problems, don't we?"

"Is there a town near here? Will another bus be along?"

Jack grabbed her arm and pulled her to the middle of the road, and then pulled her around so that she faced the other direction.

Joan saw nothing but wilderness. He leaned very close to her; his blue eyes flashed.

"And this is rush hour," he quipped.

Jack scanned the sky above and saw the storm clouds gathering. He rushed back to his jeep and quickly gathered his things.

"I *must* get to a phone. I'm supposed to be in Cartegena!" Joan must be coming unglued.

"Cartagena? You're hell and gone from Cartagena, angel. Cartagena's on the coast."

"But I was told this bus—"

"Who told you that?"

Joan thought for a moment. "The man who . . ."

"Pulled a gun on you? What else did he tell ya?"

Jack turned his back on her and walked up the road. Joan grabbed her suitcase and though it was heavy, she wasted no time in catching up with him.

"Please," she said, "I need your help."

"Is that my new career?"

"If you could just get me to a tele—"

"Half a year's salary just flew south for the winter, my jeep would win first prize at a scrap-metal convention, and in five minutes everything I got left in the world is gonna be soaking wet. So lighten up lady. I haven't got the time."

Joan determinedly kept pace with him. "You don't understand. My sister needs me. It's a matter of life and death—if I don't get to her." She paused. *"I'll pay you!"*

"How much?" Jack asked.

"Fifty dollars."

Jack turned just enough to laugh directly into her face and then continued walking.

"I thought you just lost everything," Joan countered.

"Not my sense of humor."

"Well, what d'you want? I'll give you a hundred dollars. Two hundred dollars."

"I'll do it for five."

"That's ridiculous. I'll give you two-fifty."

"Lady, my *minimum* price for taking stranded women to telephones is four hundred dollars."

"Will you take three seventy-five in traveler's checks?"

"American Express?"

"Sure."

"Deal."

Chapter Six

In 1948 a small area of the jungle had been cleared away by an escaped Nazi who had planned to spend the rest of his days hiding in Colombia. Painstakingly, he had built a large wooden structure for the main house, horse corrals, and a barn. In an outlying circle he erected adobe buildings for storage of food, a workshop, and kitchen. At one time there had been vegetable gardens and carefully pruned shrubbery and flowering plants.

The Nazi died of dysentery in 1952 and a year later the local police confiscated the area for use as their outpost. Since that time, not a single human hand had been lifted to maintain the compound.

The sun had baked the gardens until all that remained was dust. The roofs leaked, floorboards had warped, and garbage was piled in mounds beside each building.

The faces of the policemen that lounged in the hot sun reflected the inherent apathy of the compound. One man sat in a rickety jeep, his feet propped up on the steering wheel, a hat pulled over his face. Another snored loudly as he slept with his back against a box filled with rubbish.

Santos, the *jefe,* sat in a chair outside his office, fanning flies away with an old newspaper. He heard the sound of an approaching car but paid no attention. He swatted another fly and then picked the insect off the newspaper.

The Renault convertible pulled up in front of Santos. With lumbering movements, the overweight Santos stood up. As he walked toward the driver, he hitched up his pants to impress the driver with his rank. He leaned over to speak to the driver, a menacing look on his face, when from the passenger's side of the car emerged Zolo.

"Assemble your men," Zolo commanded him in Spanish.

Santos immediately snapped to attention and saluted his superior officer. Santos began shouting commands to his men and everyone jerked to attention. Santos shouted again and the men raced about the compound gathering guns, ammunitions, and provisions.

While the policemen scurried about the buildings and Zolo was conversing with Santos, Ralph stole inside the main building. The desk was filled with tin plates covered with dried beans and meat bones that even the flies did not want. Papers were scattered over file cabinets and chairs. A missing pane of glass had been patched with a soiled shirt. An oscillating fan was the only relief from the ovenlike temperatures.

On the far wall, which was papered with "Wanted" posters, was a telephone. Ralph nearly leaped across the floor. He held the earpiece and wound the crank on the antiquated piece of machinery.

As he turned around to face the three jail cells on the farthest wall, he spied a wild-eyed American. The man was nearly emaciated, his clothes were shredded, and he looked as if he had been beaten. The American kept begging him for help, but all Ralph wanted was to make his call. Very politely Ralph excused himself and told the American he was on long distance.

Finally, his call went through to Ira, who was still on the freighter with Elaine.

"Hiya, Mom? It's me—Irving," he said, hoping Ira would understand his code.

"Ralph, you little pussy, where are you?" Ira answered.

"Calm down, Ma, will ya? Who says I never call?"

"Ralph, will you for chrissake tell me the story?"

Ralph had to pause for a moment as two of the policia entered the jail and rummaged around for papers and guns, which they finally found in the drawer of the desk. Ralph let out a sigh of relief when they left.

"As usual, cousin, you've got us in serious shit. The stupid dame got on the wrong bus. I'm stuck in some kinda spiko military compound. They're mobilizing for Iwo Jima here."

"Do they know who you are?"

"Whaddya think? I'm an announcer at Radio

City? I'm keepin' a low profile."

Ralph then made the sign of the cross over himself and looked upward toward heaven and froze. There on the wall was a "Wanted" poster of himself! It was all he could do not to pee in his pants. He tried to reach up and pull it off the wall but it was just out of reach. He grew more panicked with every passing minute.

Ralph dragged a chair over to the wall and climbed on top, trying to reach the poster. He continued talking to Ira at the other end of the line.

"And the other little tidbit, Ira, is that *Zolo* is after her, too. You got that, brains? Not only are we kidnappers, but I'm about to have a close encounter with a cattle prod."

This time Ira's voice was nearly as frenzied as Ralph's.

"Zolo . . . Zolo is after her? Has he got his squad with him?"

"Not yet. He's makin' do with these local yo-yos."

"Ralph, goddammit. I don't care what you do, just get me that map. Just get it!"

"Don't yell at me, Ira. I told you this idea sucked from the word go!"

Just then Ralph fell off the chair, cutting his connection with Ira.

Inside the stateroom on the freighter, Ira and Elaine were seated at an elaborately set table. Pink and white Limoges china serving pieces held bacon-wrapped filet mignon, *pommes au beurre* and julienne carrots. Waterford goblets were filled with a delicate Perrier Jouet.

Elaine could only pick at her food, for she was unnerved by the pair of baby alligators lounging next to Ira's plate.

Elaine couldn't decide which was worse, her morbidly eccentric jailer with his affinity for reptiles or the fact that for the first time in her life she was dependent on Joan. How was it that fate had done an about-face on the Wilder sisters?

Elaine had always cared for Joan, especially since their parents had died. There had been times when she wondered if Joan would ever mature emotionally. She had been partially at fault for that, being the decision-maker in the family. Joan had always been shy, and when they were younger Elaine had had a devil of a time persuading Joan to join in the simplest neighborhood games.

Something inherent in Joan's nature had kept her perpetually frightened of life; whereas Elaine seemed to plunge in head first. Too often she had not thought things through enough, she realized, but at least she had acted. That had to count for something.

For Joan, ordinary tasks—like banking, marketing and job interviews—were overwhelming. When Elaine had taken Joan shopping for clothes to wear at the book-signings Avon had arranged, it had been an all-out battle. Joan fought the idea for two weeks before Elaine badgered her into agreeing to the outing.

Twice during the afternoon at Bonwit's and

Bergdorf's Joan had pleaded headaches and asked to go home. It was bad enough that Joan refused to purchase any of the newer styles that Elaine thought so becoming on her.

"You're becoming a famous person, Joan, and you should look the part," Elaine had said.

Elaine still could not understand Joan's aversion to the limelight. If it had been she, Elaine would have played it up for all it was worth. After all, who knew how long it would last?

Instead of being proud of her talents and the fame she had worked long hours for, Joan pooh-poohed the whole thing and went straight back to the typewriter and her dreamworld.

Many times Elaine worried that perhaps Joan's writing was not good for her. True, it paid her bills and fulfilled her creative nature, but it kept Joan cut off from living. And Elaine was a full believer in living.

Joan was young and quite attractive when she let herself be. It was Elaine's hope that one day she would relax and the real Joan Wilder would emerge.

Elaine had seen glimpses of that person from time to time. There was the time when Joan had been a sophomore at NYU and had come home all dreamy-eyed over her new Eighteenth-Century Lit. professor. For two months Joan looked, felt, and acted like a different person. Elaine knew all along it would not last, but the incident gave her a different perspective on her sister.

Then there was the time when a history class had

taken an excursion to Stratford-on-Avon in Canada. Joan had been reluctant to go, though Elaine explained that seeing the Shakespearean plays performed in the out-of-doors would be a broadening experience. When Joan returned she spoke of nothing else for over a week. Joan absorbed the experience like litmus paper. With flamboyant gestures, Joan described the bus ride to Canada, the people she met, the countryside, and the food she ate.

Elaine thought then that underneath Joan's prim exterior was the soul of a Marco Polo and the womanly desires of a Fanny Hill. They were blood kin, and that much different they couldn't be!

More important, Elaine believed it impossible for Joan to write the kind of torrid romances she did without having some of those feelings locked inside her. Though this was the nineteen eighties and not the eighteen eighties, Elaine hoped, foolish romantic that she was, that if the right man came along . . .

Perhaps that was Joan's problem. Perhaps her sister was waiting for the day when Mr. Right would literally ring Joan's bell and announce his presence. Elaine knew that would really be a fairy tale!

Elaine certainly had not set a good example for her sister to follow. Now that she had discovered she'd known nothing about the man she married, she was torn between grief over his death and anger at his betrayal of her trust. How could he have become involved with smugglers and thieves; even kidnappers? When had it begun? Before their marriage or after? She guessed that it was long before, since he had owned the bookstore for over three years before she met him.

She berated herself for being blind to his "business dealings." As she thought about it now, she remembered the phone calls late at night, which he had explained were from old fraternity brothers. He had always made it a point to work late on the nights when she'd done the same. She had naively believed him when he told her he arranged matters that way so they could spend their free nights together. It had sounded plausible at the time.

What kind of smuggling had he been involved in? Had he been part of the "Colombian Connection" she'd seen reported on television? Even if she did get out of this alive, would she be pursued by drug dealers, the mob, the FBI? If he had loved her, how could he expose her to such danger? Had she only been a cover for him? What purpose could he have had in mind when he married her?

Now that he was dead, she would never know the truth. She would never know if she had only been a pawn. She wanted to believe in love as much or more than Joan, but now she wasn't sure about anything.

Perhaps her near-recluse of a sister was truly wiser than she, and the risks were not worth the pain.

She watched the tall gold-and-crystal pendulum clock move its hands ever so slowly.

Elaine was more worried about Joan at this moment than she was about her own safety. Something told her that Joan should have been back from the airport hours ago. She wondered if Ira had any idea how much she hated him for forcing her sister to fly here and expose herself to this danger.

Had she not been worried about what the other man, Ralph, might do to Joan, Elaine would have gladly lunged across the table and slit Ira's throat with her steak knife.

Ira slammed down the ship-to-shore receiver and glared at Elaine.

"Little sister took the wrong road and that third party I told you about . . . he's tagging along."

"The man who killed my husband," Elaine said, fear and anxiety coursing down her spine.

"The *butcher* who killed your husband. A very powerful man with his own private army to back him up. Whether he calls himself Dr. Zolo, 'Minister of Antiquities,' or Colonel Zolo, deputy commander of the Secret Police, he's still just a butcher. And right now Joan Wilder is New York sirloin," Ira said as he plunged his knife into Elaine's unfinished steak. "I certainly hope that girl learns to get her ass in gear."

Ira tossed the steak through the porthole to the snapping, yellow-striped king crocodile below.

Chapter Seven

A COLOMBIAN "RAINSHOWER," Joan found, was equal in a gallons-per-minute ratio to the Johnstown flood. She knew he was somewhere in front of her, even though she could not see or hear him. Somehow she just sensed his presence, she told herself, not wanting to admit to wishful thinking. She was completely drenched, her shoes were ruined, and her suitcase was caked with mud. She thought that at any moment her arm would fall off from its weight.

Jack paused in the road and watched as Joan struggled vainly toward him.

"Y'got any valuables in that suitcase?" he called over the rain.

"No. Well . . . my things . . . my clothes."

"Y'got a raincoat?"

"No."

"How 'bout a comfortable pair of walking shoes?"

"No, I . . . these are the only ones I brought," she said, swallowing a mouthful of rain with her statement.

"Uh-huh," he said, eyeing her again. He sighed. "Okay."

Jack walked over to her and smiled. He offered to take her suitcase and Joan gladly accepted. He patted her shoulder comfortingly, and then promptly walked away from her and flung the suitcase far into the underbrush.

"Now maybe we can make some time together," he said and walked on.

Joan was astounded and had to consciously shut her gaping mouth. The bastard! she thought. She couldn't decide whether to beat him with a string of obscenities or with her fists.

Joan had taken one step forward, when suddenly the ground beneath her feet gave way and swallowed her up! A terrified scream roller-coastered out of her throat. In less than a second Joan had vanished.

Jack heard the scream, glanced over at the mountain behind him and then looked down at his feet. A crack in the earth zigzagged around his feet.

"Sonuva—" And Jack vanished too.

Head over heels, Joan tumbled down the landslide, rocks, mud, and debris forming a waterfall around her. Her mouth was caked with dirt, her only screams were voiceless ones. As she careened around a curve for an instant, she spied her "savior" rolling like a sledless racer behind her. Joan knew without a doubt that she was falling straight into hell. She could see nothing around her but rock and mud. She struck her head on a falling boulder, but jerked away quickly and avoided serious damage. Frantically she tried to grab on to something to stop her downward plunge, but there was nothing to save her. The force of the slide plummeted her down farther and farther. It was like drowning in a powerful undertow, she thought, but she knew she was not being carried out to sea. She was going to be buried alive!

She felt her clothes being ripped as if a thousand tiny razors were slashing at the fabric. Her arms would flail out and then a mass of mud would shove them over her head. It felt as if her legs were being ripped from her hip sockets. She tried to steer herself so that she took most of the slide on her back, but it was no use. One moment she was on her stomach, her legs behind her, and the next she was rolling sideways in a ball.

She almost gave in to hysteria, but she thought about Elaine. She had to make it through this and get to Elaine. She focused her mind on a picture of her sister and when she did, the ravages of the rockslide against her body seemed to diminish.

Elaine . . . Elaine . . . her mind repeated.

Mercifully she crashed to a halt at the bottom of the mountain. Seconds later Jack tumbled on top of her.

"Whoo!" he exclaimed as he rolled off her. "This turned out to be one helluva mornin'!"

Joan was so stunned she still was not sure she wasn't dead.

"You okay?" he asked.

Joan felt heavy raindrops pelting her face, washing the mud away. When her eyes opened, she looked down at herself. Her coat was in shreds and her skirt was hanging on by a single button. She felt no pain. In fact, she felt nothing except the rain washing the dirt out of her hair and rinsing down her clothes.

"I said, are you hurt?" She looked like a zombie, lying there not moving, only staring at him with wide, glazed, green eyes.

"What'd the fall leave you—paralyzed from the neck up? Are you hurt?" He demanded, shaking her shoulders.

"No!" she screamed back at him through the dirt clogs in her mouth.

"Good!" He grabbed her hand. "Then what's your name?"

Joan glanced at his hand and wondered if he was another of those hand-shakers she despised so much.

"Joan Wilder," she answered.

"Joan Wilder," he said with a big grin, "welcome to Colombia."

Though the rain lashed at them, Zolo and Santos continued their inspection of the bus and jeep crash site. After they finally uprighted the jeep, Zolo picked through the interior and found an American yachting magazine.

"No one pulls a gun on Zolo. No Yankee. No one."

The members of Santos's policia used ropes and pulleys to shift the bus to the side of the road. Once again the road was passable.

Just then Ralph came chugging around the bend in his Renault convertible. Spying the police, their two jeeps, and Zolo, he slammed on his brakes. He waited while the policia finished their task of moving the bus and once again got into their jeeps.

Cautiously, Ralph eased his car forward. He licked his lips nervously, wondering if he would make it through this time. As he drew closer to Zolo, Ralph's nerves began to fray.

Zolo peered curiously at Ralph as he passed by. Ralph offered a weak smile and a little wave and continued up the road.

The storm clouds rolled away as suddenly as they had come. Jack laid his rain-soaked shirt over a large rock and withdrew a clean one from his backpack. He picked up the picture of his boat, which had been lying on the rock to dry.

As he stared at the picture of the yacht, he wondered if elusive dreams would always be his anathema. Jack Colton was the only son of Carol and Don Colton, who still lived in a glass-walled beach house in Malibu. Jack's father had made a fortune in real estate and his mother had worked alongside him for over forty years, encouraging and supporting him with her cheerful, optimistic viewpoint. Jack loved his parents dearly and to this day he still went home for the Christmas holidays. This past Christmas had found him with no money, and rather than admit it to his father, he told Don Colton that "business" would require his presence in Colombia. Jack promised his mother that perhaps he could plan a trip home for her birthday in May. When his mother offered to pay for his air fare, Jack knew he had not fooled them one bit. But he had his pride—which was about all he had—and with the loss of his birds he knew now he would not make it home for his mother's birthday.

Jack had lived a typically upper-middle-class adolescence, spending his summers surfing on the Pacific Ocean, riding his jeep through the dunes, and dating blond, perpetually tanned California nymphets.

Just prior to entering college, Jack experienced his first and last conflict with his parents. Carol Colton had dreamed of her son becoming a Beverly Hills plastic surgeon. Her list of reasons were endless—all typical, he supposed, of any mother who wanted only "the best" for her son. Until the day he entered UCLA and chose finance as his major, his mother kept up the battle. Finally realizing he would not change his mind, she wisely chose to drop the argument, her son of more value to her than the profession he chose.

His college years progressed uneventfully, much the same as his high school years. When he graduated he went to work in a brokerage firm in New York.

For thirteen years he dressed every morning in three-piece pinstripe suits, ate lunch at Lutèce with wealthy clients, and went to bed with a different "girl of the year." After his fourth year in New York, he found the city was losing its glitter for him. One by one the younger members of the firm's staff got married, moved to Connecticut, and became fathers. They were no longer interested in Jack's sexual exploits from the weekend before and neither was he.

It was about that time in his life that Jack realized there was something drastically askew in his goals. He had risen to the top of his firm and found the accomplishment a hollow one. He read an article on "Corporate Burn-Out" in the *Wall Street Journal* and attributed his depression to that.

The cure for "burn-out" was rest and a change of scene. Jack decided to go to Vermont and try his hand at snow-skiing. After all, how much different from surfing could it be? After perusing the travel brochures and carefully selecting an inn that would suit him best, he booked his reservations and put in for his time off at work.

When Jack visited the sporting goods department at Bloomingdale's, he found that his vacation choice was going to cost him a small fortune, for he owned not the first piece of equipment. Since he knew it would not take him long to master the sport, he purchased the highest quality skis, boots, poles, goggles, and gloves. He did not own a parka or insulated pants, so he bought a coordinating navy outfit with red and silver racing stripes down the pant leg. Since he owned only the suits he wore to work, he had not one acceptable ski sweater in his closet. For those evenings around the fire at the inn, he needed sweaters, slacks, an extra pair of doeskin hiking boots, a wool vest, and a herringbone sport jacket. With the essential accessories, wool socks, two cashmere mufflers, insulated underwear, knit caps, and face masks, his total bill came to eighteen hundred, seventy-one dollars and fifty-two cents. Blithely, Jack placed it all on his Bloomingdale's charge and did not let out the mounting groan of pain until he went outside the store.

Undaunted, Jack filled his radiator with two gallons of antifreeze and set off for Vermont. The mountains were breathtaking and he thought he had never breathed air so crisp and clean. A snow squall had passed through the night before, leaving clear, cloudless skies and three inches of perfect skier's snow.

Jack pulled up to the "charming and homey" inn where he'd made his reservations and noted that the inn did not look quite like the brochure picture. Jack had been dreaming about the kind of place he'd seen in that Bing Crosby and Fred Astaire movie he watched every year at Christmas time, *Holiday Inn*.

This inn looked as if it had seen too many holidays. The exterior paint was chipped, and the gutters and downspouts were rusted and sagging. The sidewalks had been recently shoveled but no one had put salt on the ice-caked steps.

He opened one of the etched-pane doors and walked into the lobby. The carpeting was worn and the white curtains were badly in need of laundering. Still, there was a fire burning in the fireplace. As Jack walked to the reception desk, he thought it odd that the place was not filled with tourists. He rang the bell and waited.

Four large crewel-worked wing-back chairs were grouped around the fireplace with a cherry Queen Anne coffee table in the center. At the sound of the bell, a white-haired old woman peered over at him from one of the wing-back chairs and smiled. With lumbering movements she eased herself out of the chair and walked toward him, leaning heavily on her ebony-and-ivory-handled walking stick.

"You must be Mr. Colton," she said, beaming at him with the bluest eyes he had ever seen.

"Yes, I am."

When she shook his hand he was surprised at the strength in her grip. She couldn't possibly be more than five foot tall, and though it must have taken some effort, he noticed that she carried herself with a proud straight back and square, purposeful shoulders. Though the bloom in her cheeks and the pink tint to her lips was a result of carefully applied makeup, somehow he knew that in her youth she had never relied on them.

"I was waiting for you," she said with a twinkle in her eye that was almost sensual. It surprised and delighted him.

Taken aback by her statement, he cleared his throat. "Do you have someone to help with my luggage?"

"Why, yes, but my grandson is not home from school just yet. You wouldn't mind having a cup of tea with me by the fire while we wait," she said, more of a statement than a question.

"Uh, no."

She grasped his arm in such a manner that he felt remiss in not offering it and together they walked over to the fire.

"We are very casual around here as you can see. I can't tell you how delighted I was that you accepted our invitation to stay with us."

"Pardon me?"

"I regard my patrons more as family friends, than paying customers. It makes it easier for me." She smiled at him while she poured hot steaming tea into a delicate porcelain cup. When she handed it to him the cup rattled slightly on the saucer.

"I keep telling myself old age is a state of mind, but I'm afraid it has settled mostly in my bones," she said with a laugh.

"I think you look remarkably well."

"How would you know? You don't know if I'm fifty-five or one hundred and five."

"That's true, but I wouldn't dare ask."

"Such a polite young man, you are. But I'll tell you. I'm ninety-seven years old last Tuesday."

Jack nearly choked on his tea. "That's incredible! My grandmother was sixty-eight when she died and you look much younger than she did."

"I always did love men who lie." She smiled again.

Jack knew he wouldn't be able to convince her, but he'd never been more serious in his life. Now that he was closer to her, he realized that she still had all her own teeth, her eyes contained none of the gauzy film connected with old age, and her skin was webbed only around her eyes and throat. She must have been stunning when she was young.

Just then the front door flew open and a young boy of about thirteen walked in. He slapped the wet snow off his parka and pulled off his boots, mittens, and knit hat.

"Hi, Grandma Jeannine!" he called exuberantly. The cold air had painted his cheeks and nose a bright red.

"Billy! How was school?"

"The same," he answered, and sat down in one of the chairs, reaching for a frosted cookie which sat in an epergne on the coffee table.

"This is Mr. Colton, our guest, who is planning to be with us for a whole week."

"I guessed. You need some help with that ski equipment?"

"Yes, I do, Billy."

"Well," he said, shoving the cookie into his mouth and standing again, "I guess we'd better have at it." Billy leaned down and kissed his grandmother on the cheek.

Jack excused himself and followed Billy outside where they began untying Jack's newly purchased skis from the top of his MG.

"Man! This is great stuff! I've never seen skis this fine!" Billy said, admiring the equipment.

"No kidding? You like to ski?"

"Love it! I'm practicing the slalom, and someday I'm going to be in the Winter Olympics."

"That's admirable. Do you think you could teach me how to ski?"

Bily looked at him incredulously. "You can't ski?"

Jack laughed under his breath. "I figured it can't be too difficult."

"Well, you must know something about it, cuz you got all the right stuff here!"

As they walked back inside Jack knew he would never shop anywhere but Bloomingdale's.

Snow-skiing, Jack found, was about as close to surfing as California was to Vermont. He spent the first day on the slopes "riding his ass," as Billy termed it. The sun had nearly set behind the mountains when Jack insisted on one last try. This time when he manuevered down the "bunny hill," he was successful.

With the pride of a returning conquistador who had just found the Incan treasure, he entered the inn that evening.

While Janice, the cook, prepared the evening meal, Jack sat by the fire relating his exploits to Jeannine.

In the two short days he'd been at the inn, Jack had never felt so much at home in his life. He didn't mind the fact that there was no hot water for his shower in the morning, nor that his room temperature was somewhere just slightly above freezing, for the thick down comforter kept him warm. His room was sparsely furnished but the antiques it contained, the four-poster bed and armoire, were exquisite.

He was glad there were no other guests, for that meant he had Jeannine and Billy all to himself. In the morning, Janice prepared mounds of sausages, eggs, pancakes, and maple syrup. And now, for supper, he could smell chicken frying in the kitchen.

The huge oak trestle table was laden with food when they sat down to eat. He helped Jeannine with her chair and sat next to her, Billy on her left. It was then he noticed that another place had been set.

"Are we expecting someone else? Another tourist?"

Jeannine laughed. "This time my guest really is family. Billy's sister is driving up from New York to spend the weekend with us. I'm very proud of Alecia. She is going to be a lawyer someday."

"That *is* admirable," Jack said.

"When our mother died," Billy said, "Grandma took care of us both. Grandma has been paying for Alecia's tuition for college and law school, and that's where the money for the new plumbing and paint have gone," Billy said with an accusatory glance toward Jeannine.

"Now, Billy. There was money from the insurance . . ."

"But not enough."

"I'm sure Mr. Colton is not interested in our family finances."

"Just exactly what is wrong with the plumbing?" Jack inquired.

"I'm not sure, but the plumber told me it would cost a lot of money to have it fixed."

"Would you mind if I looked at it in the morning?"

"I wouldn't hear of it!" Jeannine said as she passed the chicken to Jack.

As Jack glanced at Billy, he noticed the wink the young boy gave him. Jack winked back and knew in the morning they would be in the basement checking the plumbing.

They were halfway through dinner when Jack noticed headlights outside. "I think your granddaughter has arrived."

When the front door opened, Jack could only gape at the most beautiful woman he had ever seen. She was tall and slender with long blond hair and the same incredible blue eyes as Jeannine. Her smile filled her face as she embraced her brother and grandmother. Jack couldn't remember what he said as they were being introduced.

She doffed her double-breasted camel hair coat, brown leather high-heeled boots and matching gloves. She wore a white angora sweater and apricot wool slacks.

Jack sat across the table from Alecia, listening to her chat with her grandmother, thinking he'd died and gone to heaven. There was a glow about her face that he refused to admit was due to firelight playing with the wispy angora of her sweater.

After Billy went to bed and Jeannine had retired for the night, Jack entreated Alecia to have one last glass of brandy with him. They talked for over an hour about the mountains, the history behind the old inn, and their lives in New York. When Jack said good night and went to his room he knew that he was in love.

Jack's stay at the inn found him not only learning to ski with skill equal to amateur-rank status, for he was glad he could ski standing up rather than sliding down the mountain; but he also patched holes in several pipes, fixed two leaky faucets, and repaired the hot water heater. He regulated the thermostat on the furnace and tied up the sagging gutters. On the sly he went to town and hired a man who agreed to paint the inn in the spring and send him the bill. He spent the rest of his time trying to get into Alecia's bed, but he never succeeded.

It was true what they said about love, for he was doing the craziest things.

After the weekend, Alecia went back to New York and Jack remained on for the last two days of his vacation. He was counting the minutes until he returned to the city and could see her again.

When he left the Vermont inn, he left his skis, boots, and poles with Billy, who promised to practice even harder for the Olympics. He hugged Jeannine and kissed her. When he walked to his car, turned, and took one last look at the old woman standing with her shawl around her strong shoulders and leaning on her cane, he went back and hugged her once again.

"I'll be back," he said.

"I'll live for that day." She smiled and again he was unnerved by the sensuality she emanated.

For six months, he and Alecia dated on weekends when she was not working as a paralegal or going to school. Every Friday she met him at his apartment, bathed, dressed, and ready to go out. They went to the theater and dinner; they danced at every discotheque in Manhattan, and when they returned to his apartment they made love until well into the night.

Twice in March, once in April, and three times in May they traveled to Vermont to visit Jeannine and Billy. All six of their trips had been at Jack's insistence, not Alecia's. In May, Jack had the excuse that he was supervising the painting of the inn. He didn't tell Alecia that the painter had finished sooner than expected and so he hired him to put a fresh coat of paint on the interior. The color selection he left to Jeannine, who was ecstatic over her "redecorating" projects.

The first weekend in June, the painting was complete, Jack proposed to Alecia, and Jeannine died in her sleep.

After the funeral Alecia remained in Vermont while the will was read and the inn was put up for sale. When she returned to New York, Alecia had changed.

She now insisted that they attend the parties she had been invited to by the other attorneys in her office. She wanted to meet "all the right people," and she pushed Jack to be more sociable when all he wanted was to stay at home and cuddle with her in front of the TV.

As the months passed, Jack began to realize that something was missing in his relationship with Alecia. For a long time he had fooled himself, thinking that he had been satisfied with their lovemaking, when in actuality he had been left with an inexplicable loneliness. The tension between them mounted and they fought constantly. The day that Alecia gave him back his ring and told him that they wanted different things out of life, he was relieved.

It was not until a year to the day that he'd first gone to Vermont that he realized that he had fallen in love all right, but it had been with Jeannine and not Alecia. He was now convinced that modern girls lacked a certain compassion that he'd found compelling in someone like Jeannine. Whether it was depth of character or a zest for life, he was not sure, but he knew he would never find it again.

Jack saw Alecia every once in a while when he would go to her apartment to see Billy. He and Billy continued to ski in Vermont and even took a couple trips to Colorado. A year or two later Alecia married a noted attorney from Los Angeles and Billy moved to California with her. Jack gave Billy his parents' number and address in case he couldn't get in touch with him in New York and needed him.

Jack missed Billy tremendously and when his friends at work asked him why he'd lost his enthusiasm for skiing, he told them he had injured his knee on one of the slopes at Vail. He joked about his lack of coordination and no one ever guessed the truth.

With his life boiled down to his work and an occasional weekend with married friends who were constantly trying to match him up with a single cousin or in-law, Jack knew the time for a major change had come. He wanted a challenge and adventure. He wanted to *live*.

He sublet his apartment, sold his car and three-piece suits, and set out for South America.

It had seemed a good idea at the time, but after having lived in the wilderness and impoverished towns for the past three years, Jack longed once again for the luxuries in life. It hadn't taken long to deplete his savings, since his main source of income—the sale of wild, exotic birds he captured—was equal only to two months' pay in the States.

He knew he could never go back to the headache of Wall Street again, but there still was something out of sinc in his life. He looked down at the picture again. This yacht would give him the challenge of pitting himself against nature, which would stimulate and thrill him and at the same time afford him luxurious quarters in which to live. It was the perfect melding of his needs. And it was about as attainable as finding buried treasure.

Dolefully he folded the picture and put it away. He looked around for Joan but did not see her. Where had she gone to now? Women had always caused him one kind of trouble or another, but this one was a real pain in the ass. He stood and began searching for her. Just then he heard a crashing noise coming from behind some trees.

She was leaning over, and with a concerned look on his face he asked, "What's the matter? Are you sick?"

"I lost my laundry key."

"What?"

"The key to my laundry room. I dropped it."

"Are you outta your mind? Nature just did your goddam laundry!"

Jack pointed to the rocks where their clothes and her shoes were drying in the sun. He stalked over to the rock and pulled out the machete that he carried in a sheath on his belt. He firmly grasped one of her shoes and with lightning-quick speed, hacked off half the heel. With another similar swipe, he did the same to the mate.

Joan was horrified, watching him butcher her shoes so ruthlessly.

"Those were Italian!" she cried.

"Now they're practical."

Joan stumbled to her feet, holding her skirt up about her. What kind of maniac was he, she thought as he advanced toward her, machete in hand. She started to back away from him, but he grabbed her arm and held her steady. With a quick, clean cut, he ripped her skirt off and then tied it sarong-style around her hips.

As he tucked the ends of the knot inside the sarong, she felt his rough hands slide against her abdomen. She kept her head down and watched as his hands moved languorously across her abdomen. The muscles beneath her skin moved out to meet his touch as if they had a mind of their own. His fingers delved deeper as they secured the knot ends. Then slowly and deliciously, they tugged on the cloth to test its security. One of his hands rested on her hip, but only momentarily, causing a blush to rise to her cheeks. She dared not look into his eyes, afraid more of what he might read in her face than what she would see in his. It took every ounce of control she had to remain motionless and pretend that nothing was happening to her. She liked the possessive feel of his hands and fingers on her body and the thought unnerved her more than she cared to admit. When he had finished his task and turned away from her, she told herself the tingle she felt was due to hunger.

"Is nothing I own sacred to you?"

"Only your three hundred seventy-five dollars."

Jack turned his back on her and started away.

Joan glared at him, her green eyes seething with anger. Her appraisal of him had been accurate. He *was* a bastard!

Joan picked up one of her shoes and sat down. That instant six bullets ripped into the tree directly behind the place where her head had been not a second ago!

Jack dived forward and flew into Joan. The force of his body against hers sent them both rolling behind a boulder. After a second to catch his breath, Jack peeked over the rim of the rock.

At the edge of the road were six policia and the obese Santos. Another round of shots rang through the air and zinged off the edge of the boulder.

Jack ducked again.

"Cops? What the hell do they want! I haven't even done anything . . . lately."

Jack reached around the side of the boulder and retrieved his backpack before another volley of shots could hit him, and withdrew his binoculars.

Joan was nearly ecstatic at the mention of the police.

"Police? Thank God! They'll get me to a phone."

Jack wrestled with the binoculars and finally focused them. Standing inside one of the jeeps, peering down at them was . . . Zolo.

Jack did not notice Joan raising her hands over her head as if in surrender and starting to stand. Suddenly another round of bullets was fired. Jack tackled his feebleminded benefactress, this time blaming himself for agreeing to their bargain. He didn't need three hundred seventy-five dollars this bad!

"Goddamm it! *Stay down!* Don't blink, don't breathe unless I tell you to."

Joan nodded.

"The guy who was after you from the bus . . . he's up there . . . he's a cop! I was shootin' at a cop!"

Was there no one who could save her now? They were doomed, she knew. Her eyes were as wide as saucers as a continuous barrage of fire commenced.

Jack ran his hand through his dark hair, trying to

understand the lunacy that surrounded him. He stared at Joan, her shredded Bergdorf blouse matted against her skin. His brain clicked.

"It's you! He was tracking you! Who the hell *are* you?"

"I'm a romance novelist."

"What the hell are you doing here?"

"I told you! My sister's . . . life depends on me!"

"Don't gimme that shit. I thought you were donating a kidney or something!"

He looked at her with such blazing anger that Joan cringed away from him. Then she noticed that everything was quiet. The police were not firing at them any longer.

Jack dared another peek through his binoculars.

"Damn!"

The policia were dropping long ropes over the side of the cliff where the landslide had begun. One by one they rappeled their way downward. Jack turned the binoculars and focused for a closer look. Not only were the police carrying machetes, but the latest in rapid-firing rifles. He knew from the way their backpacks sagged at the bottom that to the man they were overloaded with ammunition. He wondered if they could outrun the police long enough to make such provisions necessary.

The two jeeps that remained on the top of the road were manned by one policeman each. Just as Santos and his men reached the bottom of the cliff, the two jeeps backed up and then raced away. Instinctively Jack knew they were going for reinforcements.

Zolo was the last of the men to reach the bottom and the four policemen and the overweight Santos awaited his orders.

Jack dropped his binoculars and looked at his companion whom he now viewed as the green-eyed angel of death.

"If you could try on the shoes now, it would be a big help."

Taking no time to comment on his sarcasm, Joan quickly placed her mutilated Italian shoes on her feet.

Jack jumped to his feet, grabbing his rifle and backpack in the process. He turned for an instant and fired a round of bullets at the advancing policia. Joan dashed after him, leaving the clearing behind. Just as they plunged into the cover of the jungle, a rain of bullets pelted the ground they had left only seconds ago.

As they charged through the trees, branches slapped against Joan's face. She tried to duck out of the way, but the growth was thick and dense. The sleeve of her blouse caught on a limb that savagely ripped the delicate fabric. It seemed light years before she managed to disentangle herself. At one point she thought their pursuers had caught up to them, for she felt her hair being grabbed from behind. Her arm flew up to her head and she yanked on a light brown lock that had become entangled in a prickly vine. As she pulled away, she declared the vine the victor, for it retained nearly half a handful of Joan's hair.

The undergrowth became denser. Jack slung his rifle over his shoulder and withdrew his machete. Joan could hear his mumbled curses, but she said nothing. With clean true slices, Jack cleared his way through the vines and tree limbs. Fear spurred him on as his arm whipped through the underbrush with lightning speed.

Joan caught her ankle in a vine that held her in a viselike grip. Every time she twisted her foot to gain freedom, the thorns cut into her skin. She had no knife to cut through its thorny stem, so she methodically sawed it with her thumbnail. When she finally escaped from her botanic imprisoner, she could not find her "savior."

In a panic she looked around, stumbled again and moved toward the ringing sound of his machete.

"Wait!" she cried, out of breath.

"The deal's off, lady!"

Zolo, Santos and four of his men finally arrived at the clearing. Zolo took note of the clothes still drying on the rock. Since he had not seen which way the Wilder woman and her companion had entered the jungle, he instructed the men to circle the area looking for clues.

Zolo tapped his foot on the ground and slammed his gloved fist into the palm of his right hand. He was impatient to kill.

Each of the men took a different direction. After what Zolo claimed as wasted precious time, one of the men returned with a piece of a woman's blouse.

Zolo called in the men and they proceeded into the jungle with machetes drawn, ready to slice away at vegetation and humans alike.

Chapter Eight

LIKE RED-HOT POKERS, the sun brandished its rays on Joan's back. The tropical jungle at midday was like a Turkish steam bath as she followed him. Her arms and legs were scratched from the vines and underbrush. There was a low-growing palm indigenous to the region whose fronds could cut through human skin like razor blades, he told her. He needn't have bothered, for the dark green plant had already introduced itself to Joan, and her left knee wore a deep slit to remind her of the encounter. Joan tore off a piece of her blouse to bind the wound and stop the bleeding. Her minor medical emergency nearly separated her from him—permanently.

She thought she had been quick and efficient when she had knelt to wind the silk around her knee, but when she looked up she could not find him at all. She didn't dare call out to him, afraid she would announce their location to the policia. The jungle was so dense she was barely able to distinguish telltale signs of the path he'd hacked away with his machete. For a moment she wondered if he had left her on purpose. As she examined the plants more closely, she found his markings, followed them, and caught up to him. But the incident taught her to be much quicker and never to lose sight of him.

For the first time in her life, Joan found herself hating the role she played of the dependent person. She had always been dependent on someone. First her parents, then Elaine, and now him! Then she decided it was not dependency she hated, *just him*. She liked him even less than the predicament she had stumbled into. The situation couldn't be helped when one looked at it realistically, logically. Things just happened sometimes. *He* on the other hand was a different matter.

She knew he was none too thrilled with the situation she had unwittingy involved him in, and he was cruel and self-centered enough to let her die in the jungle, too, if it meant saving his own skin. Joan had analyzed him enough by now to know that he was no savior, only a soldier of fortune, a mercenary. As long as he got paid, he wouldn't give a flying damn what happened to her or to Elaine.

He was like all men, out for what he could get. She was lucky she had pegged his number this early in the game, before it was too late.

Just then she heard the ringing of machetes. The policia were gaining on them! She could not tell from the noise the direction they were coming from. It didn't matter. Nothing mattered now, because the policia—if they *were* lawmen—could move faster.

She wondered if Jack knew where they were going. Until now she had assumed that because he lived in this country he had some destination in mind. What if they just hacked themselves around in a circle for days? They could starve to death out here with no food and no water!

She would have to tell him about her nervous condition and explain she could not withstand pressures like this. But she was no delicate Southern magnolia, afraid of her own shadow, either. She could hold her own! After all, he was no better than she, even if he thought so. She was determined to prove that to him.

Jack could hear her stumbling a few paces behind him. The jungle was like a blast furnace, he thought as he hacked away at a thick vine and sweat poured down his face, a small relief from the heat. The muscles in Jack's arm ached and were knotted from the constant tension. He had news for his buddies back home: a day in the jungle could do more for their physique than a year at Vic Tanny's gym.

He was beginning to think the machete was permanently fused to his hand. He didn't dare flex his fingers for fear he would lose his grip, and every swipe at the limbs and vegetation was crucial. He developed a rhythm of raising his arm, aiming for three-quarter cuts, then following through with a backhand hack, using his left hand to clear away the chopped limbs. He could not afford to miss even one cut, for every inch of pathway he carved in the jungle kept him from death. He tried not to think of the consequences should the policia overtake them.

He made a mental note that when he returned to civilization he would become celibate. One thing this "expedition" had taught him was never to come within two hundred yards of a woman again. If they weren't trying to break your heart or take your money, they were after your ass—literally. He didn't know who he wanted to get away from more, the policia or Joan Wilder.

He could hear her sharp intakes of breath whenever a branch slapped her in the face or she stumbled. But she was still trailing him like a Baskerville hound.

He wanted to believe that if he got rid of her, the policia would leave him alone, but he knew better. They wanted his hide just as much as hers. Damn her! He still couldn't believe he'd walked down off that mountain and started blasting away at a cop! He'd done some pretty wild things in his life, but he must have lost his mind to do something that stupid. But how could he have known? All he'd seen was a crashed bus, a nice-looking lady sitting on a suitcase and a sinister-looking character pointing a gun at her head. It seemed the right thing to do at the time. Skirts!

"Y'know what I like about you?" he said, glancing back at her.

"What?"

"Nothing! What'd you do, wake up this morning

and say, 'Today I'm gonna ruin a man's life'?"

Joan glared at him and he shot her a cruel look. He was about to say something else, when he heard men shouting at one another. Their echoes seemed to surround them. Jack doubled his efforts, slicing into the growth with long, arclike movements.The ring of whizzing machetes sent shivers down his spine. The policia were moving in closer.

The undergrowth began to thin somewhat and Jack took off running. Joan followed as best she could.

"I didn't park your jeep in the middle of the road!" she yelled at him in self-defense.

"You were bad news comin' my way!"

Jack looked back over his shoulder and saw glints of silver flash through the dense greenery. Up and down they swooped, their eerie ring zinging through the air. Slicing faster and faster, the police were gaining ground.

Sweat was running down Jack's face in rivulets and he could barely see. He wiped his eyes with his shirt sleeve, and stumbled. Precious seconds were lost. He got up and raced on, listening to the machetes' ring grow louder in his ears. A weaker man would have succumbed to fear, but not Jack. He was petrified!

"You know where you're going?" Joan asked, trying to be nonchalant and yet fearing his answer.

"I dunno! It's some kinda trail, isn't it?"

As the sound of the machetes grew louder, Jack knew that their pursuers must be using a knife in each hand, now making even better time.

A tall thicket impaired Jack's forward thrust, so he sliced at it with more aggressive swipes. Suddenly he came to an abrupt halt and threw his arm out sideways just in time to stop Joan.

Joan's eyes tripled in size as she looked over his arm and down a seventy-foot drop to a wildly raging river below.

"Lady, you are a jinx."

"But there's a bridge."

The sides of the cliff were covered in a gnarly growth and a few feet off to the left of them was a rickety, vine-covered bridge. Even when newly constructed it probably hadn't had the strength to hold any more than two underfed Indians at any given time. The bridge was rotten from wind, rain, and sun, and the majority of its boards were missing or broken in half.

"That's not a bridge," he said, "that's pre-Columbian art."

Jack pulled out his rifle and reloaded. He knelt behind a tree trunk, trying to spot the exact position of the policia. He listened to the undergrowth and thicket being trampled and thrashed. In seconds they would be on him. His only chance was to pick them off one by one. He'd never been so unsure about his markmanship as he was at that instant.

"I only wish I knew what I was dying for."

Joan refused to die by gunshot or by any other means until she was very old. And she was bound and determined not to stand there and wait for the fatal bullet to hit her and end it all. Carefully she manuevered herself across the woven wall of vines to the bridge. Tentatively she stepped out onto the first board. It groaned under her weight, but mercifully it held.

Jack was still aiming his rifle in the direction of the silver flashing machetes. He was shaking his head, bemoaning his fate.

"Why don't we listen to our mothers . . ."

Joan had worked her way across almost a third of the bridge. This was suicide! She wondered which was worse, being killed by a gun or by falling into the craggy rocks and violent waters below. She watched as the boards behind her fell off and went scurrying down into the river where they were mutilated by the impact. She cringed at the thought that she could be the next thing to fall off the bridge. She had been afraid before when they were running in the jungle, but this was terror!

Jack peeked over the tree trunk. The machetes were very close now. He was still mumbling to himself.

"Coulda been a cosmetic surgeon by now. Five hundred thousand a year—knee deep in tits and ass . . ."

Jack raised the rifle and cocked it, preparing to fire.

"Playmates of the year comin' and goin' . . . But no. I'm here with a romance novelist. I hope you've been keepin' notes, lady," he mumbled, " 'cause you got a real live death scene going on right here."

Oblivious to Jack, Joan took another tentative

step. Then another. She placed her foot on the next board. She was praying. Then suddenly . . . *snap!*

Jack turned just in time to see the board give way and go tumbling into the river. In a panic Joan clutched at the vine on the side of the bridge. He watched with a gasp as she swung out over the gorge. She held firmly to the vine with both hands, raised her knees up to her chest and, in a swing worthy of Tarzan himself, cleared the dangerous gorge and aimed for the far cliff. She went crashing through a wall of vegetation and landed safely on the other side.

Jack was astounded at not only her daring but the agility with which she moved. He glanced once more at the silver flashes coming toward him through the jungle. He adjusted his backpack and slung his rifle over his shoulder and tightened the strap.

She had found a way out and was successful. There was no reason to think he couldn't do the same. He'd be damned if some broad was going to show him up! He reached out and grabbed a vine. He gave it a strong tug to test it and it held. He moved backward, knowing he would need whatever speed he could pick up to make the leap. He positioned himself, and just as he started to take the first step, the vine fell.

He looked at it lying in his hands like a limp noodle. "Shit."

He dropped it immediately and glanced backward over his shoulder. He groaned. He could see a machete not fifteen feet away.

Quickly he grabbed another vine, tested it with an even stronger tug. He knew this one would hold. Even if it didn't, either way he was a dead man.

He got in three good running steps before he took the leap. He held onto the vine with a strong grip but try as he would he could not bring his knees up like Joan did. His backpack and rifle were weighing him down. In a clean swift sail he cleared the gorge.

Not until he was over halfway across did Jack realize that his vine was too long. His eyes widened in terror. He tried again to pull his legs up but failed. The wall of the cliff was coming closer. With a thud he smacked into the wall.

Jack looked up and saw the lip of the cliff only eighteen inches away. He scrambled for hand and toe holds in the rock and, securing himself, he dropped the vine. Holding on for his life with one hand and one foot he tried to dig into the rock with his free hand. He felt his rifle slipping, but he didn't dare try to fasten the buckle on the rifle strap that was becoming unloosened.

His voice was hoarse as he leaned his head back to call her. "Joan? Joan?"

Still tangled in the wall of vegetation, Joan was in shock. Her knees were scraped and bleeding, her hands had been burned by the vine; her palms a mass of cuts, blood, and raw flesh. Her eyes bulged out of her head. She couldn't remember where she was or why she was in such pain. She ached all over and her head pounded. She kept staring at her hands and tears streamed down her face.

Then she remembered him. She was certain she had heard a man scream. That must have been when the policia caught up to him and cut of his head with one of their menacing machetes. She was alone now with no one to protect her or save her but herself. She would be safe on this side of the river . . . for a while.

She was trembling uncontrollably. She must do something to calm herself. That little bottle of brandy she'd taken from the plane! If ever she needed a drink it was now. She still carried her shoulder-strap purse, which had come through the ordeal virtually unscathed. Shows what paying for quality will get you, she thought, knowing now she was nearly hysterical. She fumbled through her purse and found the precious bottle.

Her hands were shaking and painful as she tried to untwist the cap. Absorbed in her duel with the cap, Joan was unaware of Jack's dilemma.

Jack was inching his way upward when the buckle gave way and his rifle fell into the river. Jack steadied himself and looked down in time to see the rifle crash onto the rock and break into a hundred pieces. In less than three seconds, the torrential river washed it away.

Doubling his efforts, Jack clawed at the rock and successfully grasped the edge of the cliff with his right hand. Carefully, he dug his foot into another toe hold. Jaw clenched and muscles straining, Jack succeeded in pulling himself up and then reached his left arm up to the cliff's edge. Pulling and clutching he eased his body upward until he had a firm grasp on level land.

As he looked straight ahead into the thicket, he realized he could not see Joan and he'd not heard her either. Perhaps she had died in the fall.

"Joan . . ." His voice was raspy and it was all he could do to barely whisper her name.

He manuevered his body onto flat ground and took a deep breath. He massaged his legs, thinking he might never be able to stand up again, the muscles were so tense. Once the leg cramps eased, he took one last look at the deadly river below and then broke through the thicket in front of him.

When he saw Joan sitting on the ground wrestling with a tiny bottle of brandy, he stalked toward her and grabbed the container.

"Liquor?!" he yelled and lobbed it high and away into the trees. "I coulda been killed!"

Before Joan could answer his uncalled-for tirade, two bullets zinged the ground in front of them. On instinct Jack dived for cover into the jungle and Joan followed him.

Chapter Nine

It was the roar of rushing water that caused Santos to hesitate before plunging into the last thicket. Zolo, certain that he had caught the Americans and thirsty for their blood, came rushing through the underbrush and nearly fell to his death. Santos grabbed his arm just in time to jerk his superior officer back toward safer ground.

Zolo did not thank him, only peered at the tempestuous river and jagged rocks below. Thinking that the jungle had cheated him out of his revenge, his temper boiled and he cursed at the men and shook his fist at the river.

Zolo called for his binoculars and searched the waters for any sign of bodies. Passing over the rockstrewn area below, he focused his binoculars for a closer look. Teetering on the edge of one of the rocks was the barrel of a rifle. He scanned the area a bit longer but found nothing else. Experience told him he should have found something, a last clue.

Santos indicated the bridge and suggested that

they had fallen from the bridge but Zolo stated that their weight would have caused the entire structure to collapse. It was agreed that it was impassable now, but he disagreed with Santos that they had fallen in the river.

He turned his attention to the cliff across the gorge from them and spotted a dangling vine. It was improbable—but possible. The Americans were more courageous than he would have believed if they had escaped him by using the vines.

He scanned the area where the vegetation was thickest. For an instant he was certain he saw something—a flash of clothing. He continued his search and was rewarded with a clear but momentary view of the American man.

He called one of the men over, reloaded his rifle, and aimed. He pumped off two bullets in the exact direction of where he had spotted the American. He jerked the binoculars up to his eyes once more and found he had missed.

He ground his jaw and his eyes were white-hot with anger when he looked at Santos.

"I know another way around," Santos said.

Santos signaled his men, and the small band of policia followed him along the edge of the gorge.

Joan wouldn't have dreamed it was possible, but this part of the jungle was even more dense and foreboding than the area they had crossed on the other side of the river. To make matters worse, it had begun to rain and it was the strangest rainfall she'd ever seen. When the raindrops hit the sun-baked treetops, they sizzled, creating a rising cloud of steam around them.

Insects swarmed around her and she knew she was losing precious time swatting at them. There must have been a hundred different species of mosquito whose target was Joan Wilder. Flies, gnats, and moths darted around her face and flew into her eyes and mouth; she could feel them crawling in her hair and on her neck.

The rain shower seemed to invigorate the jungle, causing limbs and vegetation to reach out and grab at her clothes. Her sarong offered little protection against the onslaught, and her thighs bore a hundred tiny scratches.

She was more frightened now than she'd been before, since she now knew that Jack had no destination in mind. They were running away from the policia, but into what?

She heard the mating calls of the cockatoo and toucan and parrot that Jack would sometimes identify for her. She asked him about the other animal sounds she heard, but he told her it was her imagination. She was convinced he was lying. She hadn't gone crazy—at least, not yet. She was certain she had heard a low groaning that sounded like a dying horse.

Then at other times she thought she heard something like a lion growling and then later, a laughing hyena. Jack told her there were no such animals in Colombia. All the same, she could never be sure. Something was out there.

By late afternoon the rain had stopped and the terrain had become less dense. Jack found it easier to plow through the jungle as he called on the last of his physical reserve and slung his machete with renewed effort. He could still hear Joan behind him, her panting and footfalls a comfort now—he wanted to know that she was near, that way he wouldn't lose any time because of her ineptitude.

For over an hour Jack hacked away at the vegetation, pushing himself and Joan to their limits. Breathless and exhausted, he found he could not move another inch and sank to the ground. Sweat poured from his forehead and his shirt was soaked. His knee still ached from his crash against the rocky cliff by the river and as he rubbed it he thought of Joan's callous indifference to his plight. She was a coldhearted bitch who thought only about herself first, last, and always. Women like her made him glad he left the city and lived in the wilderness!

Joan had caught up with him and when she saw him sitting on the ground, she almost wanted to kiss him, she was so grateful for the rest. She sank to her knees knowing they couldn't rest for long. But one moment, one blessed moment, was all she wanted.

The instant Joan sat down, Jack rose and went back to his work. She hung her head resolutely, took a deep breath, and followed him as they headed further into the jungle.

By dusk they had reached the lower riverbank.

Jack was standing on the river's edge, watching the last moment of the sun. It was a magnificent sunset, the red ball of fire being swallowed by the mountains. The skies turned from red-gold to deep purples, lavenders, and mauves. White clouds streaked across the horizon, creating a filmy curtain. A flock of exotic birds feeding in the water soared into formation, giving benediction to the end of the day. He thought it almost worth their arduous trek through the jungle just to watch the color display.

Joan, out of breath, came dragging up behind Jack and collapsed at his feet. He glanced down at her.

"You can wash in the river. I'll be upstream."

If she had any energy she would have cursed him for being so callous. God! Did the man possess a heart at all? How was it that he was able to stand when she could barely crawl? She wondered if he'd found some magical potion from a South American witch doctor that gave him his strength. If she could only find the recipe, she could publish it and make a fortune!

She had to admit the waters looked cool and inviting. It was that nebulous time of day when the moon is indefinite about its cue to enter and the sun is reluctant to exit. Their shafts of half-light, one silver and one gold, cast an eerie twilight over the jungle.

Joan watched as a flock of small white birds took to the trees high above her on the mountain. She was mesmerized by the rippling water and the different colors of light as they pirouetted across the river's surface. As she untied her sarong, she remembered the touch of his hands when he'd placed the skirt around her hips and allowed his fingers to explore her soft skin.

Once again she experienced that tingle deep in her stomach that caused those same chills to course down her thighs and legs. She shivered and rubbed her arms.

Joan knew she was reacting sexually to him, though he had not given any indication, other than that one momentary encounter, that he was attracted to her. In fact, he'd spent most of the time trying to ditch her in the jungle. Every time she caught up to him, he had a look of disappointment on his face. How was it then that her body was winning out over her mind in sexual matters? She wondered if she was becoming oversexed now that she was getting older. She'd read an article in *Cosmopolitan* that stated that most women reached their sexual peak in their thirties. It relieved her to know she had something to look forward to! Elaine had often teased her that she had a sexually repressed psyche, and Joan wondered now if perhaps she hadn't been right.

If that were true, then what explanation did she have for her reaction to *him*. Joan kept telling herself it was only a common human reaction to a stressful situation. Perhaps *Psychology Today* could phrase it better and use snappier jargon, but it was an answer that satisfied her.

Looking once more at the river as it sensuously undulated its waters around the curving banks, she decided not to shed her blouse, panties, and shoes. She didn't fear wild animals as much at this moment as she did her own feelings.

Tentatively, she entered the water and was surprised that it was not cold. She ventured in further, marveling at its warm, almost bathwater temperature. The river was clean and clear, and though moonlight was the only illumination, Joan could see the river bottom. Tiny red, blue, gold, and green tropical fish swam in schools and darted round her legs. She giggled when they nibbled at her toes, and when she wiggled them, the fish bolted away.

A soft breeze wafted through the trees, tickling their branches and causing the palms to sway. Joan let the balmy night seep into every pore as she inhaled the perfumes of jasmine, orchid, and wild flowers, and listened to the birds coo to their mates. The warm water beckoned to her. Joan relented to the jungle's sultry onslaught to her senses and discarded her shoes, blouse, and panties, piling them on the riverbank.

Angelina would have approved of her, she thought as she luxuriated in the warm water. She dived underwater and darted just below the surface, then quickly spun around when she narrowly missed a big rock. She floated on her back, staring up at the stars and the moon.

How many times had she written about a scene just like this and never known, really known, what it was like to swim in a river like this—naked! She'd missed so much in her life, but there were other things she certainly preferred to being stranded in the wilds of a South American jungle!

Still, she could not resist immersing herself in this moment of solitude and peace.

She did not think about Elaine and the fact that some kidnapper was probably holding a knife to her throat at this very moment. She did not think about the policia and the crazed maniac who was after her map. Instead, she reveled in the natural wonders about her and the mystical Colombian night.

She stood in the middle of the river, leaned her head back, and rinsed her hair in the crystal waters. What she wouldn't give for a bar of soap! She washed herself as best she could, wondering if *he* didn't have some shampoo or soap tucked away in his backpack. Still, she was grateful for the river water and rinsed her hair once again.

Jack walked along the riverbank. Suddenly his eyes were drawn to the spot where she stood by the river. She look incredible in the moonglow, he thought. He stared at the water droplets that glistened on her eyelashes and in her hair. The water ran in silver streams down her neck and between her breasts. He clenched and unclenched his fists, his hands eager to reach out and touch her breasts. He wanted to massage and caress their voluptuousness. As he felt his mouth go dry, he forced himself to remember the trouble she had caused: the loss of his Land Rover and his birds—his only income.

He tried not to get lost in the depths of her jade-green eyes and pretended not to notice how her hair glistened and fell into a dark veil down her back. He told himself her skin was not *that* creamy, nor her lips *that* sensual; but he didn't believe himself.

How was it possible for a prim-looking, reclusive-type woman to become this alluring and beautiful? He'd lived too long in the jungle to blame it on the surroundings. No, he wasn't stupid—he may have been blind before not to see it—but he wasn't stupid. Standing this close to Joan Wilder he could definitely attest to the fact that she was *the* most sensual woman he'd ever met.

Her sensual appeal was more than just the way she parted her lips, as if she wanted to say something but was only able to draw in a breath; or the way her thickly lashed eyes would lower and then take agonizingly long, languorous moments to come up to him again. He nearly succumbed to the smile that fluttered on her lips, teasing him with the promise, and then ultimately rescinding the offer and dashing his hopes.

How much of her was the coy flirt, the kind of woman he'd known all his life? He peered deeply into her eyes and found not a trace of insincerity. She wanted him as much as he wanted her, but something held them both back and it made no sense to him. Physical attraction was physical attraction, lust was lust. Nothing had ever stopped him before; why suddenly should anything be different?

Just what was her game, he wondered, and then he realized that Joan *was different*. She was not one of his Manhattan ladies more interested in his position in the corporation than in Jack Colton. Nor was she one of the Colombian natives who saw him as a ticket out of Colombia to the United States. There was something other than her physical attributes that appealed to him, which conflicted with his opinion that she was a coldhearted bitch. The moonlight must have dulled his perceptive powers, because she couldn't be both. Getting to know her better would be a challenge, he hoped a rewarding one.

Joan was suddenly aware that she was no longer alone. Jack was staring at her. "I thought you said you were going upstream," she snapped.

"What? In that water? I wouldn't go in that water if you paid me."

Joan knew he was teasing her, but she found herself uncomfortable and twitchy. She kept trying to see beneath the surface of the water. "If you don't mind, I'd like to get out now. I'm starting to get cold. Please turn around." She could hardly bear to imagine what might be lurking in the water. "I don't think I'm alone in here."

Jack turned away and began arranging some palm fronds he'd been carrying over a framework of vines.

Joan snatched up the clothes which she had stretched out to dry on some nearby ferns and ducked behind a tree to try to get dressed in what little privacy the narrow tree afforded. She was unable to convince herself that it hid her from his view, so she dressed as quickly as possible. Pulling her blouse together, she stepped out from the tree. "How far is Cartagena?"

"A couple hundred miles," he said nonchalantly.

"Oh, God. We really are in the middle of nowhere." She worked to secure the fastener on her still-damp skirt. As she fumbled with it, she realized that Jack was removing his shirt, though he left on his trousers and T-shirt.

He felt her eyes on him and smiled. "Well, we're in the jungle." He moved away from her to the far side of the shelter, sat down, and began to take off his boots. After removing them, he eased his body under the framework of ferns.

Joan peered at him anxiously. He really meant for her to sleep there on that rigged-up arrangement of a ground sheet and some vines. It wasn't exactly a king-sized bed, she mused. Not really room for two adults to sleep together—that is, not for two adults who weren't sleeping together.

Jack made a pillow of his shirt and backpack, lay down, and was comfortably reclining inside the sleeping bag when Joan walked up. He looked up at her and grinned. Her face was expressionless and so he yawned.

Joan looked at the bedroll and the very narrow space that would be hers. He must have read her mind, for he slid over and then patted the ground next to him.

"You really don't wanna sleep without ground cover."

Joan looked at the sheepish smile on his face and knew she needn't have worried about her lack of sexual attraction. She felt like Daniel walking into the lions' den.

"Uh-huh," she answered him.

"Joan, this isn't about sex. It's about things that crawl in the night."

She stepped back from the shelter and leaned against a tree, then slowly sank down on her heels. "I'm, uh, not actually all that tired really. Strange, isn't it?"

"Yeah," Jack said, amusement clear in his voice. "Real strange."

"Really, I'll be fine right here. This is comfortable." Desperately trying to convince herself that she was comfortable, Joan shifted her weight against the tree trunk and tried to ignore her cramping muscles and the fact that the temperature was dropping. It was especially hard to do because Jack *did* look so comfortable stretched out on the ground, sheltered by the vines, but it just didn't seem like a good idea . . . Telling herself she was drowsy, she reached out to find her purse and shoes, then screamed as something huge and fuzzy met her hand. Shrieking, she jumped to her feet, shaking her hand wildly— A black wooly centipede fell to the ground. She lunged toward Jack and the shelter.

"I'm coming!"

"You're not even breathing hard," Jack mumbled as he turned away from her.

Joan decided to pretend that she hadn't heard

him. She slipped into the protection of the vines and stretched out next to him, still clutching her purse. In a few minutes, she actually began to relax.

As though he sensed that her guard was down, Jack suddenly turned to her, and pinned her arms near her shoulders. His face loomed over hers in the darkness. His voice was very, very low: "Why don't you tell me about your sister?"

Joan struggled slightly against the pressure of his hands. "I already did," Joan answered, wondering how it was possible for a man to look at a woman like that and not become a raging sexual beast! She had always prided herself on her self-control, which was being tested to its limits, but this man could give lessons!

"Yeah. Come on, Joan. I want to know what I've gotten myself into."

"Our deal was for you to get me to a telephone," she said stubbornly. "That's all there was to it."

Jack stared at her, knowing he had to find a way to get through her barriers. He'd been aware for some time that she was hiding something, and it was time he got to the truth.

"Her husband died. I've come to . . . comfort her."

Jack was infuriated. "You expect me to believe that?"

Her gaze was steady as it met his. "It *is* the truth."

Jack stared at her, then slowly lowered his face to hers, starting to kiss her. In spite of herself, Joan turned her head away. "What are you doing?" she asked peevishly.

"Don't you trust me?"

"No." Do I? she wondered.

"You're trusting me with your life."

"I trusted the Pan Am pilot with my life, but that doesn't mean I have to sleep with him."

Jack pulled away, but she could see he was amused by her retort. "That's good," he said, "that's good." With that, he rolled onto his back and settled down again. "Well, Joan, I've gotten too old for this stuff."

Joan turned away from him, smiling. She couldn't believe what she'd said. Angelina would have been proud of her, she knew.

It took Joan less than three minutes to fall asleep. Jack knew she had been more tired than she was willing to admit. He unzipped the bag so that he could maneuver his body, and then rolled over to face her. Tiny wisps of hair around her face had begun to dry and he noticed how they curled with a natural wave. He wondered if the rest of her hair would curl that way when it dried. He had assumed her hair was straight since she'd worn it that way. He wondered what there was about women that they always wanted to reverse what nature had given them. Those with straight hair wanted curly hair and those with curly wanted straight hair. Tall women wanted to be short, short ones dreamed of being tall. Buxom women were always getting their breasts reduced . . . and . . .

His hand crept up and unzipped the bedroll, just enough for him to see her breast. He could still see her nipple through the damp silk blouse. A gusty wind blew through the area and he watched as she shivered and then moved closer to him. He smiled to himself.

What was there about her that made him think of fireplaces and wing chairs? He wished they had a campfire and that they could sit around it and talk leisurely. He wished he could wake her up and they could hold each other and give each other comfort. He wished she weren't afraid of him, but she was. There were times when he looked at her and saw real terror in her eyes. Not the kind of fear that even he felt being chased in the jungle, but something else—an unwillingness to trust.

What the hell did a guy have to do to prove himself to her? Without a doubt she was the most impossible woman to unravel. She sure as hell had him coming and going until he didn't know which end was up. One moment she was the quintessential Boston schoolmarm and the next moment she was a river goddess flaunting her sexual powers over him. She could look at him with eyes that would make iron melt and the next moment shoot him with a look that was meant to kill.

It would take a hell of a man to tame her and not go crazy in the process. Jack stifled a yawn and was finally unable to resist sleep any longer. As his lids closed for the last time he wondered if there was such a man in New York waiting for her return.

Joan woke with a start and found that he had rolled over and his hand firmly cupped her breast. She noticed that the bag had been unzipped further and wondering just how much protection an opened bedroll was against crawling "things."

His face was buried in the crook of her neck, locks of her hair wound around his neck. She navigated a turn and her face was only inches from his. He seemed as if he were asleep, but he still held her breast with a firm grasp. One by one she pried his fingers off and realized then that about the only place for his hand to go was over her hip or in between their legs. From the frying pan into the fire she thought, when suddenly . . . *snap!*

Joan glanced off to the right in time to see lights flickering in the trees. Like tiny Tinkerbells they danced toward her. When she heard another twig snap, she knew the nightmare had begun again.

Her body tensed and stiffened as she watched the policia move closer toward them. They were sure to find them and this time they had no chance of escape. If she made the slightest move, it would alert the policia.

Uncontrollable tears etched a path down her cheeks and she felt a sob try to run up the tunnel in her throat.

At that moment a hand clamped down over her mouth! Her eyes wide with terror, she choked back her sob and held her breath. Would her assailant plunge a knife in her back or hold her captive for torture? And what about Jack—was he already dead?

Just when she thought about him, Jack moved over her and their eyes met. It was his hand across her mouth! He signaled to her not to make any noise and then he listened to twigs snapping and the sound of footsteps drawing closer. Stealthily, Jack went for his machete, keeping it close to his body and making certain it was covered and would not reflect any light. Jack held his body in tense anticipation, ready to kill.

Joan and Jack watched in alarm as a strong flashlight beam inched toward them. Like a silver snake it slithered across grass, leaves, and moss, seeking its target. Creeping soundlessly toward the sleeping bag, the beam of light searched every inch of ground in its path.

Jack could hear the footfalls of the man who accompanied the beam of light. He stood not ten feet from Jack's head and used his flashlight to comb the ground carefully before moving on. Jack gripped the machete even tighter and prayed he would have a chance to use it. He hated the thought of dying by a bullet without a fight.

The beam of light was only an inch away from the foot of the sleeping bag. Jack watched as it miraculously moved farther to the left and on into open ground. He was just about to turn back to Joan when the light darted back over to their position, missing his head by a fraction. He felt Joan tense beside him. If either of them so much as breathed, they would be dead.

With excruciating slowness, the policia moved away, their beams of light looking like bloodhounds on a leash, leading the way. Jack waited until they were far away before he so much as exhaled.

When he looked at Joan he thought she was going to crumble into a thousand pieces. There was terror and relief in her eyes and a conscious awareness that the policia could return.

She buried her head in his chest and threw her arms around him. He ran his hand through his hair, trying to soothe her muffled cries. He whispered softly to her and held her close while he kept one ear cocked to the jungle. More than ever, he knew he must wrangle the truth out of Miss Joan Wilder and discover the mystery behind her presence in Colombia. He'd been here for three years and he knew that the lazy outpost policia did not conduct manhunts over this kind of terrain for nothing. There was *a lot* Joan Wilder had to explain to him and he intended to get the right answers.

Chapter Ten

RALPH PARKED THE Renault convertible on the side of the mountain road and put the top up for the night. With an old tablecloth and a new plastic-encased bedspread with the sales slip still attached, Ralph made himself a bed in the backseat of the car. He would have to explain to Ira that he needed the bedspread more than Ira's suite on the freighter.

He turned on the dome light, so that he could read before going to sleep. As soon as he did, mosquitoes, with accuracy of air force commandos, dive-bombed through the open windows and landed squarely on target—Ralph's neck. In retaliation, Ralph rolled up the windows and quickly engaged in a counterattack, armed with a can of bug repellent. In moments the war was ended and Ralph was the victor.

Once again he settled himself down to read his book:

Angelina gasped upon seeing his full manhood exposed . . .

Quickly Ralph turned the page and in his excitement he cut his finger on the paper. "Damn!" he cursed, sucked his finger and continued reading.

Like the redwoods she had known as a child . . . Ralph looked down between his legs, tossed the book aside, and said, "What a piece of crap!"

Ralph had just switched off the domelight when he heard a roar and an odd flapping coming at him from overhead. Ralph rolled down the window and stuck his head out to get a better look. The noise moved closer but he was still unable to determine its direction. Then he saw bright lights fluttering in and out of the treetops. Rocketing out of the distant foliage he saw a flare rise into the sky to meet the helicopter.

Ralph guessed that the military helicopter had found its target.

Zolo scanned the skies above his makeshift jungle bivouac. On the border of a clearing he had instructed the men to hang their flashlights from the trees. A small campfire was started and Zolo hoped that between the flashlights and fire, they would be easily spotted.

Santos, having spent many long years in the jungle knew that with foliage of such density they could be lost in the wilderness for years and never be rescued. Fortunately for him, he was not looking for a rescue. He had informed Zolo that this was the edge of his domain and he would not go any further with him. Using his shortwave radio, he had ordered his men from the outpost to meet him at this specified clearing with jeeps and a truck to take them back to his command post.

There was static on the radio when he tried to reach the post. The trucks should have arrived by now and he had no intentions of spending the night with Zolo. Just as he was about to try the radio again, the trucks arrived. Santos ordered his men to pack up their gear, stow it in the truck, and prepare to leave.

The sound of the helicopter stopped all progress in the jungle bivouac. Zolo's neck craned as he used his binoculars to search the skies. He shouted an order to a policeman to fire a flare and when the man was hesitant, looking to Santos for the final command, Zolo's temper raged. He dropped the binoculars, tore the flare gun out of the man's hands, and fired it himself. He shoved the flare gun back into the man's hands and again held the binoculars to his eyes, searching for the helicopter. This time when he motioned to the policeman to fire the flare, the man quickly pulled the trigger.

The light of the flares suddenly illuminated an ocean of vegetation around them and pinpointed their position to the helicopter, for at that moment it turned slightly to the northeast and headed in the proper direction.

Santos had nearly completed his preparations for disembarkation, now that the helicopter was due in. He stood by the campfire placing the last of his notes in his ever-present notebook.

Santos paid no attention as Zolo passed by him, stopped, glanced over his shoulder at what he was writing, and snatched the notebook out of

Santos's hands.

Santos was astonished at the action. "Notes for my report," he tried to explain to his superior.

"You will make no report," Zolo said, and dropped the notebook into the fire.

Santos could not believe his eyes. Not only information about this expedition, but his daily reports for the past three weeks were contained in that notebook. He reached into the fire, hoping to save it.

"But I always—" Santos said, fighting the flames.

Zolo quickly moved forward and planted his black polished boot on Santos's arm, pinning his hand in the flames.

Santos refused to cry out, but his face contorted in pain.

"No report will be filed. *Comprende?"*

"Si. Si. Si." Santos nearly screamed in pain but he held back, his machismo not allowing capitulation.

"Ever," Zolo said between gritted teeth as he pressed harder with his foot.

"Si. Comprendo."

"Gracias." Zolo stepped off his arm.

Santos was in such pain he could only lie on the ground holding back his screams. Zolo placed a hand under Santos's arm and helped him up.

"You see, Santos, this is a personal matter, not official business. You and your men will forget this day, *comprende?"*

"Si. It is already forgotten."

Santos stared at his scorched hand and fought the pain. As Zolo threw a brotherly arm around Santos's shoulders, his thin cruel lips parted in a malicious smile. Though his flesh was charred and his fingers burned, Santos felt a chill race down his spine as he looked at Zolo. He was glad they were parting company. Zolo guided Santos toward the parked truck and his jeeps.

As Santos climbed into the first jeep, still holding his throbbing hand, Zolo patted his shoulder as if they were the best of friends. Santos glared at Zolo's hand and then removed it from Santos's shoulder.

"It is good you have forgotten the report, since I know where your children sleep," Zolo said.

Santos did not answer but signaled the driver to leave.

Just as the jeep's engine started, the helicopter hovered over them, drawing everyone's attention. The helicopter signaled that it was about to land and the area was cleared. Jeeps pulled out of the way and men scurried alongside them.

The helicopter blades tossed grass, leaves, twigs, and dirt into the air, causing Santos's men to shield their faces with their hands and arms. The roar of the engine and propeller were deafening.

Santos watched from his jeep as six men dressed in charcoal gray and black uniforms alighted the helicopter. They wore black berets, black gloves, and shiny black boots, all bearing the white, gold, and black insignia of Colombia's elite corps.

Santos had heard of Zolo's personal death squad,

but until this moment had believed it was another jungle rumor, much like the stories told by witch doctors. Though not in formation, these men marched with precision-measured steps. Their silver buttons and buckles gleamed in the light from the flares. Santos wondered if it were true that the bullets intended for particularly important victims were made of silver. As he inspected the latest weaponry they carried—their pistols with infrared sights and automatic rifles with similar features—Santos believed that Zolo's ego would ensure his men were provisioned with silver bullets. Santos put nothing past the maniac who stood beside him, saluting his men.

Zolo advanced, displaying the same marching step his commandos had used, and was saluted by his squad. The lead soldier took one stiff step forward and with an outstretched arm delivered Zolo's own charcoal and black uniform, still clean and neat inside a plastic dry-cleaning bag.

Joan awoke the next morning to the sound of the river water busily churning its course downstream. It took her long moments to open her eyes and focus. She rubbed her eyes and as she turned her head, she found the zipper on the sleeping bag was stuck to her cheek. She pulled it away, felt the deep impression it had left and wondered what he would say when he saw her zippermarks.

She stretched her arms over her head, smiling to herself as she remembered sleeping with him the night before. She could still feel the pressure of his body next to hers as they had fallen asleep. She had found to her surprise that she liked the feel of his hand on her breast and never again would she intentionally move it away. Sleeping with him could be an addicting experience.

She rolled over to wake him up and found he was gone. Quickly she scanned their small campsite and discovered that both he and her purse were missing. Why would he leave his bedroll here with her in it? She jumped to her feet, stopped momentarily to wonder which direction he had chosen, and then tore off into the jungle.

Why was he continuously abandoning her in the middle of nowhere? What did he want from her? At first she thought he wanted her money; then she thought it was her body. Perhaps it was neither. He made no sense to her at all.

She darted past a clump of trees and cleared a path through thickets and low-growing vegetation. She stopped to get her bearings, then turned and started in a more westerly direction.

This was insane! She could be lost forever out here, not knowing where she was or how to live off the land. As she trudged through more undergrowth, she realized how hungry she was. Her stomach growled so much she was certain it had devoured itself. If she ever found him, she would insist they catch some fish by the riverbank and shimmy up one of these trees for some dates or bananas.

Just as she cleared a second clump of trees, she came to a halt, for there he was, sitting on a rock a short distance away from her. He was so engrossed in studying the map he'd taken from her purse that he didn't hear her walk up. Joan was furious when she saw how he'd scattered her things around with such blatant disregard, but then, what could she expect from a thief? She stomped toward him.

"Put that down! Give me that! You've no right—"

Joan tried to grab the map but he jerked it away from her. When she repeated the move, he sidestepped her lunge. She was more shocked by his unwillingness to return her property than she was by the fact that he'd taken it in the first place.

"Give it to me! God damn you—give it—" Her temper flared; she was in no mood to play keep-away. She sprung at him again, trying to snatch the map away from him, but he jerked his arm in the air far over his head and well out of her reach.

His eyes looked at her curiously. "What is it?"

"It's mine!" She did not feel he deserved any more explanation than that. Who ever heard of giving a thief detailed descriptions of their booty?

Jack stepped away from her, keeping the map close to his chest. He read the title. "El Corazón?"

"I don't *know* what it is!"

Joan was so frustrated, arguing with him about the map, about everything, that she finally broke down. Tears welled in her eyes and she felt the energy draining out of her body. She sank to her knees and began gathering her things. She picked up her lipstick, brush, and flowered compact. She was tired and very hungry and she felt as if she could not fight anymore. She was no match for the policia or the kidnappers or the maniac who wanted both her and her "savior" dead, and she was no match for *him* either. She couldn't wrestle with her conscience or her body anymore. She relinquished all her power to him.

She wiped the tears away and sniffed as she put her mascara and breath mints back in her purse. Strange how inconsequential things like her makeup meant so much to her. Maybe the jungle was driving her insane.

She looked at him once more and realized she would have to tell him the truth. She'd been naive to believe they could travel three hundred miles together and not reveal her purpose for her trip to Colombia.

"Someone's kidnapped my sister. If I deliver the map, then she goes free. That's all I know."

"Ransom. They're holding your sister for ransom? For El Corazón?"

His voice was incredulous as he digested the information. He crouched down next to her, looked into her tear-filled eyes, and smiled as he handed her the map. Gratefully she accepted it and placed it in her purse. For some reason she didn't have the energy to smile, and when she looked at him her eyes flooded again.

Everything seemed so hopeless to her. She couldn't be sure they hadn't already killed Elaine, and she was stranded in the middle of the Colombian jungle with no means of communicating with her sister.

Gently he wiped her tears and helped her pick up the last of her things. He handed her an eyeliner pencil—dark brown—and said, "Why didn't you tell me?"

"I don't know. Didn't know if I could trust you. I . . . I still don't know," she said as she looked up and saw he was holding her checkbook. She shot a vexed glare at him, seized her checkbook, and stuffed it securely in her purse.

Jack thought his frustration level was about to break its limits. He'd about had it with this New York prima donna.

"I nearly died back there for your sister. Anywhere back there. Pick a place!"

"I was told to tell *no one*. All right?"

"Fine! But if we're taking ransom, what's with all the cops?"

That was a question she'd been asking herself and she still had no answer. She was hoping he could tell her! He was the resident and she the tourist. Nothing made any sense to her any longer.

"I only know I'm supposed to be there already," she said, shaking her head and fighting back her tears. "What . . . what if they've killed her?"

Jack stood up and took her arm. "Don't worry about that. As long as you've got the map to El Corazón, your sister's gonna be just fine." Joan smiled wanly as she stood next to him. "You'll come through for her—Joan Wilder."

Joan searched his eyes, hoping that she hadn't made the wrong decision by telling him the truth. What secrets did he hold behind his crystal blue eyes? Would he really help her free her sister? Did he know a way back to civilization? She felt she had to trust someone and he had risked his life for her many times over in the past twenty-four hours, and he'd done so without asking a lot of questions. Instinct told her he was after something more than the three hundred and seventy-five dollars she was paying him. What did he really want from her?

She peered into his eyes once again. "Do you know what this El Corazón is?"

He immediately turned away from her, avoiding her eyes. "Haven't got a clue."

Joan watched as he walked back to camp to gather their gear. She didn't believe a single word he said. By process of elimination, Joan deduced that he was not involved with the kidnappers nor was he sent by the policia to spy on her. He could be from the CIA or the FBI, but she doubted it. Joan had never relied much on gut instinct, but she was certainly giving it a workout on this trip! Joan would have to be wary of him and make certain she did not give him any more information, though there was not much to tell. She believed that he was out for himself, but what puzzled her most was that she could not understand how there could be anything for him to gain other than the fee she was paying him. She looked down at the map once more tucked safely away. Just what was El Corazón and why were so many willing to murder to find it?

Jack finished rolling up the sleeping bag and put

the ground sheet in the backpack. He picked up the folded picture of his dream boat and gazed longingly at it. There was still a chance . . .

Chapter Eleven

A BRIGHT GREEN and blue parrot swooped down out of the sky and came to rest on a branch of a Cinchona tree. He stared down at the mountain road below, cocked his head to the left and then to the right, and began a high-pitched chatter. Presently, an orange-billed and gray winged cock of the rock flew into a neighboring dyewood tree and joined in the serenade to dawn.

On the mountain road, just beyond the singing birds, parked underneath a clump of laurel trees, was the Renault convertible. To any passersby, the automobile appeared to be empty.

From the distance the roar of a helicopter interrupted the singing birds and they took flight seeking another audience. The helicopter dropped down closer to the road and hovered for a moment while a spotter searched the area with his binoculars.

Ralph peeked his head out the window when he heard the helicopter approaching. He inched the door open and struggled out of the backseat as he kept his eyes on the helicopter. He tumbled out of the car and shut the door just as the chopper hovered directly over the Renault. Ralph remained hidden in some undergrowth near the edge of the road. He could only pray they wouldn't spot him. He knew they would shoot first and then ask for his identification.

Just as quickly as it came, the helicopter backed off and flew away. Ralph stood slowly, shielding his eyes with his hand as he watched the chopper disappear. He was moving a few steps backward in order to keep the helicopter in full view, when he took one step too many.

Ralph's heels catapulted out from under him as he went rolling down the incline. When he landed in a thorny vine, he groaned, knowing it would take him hours to disentangle himself. He wondered if Ira would understand.

Inside the helicopter, Zolo sat on the passengers' side dressed in his charcoal and black uniform. A pair of high-powered binoculars hung around his neck. He drummed his fingers on the dash of the chopper as he scanned an endless ocean of green beneath him. Suddenly he thought he saw something on the road ahead and signaled the pilot to drop down. He did not need his binoculars to see it was the abandoned Renault. Zolo hoped by now the vultures had eliminated the pest; he made a mental note to instruct the local policia to impound the Renault.

The helicopter moved further into the jungle, skimming the treetops. Zolo trained his binoculars on the immense expanse of foliage. Everywhere he looked, the jungle provided a mask for the living creatures within. Flying over an ocean searching for a tiny boat would have proved no less difficult.

Limbs from mahogany and laurel trees intertwined and formed a living canopy over the jungle floor. Woven into the arbor were flowering and fruitbearing vines and moss. It was a perfect camouflage for the Americans. Whether he pursued them from the ground or from the air, the Americans were proving themselves worthy adversaries. He ground his narrow jaw, refusing to admit to a single moment of defeat. He focused the binoculars and instructed the pilot to circle once again.

Jack sliced his machete through the undergrowth in a particularly dense area they'd come to. As the hours passed and morning became afternoon, his preoccupation with Joan's map had evolved into an obsession. He was careful that she did not fall behind and several times he glanced back at her and smiled.

Joan was nervous again. She was suspicious of the smiles he gave her every so often, for she couldn't tell what he was remembering: the night before when they stood naked together in the river, or was it the map? She told herself she was being silly to be jealous of a piece of paper, but she was. The only reason she clung to the stupid thing so adamantly was that it was Elaine's only chance to stay alive. After Elaine was free and they were both headed safely back to New York, he could have the damn map. She laughed to herself when it hit her that then he would be the hunter and not the hunted. Somehow she thought he would adapt to the role equally as well.

Joan helped Jack clear away an unusually twisted vine. He kept chopping with his knife while she pulled it aside. Jack noticed how her hair curled around her face in wild abandon and the sun lavished it with gold and red highlights. Dressed in her sarong and the remains of her silk blouse which she had tied securely under her breasts, she looked nothing like the Joan Wilder he'd met less than two days ago.

Had it only been two days? It seemed they had lived a lifetime already.

Joan grasped the vine firmly and yanked it out of his way. When she bent over, he could see her full, round breasts dangling in front of him, enticing and coaxing him to fondle them. The muscles in her long shapely thighs tensed as she pulled at another vine. He wondered what it would be like to nibble at them, especially on the insides where the skin was soft and tender, yielding willingly to the touch.

Jack closed his eyes and shook his head, trying to rid himself of the images in his brain. He had his work to concentrate on and there was no telling how close the policia were. The lawmen had a nasty habit of showing up just when he was positive they had eluded them.

Jack had once read that Butch Cassidy and the Sundance Kid had escaped to Colombia, but the local posse had put an end to their lawless careers.

Jack wondered if it was the same crackerjack team pursuing him and Joan that Butch . . . Naw! But they could be descendants!

Finally they worked themselves into a more sparsely planted area. Joan looked nervously at Jack and he quickly turned back to his work wondering if she had read his thoughts about her thighs.

"Y'know . . . uh . . . that map you've got there. It refers to Cordoba Province."

"So?"

"So we're walkin' through it. Doesn't that twist of fate intrigue you?"

"No," she answered tersely, cursing herself. She should have known he was only interested in the map.

"Well, aren't you the least bit curious? You've got this old map! What do old maps lead to?"

"I don't care!" she retorted, becoming quite angry with him.

"Treasure! They lead to treasure. El Corazón—that's Spanish for 'The Heart.' Your map leads to the heart . . . but the heart of what? The Heart of Hearts? Heart of Stone? Heart of . . . gold?"

Just then he turned to see her reaction and found she shared none of his enthusiasm, for her face was like a stone.

He decided to try again: "Let's do it—let's find El Corazón."

"You don't even know what it is," she said flatly.

"Well, shit! It must be valuable, we've got half of Colombia chasing after us."

Joan clutched her purse even closer, testing the

strap for security. "You're damn right it's valuable. This map is my sister's life!"

"Whatever. At the end of this map is your sister's life. Get your hands on this El Corazón, and you'll have something to bargain with."

He knew he had pushed her too far, for her cheeks became inflamed as her fury rose. She sputtered while she tried to form her words and steam seemed to rise from the sides of her jade-green eyes.

"You couldn't care less about my sister, could you? All you're after is a quick buck. That's all you are, isn't it? Some burnt-out case bumming his way through the jungle taking money from stranded women."

Jack's patience got the better of him. "Hold it *right there*. I'm out here bustin' my ass keepin' you alive so you can rescue this sister I never met, don't even know what her problem is, and in all this time you haven't even asked my name!"

Jack spun away from her and stalked over to a thick vine. He drew his machete and took his anger out on the thorny rope-looking plant. "Now that's cold, lady—you are the coldest woman I've ever met! You're like a goddam stone."

Of all the things he could have said, those words cut into Joan like the machete he used to carve their path through the jungle. Even Elaine had accused her of being a stone at times, and not in a flattering way, either. Didn't they understand it was safer that way? There was nothing to worry about, since no expenditure of emotion had been made.

She knew she wasn't perfect, but then neither was he. She had to admit she was being unfair. If she had tried to hack her way through the jungle without him, she would not only have lost the map, Elaine's ticket out of Colombia, but she might very well have been murdered in the process.

Even now he was back at work fighting against the jungle and against time. The only thanks she had given him was to be suspicious, untrusting, and impolite!

Joan was about to say something to him when suddenly she heard the roar of an engine above her. She was standing there looking into the sky when Jack catapulted across the clearing, grabbed her around the waist, and dived for cover.

They stood huddled together, Jack's arms around Joan beneath tall mahogany trees whose limbs were encased in moss and vines. They could hear the helicopter but not see it. The sound of whirling blades loomed over them when suddenly Jack noticed that he'd left the machete on the ground. The sun hit the shiny steel blade and sent a beacon of light flashing skyward.

If he'd sent them a telegram announcing their position, he couldn't have done any better. Jack cringed and held Joan tighter.

Inside the helicopter, Zolo had his binoculars trained outside. One of the soldiers whispered to the other that if Zolo leaned any further, he would tumble out of the helicopter and the men could then fly home.

Zolo heard none of this, so intent was he on finding the Americans.

Without announcing his intentions, the pilot turned the helicopter at a quick angle heading back in the direction from which they had come.

Zolo turned to the pilot, a hungry zealousness in his eyes that caused the pilot to look away, "What?" Zolo asked.

"I thought I saw something." Now he was afraid to say anything more. He had the feeling that if Zolo found he was mistaken, he could easily lose his life at the hands of this fanatic.

Zolo turned to his lead soldier, a man who was a crack shot and who had received the only incidence of respect Zolo had shown for another human being. "And you?" Zolo asked.

The lead soldier looked down at the mass of green foliage and shrugged his shoulders. "Trees, many trees."

Zolo did not take kindly to the joke and decided that when they returned to the base he would demote the man immediately.

However, Zolo was forced to admit that his soldiers, joke or no joke, had drawn the only conclusion they could. It was impossible to detect anything from the helicopter. Zolo finally admitted his defeat.

"This is useless," he said and handed the radio to the pilot. "Call for our jeeps."

Jack felt Jean's arm tighten around his waist. She was shaking as the helicopter hovered just above them and he was not about to tell her that if they were captured it was his fault for leaving the machete in the grass. Jack looked up through the trees and could see the body of the helicopter and a man leaning out of the door opening. As the deafening sound of the chopper blades assaulted his eardrums, Jack realized that while El Corazón seemed to be a very important treasure, there was nevertheless a chance that his hunch could be all wet. What if El Corazón was a fake, a cover-up for some government papers they were after, not buried treasure? It was a chance he would have to take. He still wasn't sure if Joan was telling him *all* she knew, but it was a safer bet then any. She didn't impress him as the street-smart type. She was the librarian type, he thought, and then he looked down at her. She had buried her face in his chest when the chopper seemed to inch closer to them.

Jack watched through a crack in the canopy of foliage above him as the helicopter banked and pulled up into the sky. Miraculously, they were leaving! Not until the roar of the chopper had faded in the distance did Jack relinquish his hold on Joan.

Joan was looking up at him when the helicopter finally vanished. She didn't look much like a librarian now, he thought.

Joan's voice was soft and her eyes cool emerald pools when she asked him: "What *is* your name?"

"Jack T. Colton," he said matter-of-factly, wondering why it was that when he looked into her eyes, he felt panicked and only wanted to bolt and run.

"What does the *T* stand for?" she asked.

"Trustworthy," he said as he made his way deeper into the jungle.

Chapter Twelve

Attributes like punctuality, stability, and regularity had always impressed Joan, but when the heavens opened up again at precisely 3:32, she almost screamed.

"Is it going to rain like this every day?" she yelled over the pelting rain.

"Same time, same station," he yelled back.

Jack tried to cheer her, telling Joan that if they were traveling in the opposite direction, toward the Atrato River, they would come upon an area of land that received over three hundred and fifty inches of rain a year. That was an inch a day!

It was the first time Joan felt thankful.

Jack had been working like a maniac throughout the afternoon, hacking away at the jungle. At times he thought he hadn't made any headway at all. The trees, plants, and vines all looked the same as the place where they had been and the place where they were going. His mind was almost a blank as he watched his arm swing mechanically at the underbrush, clear the path, and then take another swipe at yet another tangled vine.

He hated the goddamn rain that came every afternoon and slowed his progress. He hated maneuvering over mushy ground and getting his feet stuck in an occasional bog. It seemed his clothes had barely dried when suddenly they were wet again.

Jack was swinging the machete at yet another thorny limb when his arm doubled up in a cramp. The machete fell out of his hand and he rubbed his arm, easing the knot out of the muscle. He flexed the arm and then, cramp eliminated, he picked up the knife and resumed his work.

Half an hour later, the rain dissipated and Jack cleared the last of an especially thick-stemmed vine that was partially woven around a banana tree. He took a final whack at the vine and watched as it fell to the ground, creating a clear passage.

Jack sank to his knees, drained of all his energies. Even his bones throbbed with the pain of overexertion.

"We're stopping?" Joan asked as she stood over him.

Jack could barely raise his head to look at her, and when he did, his eyes were filled with fatigue and frustration. He gripped the machete in his hand and for an instant thought half-seriously about using it on Joan Wilder. Instead, he hurled it through the air and embedded it in the trunk of the banana tree.

"Be my guest," he said, knowing she would last about fifteen minutes—twenty at the outside.

Joan flashed him a challenging look, stalked over to the banana tree, and with both hands on the handle and one foot planted on the trunk, removed the machete with a single pull. This accomplished, she lifted the machete and swung at the undergrowth. She was glad her back was to Jack so that he could not see that she hadn't so much as cut a leaf, much less sliced through the branches. She wielded the machete once again; and then again. Finally she cut through the tall plant and held up the severed limbs for Jack to see.

He was not impressed.

Joan frowned at him but continued with her task. She chopped away at a multi-limbed vine. This time it took her five swipes before she vanquished her foe. Joan knew her attempts were clumsy, but she was determined to master the swing. She had watched Jack for two days and remembered now that he'd developed a definite rhythm to his body as he swung at the foliage.

Joan pretended she was playing golf. She swung back and then followed down, using her hips in the swing. It was just the right body movement to give her arm the force she needed to cut through a vine on the first stroke.

Jack lay back on his elbows admiring the way Joan's hips would dip a bit to the left then circle halfway to the right and quickly jerk back to the left. After about five minutes, she had developed a very sensual little dance. Jack wondered if she had any idea what she was doing—not to the underbrush, but to him.

She had a natural grace about her that reminded him of someone, but he couldn't quite remember . . .

Joan was slicing through yet another plant while Jack admired her body, when a strange noise caught their attention.

Joan stopped in mid-swing and looked at Jack, who was coming up onto his knees.

"What is it?"

Jack turned around to face her and gave her a tense smile. "Nothing," he said.

Joan knew he was only trying to protect her from worrying and the knowledge warmed her. Joan turned to resume her attack against the jungle growth. She slid the machete through the thick stem of a multi-leaved vine, cleared the fallen vegetation, looked up, and screamed!

There, at eye level, was a man's head! It was mostly de-fleshed, with empty pits where the eyes had once been and a wide cavity for a nose.

Joan literally jumped back two feet and dropped the machete when her hands flew to her face.

Jack was on his feet in seconds and dashed over to her. She was trembling, her eyes were wide in horror, and she was speechless. She tried to talk, but only garbled words escaped. She pointed to the area where she'd been clearing the vines.

Jack cautiously pulled the vines away. When he saw the man's head he was repulsed, but successfully choked down the bile in his throat.

Jack pulled at more vines and plants until he discovered a skeleton protruding from the cockpit of a crashed DC-3. The man must have tried to escape after the crash and had become ensnared in a tangle of vines and undergrowth. Jack deduced that the man must have passed out and bled to death at that point, for there were massive bloodstains on the man's clothing and on the plane.

Inside the plane, Jack found another skeleton still strapped in its seat, wearing a brightly printed Hawaiian shirt, now in tatters. The second skeleton was far more eerie-looking peering at Jack through aviator-style sunglasses. Jack reached over and pulled the sunglasses off the skeleton; somehow, it had seemed not quite dead with them on.

Joan came up behind him and together they began tearing the undergrowth from the fuselage. They edged their way down the length of the plane and found a gaping hole in the side. From the look of the hole and the way the metal shredded to the outside, Jack wondered if something had not exploded from the inside causing the plane to go down. As he and Joan crept into the fuselage he decided that until he went to work for the FAA he wouldn't worry about how or why the plane was here.

Inside the plane they saw mysterious gauze-covered bales stacked in piles along the walls. Jack took off his backpack and began searching inside.

Joan looked around her and then turned to Jack. "What is all this?"

"All this? Five-to-life." Jack checked his backpack again. "Where's the machete?"

Joan looked out the hole in the plane. "I dropped it out, ah . . . ."

"You dropped it, you get it. And while you're at it, see if you can rustle up some bananas."

Once Joan had left, Jack was leaning back on his backpack, intent on taking a much needed nap, when he spied Joan's purse. Quickly he unzipped it, rooted around for a moment, and found the map.

This time he examined it very carefully, memorizing points that would serve him well later. There were several landmarks he easily identified. The most important one was "Devil's Fork," which was located at a crossroads, but the map was so incomplete that he could not determine where the crossroads was located. Just off the side of the crossroads was a drawing of Satan with a pitchfork that was pointed in a westerly direction, but Jack couldn't tell if that was important or not. There were several Spanish verses, none of which made sense to him since they were in the Madrid dialect and not Colombian. The remaining roads on the map were drawn erratically, and almost none were labeled. By locating the water masses and mountain ranges, Jack tried to pinpoint some of the roads, but found it impossible. He memorized some of the verses, hoping that when he reached Cartagena he would ask his buddy José to interpret for him. José would do almost anything for the price of a bottle of rum.

Jack was halfway through the verse, repeating the words to himself, when he noticed a shadow creeping in front of him. The cops! They had found him and he didn't have his machete for protection. Jack sucked in his breath, clenched his fists, and was ready to spring at his attacker when he turned around and saw Joan standing over him.

She was holding a bunch of bananas in one hand and in the other was the machete. She had raised the machete over her head and was ready to strike him! Her eyes blazed with crazed panic and fury; it was a look he knew, for he'd seen it just before someone was going to kill.

The machete's steel blade gleamed in the afternoon sun as it fell to Jack's head—and then down past his ears, barely skimming the lobes, and onto the floor, where Joan successfully lobbed off the head of a snake!

Jack's head stopped spinning when he realized that he was still alive. He picked up the snake and held it in the air.

"This wasn't even poisonous!"

Joan looked at him, disgusted with his ingratitude. She wondered how sarcastic he would have been if it *had* been deadly! Frankly, she didn't care what Jack Colton thought about anything anymore! She was more than proud of her accomplishment. She had to admit that she was surprised by her own boldness, but these were extraordinary conditions they were living under and they called for extraordinary measures.

She smiled at herself, thinking Joan Wilder wasn't so dependent after all!

Chapter Thirteen

A LIGHT DRIZZLE fell outside the wrecked fuselage of the DC-3 as Joan and Jack sat in front of the warm fire. Joan watched lazily as the smoke curled in wide ribbons and seeped out through a makeshift chimney Jack had made in the ceiling of the airplane.The firelight flickered and danced on the walls while Joan watched Jack place another "log" on the fire. Smoke filled the air, covering them like a blanket. Jack sat down next to her and made another "log" out of the bales of contraband he'd stacked next to him.

Jack skinned the snake and placed the meat on skewers. He erected two V'd poles out of twigs and laid the skewers in between. Jack was proud of his backyard chef capabilities as he watched the meat brown evenly over the fire.

Jack placed another log of grass on the fire, causing a thick layer of smoke to envelop them.

"Now that's what I call a campfire," he said.

"A bit smoky, don't you think?"

Jack took a deep breath, inhaling the smoke,

and held it.

"Yup," he said, still not letting out his breath, "that's how I like 'em. That's how I like 'em."

Just as he exhaled, he leaned over took a skewer off the flames and popped a chunk of snakemeat into his mouth. He grinned clownishly at Joan while he chewed the meat.

Joan was feeling dizzy herself; rather, "high" Jack told her. She was so hungry she could and would eat anything. She reached over and carefully took a piece of snakemeat off the skewer and tried it.

"Boy, this is great!" she said as she munched. "Really good."

Jack watched as she reached for another piece and tossed it into her mouth. When her eyes met his, he found he could not look away as he'd done before. Even when she'd been in the river he remembered staring more at her naked breasts than her eyes. Jack was unsure which was more intoxicating, the marijuana smoke or her sultry green eyes.

Her eyes continued to bore into him. "I've always admired people like you. Who do what you do." Her voice was so sensual Jack thought the sailors in Greek mythology stood a better chance against the Sirens than he did against Joan Wilder.

"Burned out? Isn't that what you called me?"

"I'm sorry I said that."

Jack paused for a moment, wondering if she really meant it or if she was simply high.

"What is it you think I do?" he asked.

"Lead a life of adventure. Probably of danger."

Jack smiled to himself, privately pleased that she would think so. "You've got it. Let me tell you about the dangers of bird wrangling. Those cockatoos are a bitch."

He was being facetious and Joan was serious. His world was so different from the one in which she lived. He sometimes did seem like one of the heroes out of her books.

"Yes, but living off the land, not having to answer to anyone—going down your own road—" She was getting carried away with herself. "You're one of the last of your kind."

Jack's chest was puffed out a full two inches more than normal listening to her romanticize his very simple life-style. His smile covered his face and his eyes were now bloodshot and glassy from the marijuana smoke.

"Yeah, they don't make 'em like me anymore."

Joan became reflective as she watched him. "But what's the downside, Jack Colton?"

Her question was a sobering one and he evaded it. "Can't think of a thing."

"Get's kind of lonely out here, doesn't it?"

He wondered how it was that someone like Joan, who hadn't lived much at all—he knew that much after the first twenty minutes with her—could have so much insight. Just like that, she pegged him to the wall. He could rattle around in his brain for weeks trying to pin her down and would be floundering just as much then as he was now. Joan Wilder baffled him more than any woman he'd ever met. He's always been able to put women into neat cubbyholes, and for the most part they'd been happy with the arrangement. But Joan was different. He knew he must have said that about her at least a dozen times since he met her. There was something . . .

Joan's eyes locked with Jack's and she wondered what he was thinking. She knew she must have been prying too deeply into his private affairs. She was nothing to him, only three hundred seventy-five dollars. Perhaps he wasn't lonely at all. Perhaps he had a Colombian girl waiting for him at home, wherever that was. Just what was a man like Jack Colton doing in South America? What would cause someone to leave his country for the wilds of the jungle? If she had been writing one of her books, she would have said that a broken heart forced him to live in the wilderness. Even if it were true, a man like Jack would never admit to it. Perhaps he truly was one of life's adventurers who could not survive in a world where there was no life-and-death struggle confronting him at every turn. Was Jack a real hero or was he simply a man trying to find his way?

"Guess I better throw another key on the fire," Jack said, tearing his eyes from her.

"What were you before you came down here?"

"What do you think I was?"

Joan reflected for a moment, scanned him up and down. "Ski bum."

Jack dropped the brick of grass on the fire much sooner than he'd anticipated. The log rolled off, nearly catching his sleeve on fire. He used one of the skewers to push it back into the flames. She was positively spooky the way she came out with things like that! He knew he hadn't been successful at masking his surprise one bit.

"Still got my snow tan, huh?"

"And I bet you spent a lot of time in . . . Colorado."

This time when she hit the button, he wondered if she wasn't an apprentice in witchcraft. If she made the slightest reference to Vermont, he vowed he would send what little savings he had to the building fund for the new synagogue in Malibu and a second check to his mother's ORT chapter.

Joan watched Jack retreat into silence as she ventured further.

"Hot-dogging it drunk one day, you wrecked a knee and that was the end of that!"

"Boy, you got a way of reducing thirty-six years to the lowest common denominator." She had been slightly off in her last statement, but not by much.

Joan went over to Jack, bent down, and kissed him on the cheek. It was a sisterly kiss, containing none of the passion he'd seen in her eyes earlier nor none of the fear of him her voice had harbored during most of their conversation. He found he liked it, for it demanded nothing of him. It was a gift.

"Jack Colton, thank you for everything . . . and the snake was delicious."

Joan turned her back on him and began making a bed for herself out of the bales of contraband.

She'd never slept on a million dollars before and she wondered if it would be any softer than her mattress at home.

Jack watched as Joan stretched her long legs out and her arms over her head. Then after a long sigh she pulled her knees up to her waist and curled up into a ball. She looked like a little girl in need of a teddy bear to cuddle.

The firelight danced in her long curls and gave her cheeks a peach-colored glow. He knew she hadn't used makeup in days and yet her lips were a soft pink. She was beautiful . . . he'd known many beautiful women . . . Joan was like no other . . . Joan was like . . .

It was then it hit him. The firelight, the sensual gleam in her eyes whenever she looked at him, and the way she cared about knowing him, not just prying into his affairs. Joan reminded him of Jeannine! There was something old-fashioned about Joan and yet she had not become squeamish or demanding when faced with hardships he knew were foreign to her. Joan knew a lot about him and yet she didn't press him about his past as most women would.

He liked the way she depended on him without giving up any of her own independence. She relied on him to lead them out of the jungle, and yet she was willing to help him when necessary. He knew he had pushed her further and longer than he should and yet she hadn't complained. Gamely, she had kept going. She was there, behind him or beside him, helping to hack their way through this godforsaken place—and when had he ever thanked her? True she had gotten him into this mess, but he had to admit she wasn't *that* burdensome.

Jack looked at her once more. The dying embers cast a soft golden glow over Joan, caressing her with warmth. Jack liked the soft haze that wreathed itself around her face. He had an overwhelming urge to lie down next to her and hold her.

There were some people in this life who were innately good. Jeannine had been one and Joan was another. The only bad thing about Joan's being good was that she made him feel like a second-rate bum.

Chapter Fourteen

FOR TWO HOURS the following morning, Jack cleared their way through the jungle while Joan prayed for relief from an excruciating headache. She swore she would never come within fifty yards of marijuana again. She noticed that Jack was not laughing at her misery; rather, he was quite sympathetic. It didn't take her long to realize that he was suffering from the same affliction. Joan became nervous again, knowing that their odds for escaping the policia were dropping in direct proportion to Jack's health. Since she was not well versed in crude tribal remedies using herbs and roots, she was useless. As she watched him chop at the vegetation, she wondered if perhaps the jungle wasn't their greatest enemy.

Just when Joan thought all was lost, God answered her prayers.

Jack broke through a last thicket and on the other side was a clearing and, further on, a rise. When Jack announced they were free of the jungle, their spirits were renewed but their brains were not.

Jack mounted the rise, stopped in mid-stride, and cocked his head to one side.

"I hear bells."

Joan moved straight past him. "You'll hear more than that if you keep rolling those kind of campfires."

"No, no. Listen."

Joan decided to humor him and stopped to listen. She heard nothing and was about to tell him so, when a breeze wafted across the rise, bringing with it the sound of tinkling bells. There must have been hundreds of them, Joan thought.

Jack was watching for her reaction. When he saw the exultant smile on her face, he raced over and grabbed her hand, and together they took off running for the top of the rise.

Snuggled at the foot of the hills beyond them was a small town. Joan blinked twice, not trusting her eyes in her half-drugged state. Was it possible that out here in the middle of nowhere there actually existed a cluster of nesting humans who cohabitated for reasons of survival? A town meant food, showers, toilets and . . . telephones!

To Joan the town was an end in itself. It seemed clear to Joan: if she found a telephone and called the kidnappers they would come and fetch her, she would give them the map, Elaine would be freed, and this misunderstanding with the policia would be cleared up.

Jack could read it in her eyes, clear as a bell. Reality was going to be tough for her to swallow.

"Look, Jack, civilization!" she exclaimed as she hurried down the hill.

As he followed her, he thought he had not seen her this excited since they'd begun their journey together, and he hated himself for being the eternal pessimist.

"Maybe."

"Maybe they'll have a phone!" she cried as she walked even faster.

"Might."

"Or a car."

"Could be."

"And breakfast!"

"Let's not get too carried away here," he said, knowing he'd read her perfectly.

With the first of the hills behind them, Joan led the way as they wound their way up another incline. As they neared the top of another grassy hill, the sound of tinkling bells grew louder. When they cleared the ridge, they both stopped cold. Before them in neat, even rows were white, rock tombstones, each with a painted white cross standing guard. Around each cross hung leather strips and three bells that tinkled in the breeze.

Joan roamed up and down the rows, thinking now the bells had a morbid tone to their ring. Jack glanced at the marker nearest him. It read "Gringo."

Jack immediately grabbed Joan's hand and pulled her away. He never did like funerals or graveyards, and now he liked them even less.

On a very high ridge on the outskirts of the jungle, Zolo ordered his driver to pull to a stop. He took the binoculars from his lieutenant and peered down at the graveyard. He smiled as he recognized the Americans. Though they had been clever in escaping him in the jungle, he was more convinced than ever that their capture was inevitable, since he'd anticipated their every move. They were no match for him but he had to compliment them for giving "the hunt" an unexpected thrill.

Zolo handed the binoculars back to one of his men and ordered the driver to proceed. As the jeep bounded down the incline toward the village, Zolo's imperturbable face belied the bloodthirsty fervor in his eyes, which he'd again masked with his aviator sunglasses.

As they neared the Village of the Bells, as Joan now called it, her steps were less quick and sure. The town looked like something out of an old John Wayne movie or one of Angelina's adventures.

The main street was not wide and no more than two cars could pass each other at any given point, provided no one parked a vehicle outside a store. Neither the main street nor any of the smaller twisting streets that jutted off it were paved, and as Joan looked around she could see why. There was an apparent lack of anything automotive—a bad omen.

One-story stucco buildings hugged an occasional

wood-planked sidewalk and for the most part the buildings were dilapidated and in great need of repair. Not a single roof was exempt from missing shingles or clay tiles, and there must have been a tremendous shortage of door hinges, Joan noted as she glanced around at the screen doors that hung askew.

The further they ventured into the town, the more Joan was convinced she should rescind her earlier statement about this being civilization. There were no fire hydrants, no gutters or sidewalks, no telephone booths and she was seriously beginning to doubt the existence of electricity. She was just about to label it a ghost town when she spied a small cluster of men lurking in a doorway at what appeared to be the local tavern.

They were unshaven, with ragged hair, dirty plaid shirts, and faded jeans. As a group, they stared at her with expressionless eyes. One man with a heavily creased face and gray beard chewed on a wooden toothpick, and when Joan looked at him, he spat the toothpick onto the ground and then crushed it with the heel of his boot.

Cheaply bridled and outfitted horses were tethered at random in front of an odd building. As they progressed up the street, Joan noticed one doorway after another being filled by pairs of men. Out of the corner of her eye she noticed that some of the men carried guns in shoulder holsters or stuck them inside a belt. The chills that ran down her spine caused her to walk straighter and a bit faster.

Jack was leery about the course they had chosen

at this juncture. He knew these men lived on the fringes of the law, and he and Joan had as much to fear from the residents as they did from the policia.

If it were discovered that Joan carried an old map that, even considering the great odds against it, might possibly lead to a buried treasure, these men would kill simply to have an afternoon's entertainment, regardless of what they found.

Jack very carefully kept his eyes trained on the street ahead of them, avoiding the vacant eyes that lurked in the doorways.

Joan was behind him now and on impulse he turned to assure himself that she was still there. She clutched her purse tightly to her chest, advertising the fact that she carried something valuable. She smiled at one of the men standing in a doorway, and the man returned a sinister glare. The man standing next to him was more interested in Joan's legs than he was her purse.

"Friendly, aren't they?" Joan whispered to Jack.

"Drug runners. Just try to look mean."

Jack watched as Joan made an attempt at a "mean face," succeeding only in looking as if she were straining herself on the john. Jack groaned.

"And keep quiet," he ordered her.

As they moved up the street Jack knew his worst liability was Joan. Dressed in her sarong and what was left of a blouse, he wondered how much time he had left before the men attacked her. From the looks on their faces he ventured some of them hadn't seen, much less had, a woman in months. There had been a time in Jack's life when he would have thought it ludicrous that he would ever defend a woman's honor, believing that sort of thing died in the Civil War. If what he was prepared to do was chivalry, then it was alive and well in Colombia, South America.

Joan obeyed Jack, barely breathing as they moved up the street. She kept her eyes in front of her, no longer wanting to see the faces that leered at her or the men who scratched and fondled themselves as she walked by. She commanded her legs to keep moving, for if she stopped, she knew she would freeze. She tried to appear unperturbed by the knowledge that these men were ready to pounce on her at any second. She wondered if Jack knew how frightened she was.

Jack sensed something behind him and glanced over his shoulder. About forty paces back, one of the town's derelicts was following them. Jack continued on, hoping he was not one of the town's leading citizens. If so, they were in a lot of trouble.

After a few moments, Jack looked back again and this time another man had joined him. They followed Jack and Joan step for step, but kept their distance.

Joan looked over at Jack, who was sweating nervously. "Do you know where you're going?"

Jack craned his neck around: there were now four very mean-looking men following.

"Forward," he said gruffly and walked faster.

This time when he looked, there were six men who looked like the malcontents of Pancho Villa's renegades.

Joan glanced at Jack. "What's the matter?"

"Not a thing."

Joan stopped dead in her tracks, spun on her heel, cupped her hand against her mouth, and casually, as if she were at home in her neighborhood in New York, yelled, "We're just looking for a car!" Then she smiled and gave them a jaunty wave.

The street was deadly silent and Jack wondered momentarily if they would shoot him before or after they raped Joan.

One of the men stepped forward and pointed with a scraggly finger down a side street that ran up the side of a hill.

"Only one car in village. Juan—the bellmaker."

For a moment Jack thought Joan was going to walk over, shake the man's hand and thank him for the directions. Luckily, she turned around and headed up toward the building at the end of the road. Jack couldn't decide if Joan had nerves of steel and was more courageous than he, or if she was just stupid.

As they approached the building, Joan realized it was an abandoned church. If possible, it was more neglected than the other buildings in the town. Its stucco walls were pitted from the elements and were badly in need of replastering and paint. Two huge mahogany trees at either corner had lost most of their lower limbs and what leaves managed to draw nourishment from the barren earth grew erratically and were more brown than green.

The ground immediately surrounding the church

was littered with cracked clay molds that had once been used for casting bronze church bells. Broad-leafed weeds grew out from underneath the molds, causing them to look like fossilized flowers, eerie monuments to the decaying town.

For the first time Joan sensed that Jack was unduly nervous. "Will you calm down?"

"I've heard about this guy. He's bad."

"The bell maker?"

"Whatever you do, don't tell him what we were using for our campfire fuel last night."

"Huh?"

"The plane we slept in—I think that's probably one of his lost shipments."

"You mean he's a—"

"Just don't say it out loud."

They walked around the corner of the church and headed toward a ramshackle settlement. Besides the main house, Joan spotted two small, rickety sheds which she guessed were originally built to house tools and equipment. A larger shed almost the size of a small barn sat in between the house and the smaller sheds. The entire area was fenced in, but the fence was of little use since most of the posts leaned to the side, fence boards were broken or missing, and little of the barbed wire on top was strung correctly.

As they walked up to the house, the juxtaposition of a newly installed peep-hatch with the dilapidated, paint-chipped front door caught Joan's eye. She was about to ask Jack not to knock—perhaps there was someone else they could talk to—when it was too late. The peephole opened in answer to Jack's knock.

"*Buenos dias,*" Jack said nervously.

"Whaddayou want, *Gringo?*"

"Uh, we heard you had a car. We'd like to rent it . . . or buy it."

"For what?" the craggy voice behind the peep-hatch asked.

"To get us somewhere—get us to a town."

"What am I livin' in, a pig sty?"

"No, no, no—all I meant—"

Jack's throat went dry as he watched a Colt Navy 45 six-shooter appear in the peep-hatch. Staring down its muzzle, Jack realized he'd made a tasteless breach in social etiquette. The gun cocked.

"*Vaya con Dios, Gringo,*" the voice said with a grim laugh.

Jack backed away from the door, his hands raised against his chest apologetically.

"Okay. Thanks, anyway."

Jack glanced at Joan. Her eyes were wide as she watched the entire renegade team approach them from the far end of the street.

"Oh, Jesus . . ."

Jack turned around and stared at the Colt 45 and did the only thing he could.

"All right, your turn. Talk to them again, Joan Wilder; write us out of this one."

Just then the Colt 45 eased back out of the peep-hatch. "Joan Wilder? Joan Wilder?" the craggy voice asked. Jack watched in astonishment as the door creeped open. "*The* Joan Wilder?"

The door opened to reveal a fairly good-looking man of medium height and build, approximately thirty years old, wearing a Hawaiian print shirt and sunglasses.

Jack immediately thought of the skeleton from the fuselage the night before and knew he'd been right about the bell maker. He was no one's fool.

"You are Joan Wilder, the novelist?"

Joan was rather taken aback. "Well, yes I am."

"I read all your books; I love your books. Come in, come in."

Jack was stunned at the greeting they received and even more so at discovering this new piece of information about his traveling companion.

"Joan Wilder is the greatest novelist," their host was saying as he slammed the door and efficiently dispersed the approaching menace outside.

Joan let out a sigh, but Jack was afraid they had walked into something they would never walk out of.

Chapter Fifteen

ONCE INSIDE, JACK'S fears were alleviated as he looked around the room. It looked like a media-room in one of his father's producer-friends' homes in Malibu. The interior structure was two stories high with an open-beamed ceiling and a network of lofts and balconies above the main floor. There was a wide-screen television and the latest in stereo equipment, with a tape deck and eight speakers ringing the room. There was a VCR to tape movies, an Intellevision, two pinball machines and three video arcade games including Donkey Kong, and Space Invaders. A 1950 Wurlitzer jukebox stood in a far corner next to a screened off area where an eight-foot pool table sat.

The room was decorated in lush hunter green carpeting and peach, watered moiré sofas. An entire wall of glassed-in shelves held leather-bound books, bronze sculptures, and Ming vases. On the wall behind a group of green velvet Bergère chairs, hung a Remington painting. With the employment of transitional tables and mood lighting, the room was one of the most amiable Jack had ever seen. The only thing it lacked was an ocean view and somehow Jack knew that his host had already placed his order.

Joan was mentally critiquing the decorator's style when she remembered where she was. It must have cost a fortune not only for the decorator's expertise, but his silence. This man's Colombia was a long way from Rodeo Drive.

Their host was speaking to Jack. "Ever read *The Ravagers?* That woman, oh, she make me hungry."

An indecipherable expression covered Jack's face and Joan was unsure whether she liked it or not.

"No, I never . . . turned that page," Jack said, his eyes boring into Joan.

"Never?" Juan asked, slipping a copy of Joan's book off the shelf. "Here, read it, take it."

Jack looked down and admired the cover art. It was the picture of a woman in a wanton pose, her breasts nearly exposed as the shoulders of her Indian/Gypsy dress slipped down her arms. He flipped the book over and spied Joan's photograph. She was dressed as he supposed everyone expected a writer to be dressed. She wore her straight hair pulled back behind her ears, and very little makeup. She sat in a wing-back chair wearing dark, baggy slacks—wool, he would have guessed—and a long-sleeved white shirt beneath a crew neck pullover sweater. She did look like someone literarily famous.

She wrote this book, he thought as he gazed back at the cover. And all those others over there? He had shared his bedroll with someone who was a somebody. He looked over at her as she stood next to Juan while he proudly pointed out his Joan Wilder collection. It was incredible but they were the same person—the scantily clad, long-legged, infuriating jinx of a temptress standing in front of him and the well-known woman of accomplishment in the photo. He was surprised but not shocked. Somehow he had known she was unique, not because of her talent and notoriety, but for reasons that were special to him.

Juan was babbling on, praising his guest. "*The Ravagers, Love's Wicked Kisses*. I'm waiting for *The Return of Angelina*. And now you are here, in Colombia! You want a drink? I got Jim Beam here, Jack Daniel, anything you drink. What you want, Joan Wilder? Want to take a Jacuzzi, play some music?"

Juan stepped over to a console of buttons that looked like the instrument panel on a 747. At the flick of a switch the room was bathed in music.

Joan smiled appreciatively at Juan. "Actually what I'd really like is to make a phone call."

Juan shook his head. "No phones, no phones. I hate phones. Have a drink, let's hang out."

Juan ushered her over to a brass-topped bar. It was a testimony to the glass cutters who had artistically cut, glued, and mitered tiny mirrors and stained glass to form a modernistic mural along the fifteen foot base of the bar. Joan sat on one of the plushly upholstered stools while Juan proudly displayed his collection of Waterford brandy glasses, gold-edged Florentine stemware and solid-silver highball glasses from Mexico.

"Look," he urged her, "I got Southern Comfort, Stolie, Michelob, or, come to think of it, I got a Heineken."

Jack's face lit up. "You got a Heineken? You really got a Heineken?"

Joan was getting impatient. "Juan, where is there a phone?"

"I'll take a Heineken," Jack said, interrupting her and paying no attention to the scowl she gave him. He hadn't had a Heineken in over three years and he would be damned if he was going to pass it up.

Juan tossed Jack the beer, ice-cold from his custom-made bar-refrigerator.

"The phone is many miles from here," Juan said in answer to Joan's question.

Joan sighed deeply and looked at Jack. His eyes were glued to her purse, which she had placed on the bar. Protectively, she picked it up and placed the strap securely on her shoulder.

Jack knew Joan was still convinced he was only after her money and the map and just to tease her, he turned to Juan and said, "Say, you got a Xerox machine around here?"

Juan was quite serious when he answered. "Yeah, but it's broken."

Joan was infuriated with Jack. It seemed she was the only one around here who was still interested in saving Elaine's life. If she left everything to Jack, he'd sit here for days, drinking beer and reminiscing about the dope-smuggling trade with Juan.

"Look, Juan. Could you take us—in your car?"

"Who told you I had a car?"

"The men in the village."

"They said I had a car? They are comedians. They meant my little mule."

Jack stopped in mid-gulp, looked at the crestfallen look on Joan's face, and suddenly lost his thirst for his Heineken.

At the end of the street two charcoal-and-black painted jeeps rolled to a stop. They were specially equipped jeeps with cross-fire–injected eight-cylinder engines. While they were under construction, Zolo had specifically requested the jeeps achieve a 51:49 weight distribution, which meant that virtually an equal amount of weight was displaced on all four wheels, resulting in remarkable braking and acceleration. Both machines could do zero to sixty miles an hour in just over seven seconds and reach a top speed of one hundred and forty miles an hour. Little wonder the smile on Zolo's lips was one of victory as he rode into town.

Zolo's detachment had been increased by four men, who were now dressed in the specially designed uniforms of the death squad. To the man, they were equipped with assault rifles, tear gas, and extra shells.

Zolo instructed the driver to stop in front of the cantina. A middle-aged woman, slovenly dressed and obese, sat on the tumbledown porch. Zolo and two of his men jumped out of the jeep and went up to her. The two soldiers stood on either side of the woman while Zolo checked inside the cantina. It was completely empty.

Zolo looked at the woman. *Gringos, Americanos.*"

The woman shook her head. Zolo instantly grabbed her arm and pinched her soft flesh with his spiny fingers. With one swift movement he threw the woman inside the cantina as if she were a sack of flour. His boots clicked against the rotten wood planking as he followed her inside.

The men in the jeeps waited in silence while Zolo remained in the cantina. No one blinked when their leader walked outside, called for a handkerchief, and then wiped blood off his stiletto.

"The bell maker's," Zolo said.

Chapter Sixteen

STEALTHILY, LIKE THE inhuman predators they were, Zolo and his men surrounded the shabby settlement. Upon Zolo's orders the men aimed their rifles toward the main house, then paused momentarily, awaiting the fall of Zolo's glove, which was the signal to fire.

Zolo was about to raise his glove, when—blam!!

The rickety doors of the largest shed were ripped off their hinges and flattened by a supercharged Bronco truck that came roaring at Zolo and his men at top speed. Zolo jumped inside the jeep, narrowly missing being crushed between it and the Bronco.

The Bronco—with two roll bars, an extra bar of lights on the roof, and the words THE LITTLE MULE emblazoned on the doors—charged after a pair of commandos and ran them into a ditch. As it raced away from the settlement, the Bronco did an incredible wheelie up the road, causing Zolo's crack marksmen to miss their target.

Zolo and his soldiers scrambled into their fuel-injected jeeps and fired one volley of shots after another at the disappearing Bronco.

Crushed between Juan, who was driving, and Jack on her right, Joan watched wild-eyed as the Bronco screamed its tires to the edge of town. Joan was pitched back and forth and up and down as they raced over the bumpy streets and rutted roads.

Juan, wearing Ferrari racing gloves, jerked the Bronco onto a narrow dirt road at the outskirts of town, just missing a barrage of gunfire. Joan looked behind them and saw that the jeeps were gaining on them.

"Look over there," Juan said calmly. "See over there by the fence? That's where my mother was born."

Joan and Jack exchanged an incredulous look as another round of gunfire blasted at them.

Juan pointed off to the right. "And see the third tree up the ridge? My brother planted that tree."

Joan couldn't believe it! They were racing over hilly terrain at almost a hundred miles an hour while being shot at by lunatic policemen and Juan was giving them the fifty-cent family tour!

"This guy's crazier than I am!" Jack said to Joan.

Juan heard the comment and said, "Oh, *gracias*. Yeah, that's Lupe's Ridge. And over there, that Lupe's Long Walk."

Just then Juan gunned the engine and the Bronco was airborne, flying off a crest. Joan slammed her palms over her eyes and held her breath. The Bronco bounced three times when it landed in open terrain, tossing Joan out of her seat and causing her to hit her head on the windshield. Juan mumbled his apologies and hit the gas again as he headed for a thicket of trees. At the last second, Juan jerked the Bronco around, veering away from the trees and back into the open meadow.

Jack looked at the trees behind him. "That was cover! Those trees!"

Juan gestured off to the left. "I wanted to show you this field. Here, in eighteen fifty, my ancestors fought the Paragucchis and won the right to irrigate."

When a bullet zinged the metal handle on Jack's side of the truck, it was all he could do to keep from leaping across the seat and grabbing the steering wheel away from Juan. Instead, he wrestled with his nerves a bit longer.

Juan opened the glove compartment and withdrew a cassette and turned to Joan. "The music of Angelina!" With the high-spirited Latin music filling the cab, Juan hit the gas again and the Bronco zoomed through stalks of high grass.

Jack watched in the side-view mirror as Zolo's jeep went flying over the crest, landed, and continued on, still very much on the Bronco's tail.

Joan had a white-knuckled grip on the dashboard as they sped through the grass that was now over the roof of the cab. One of the stalks slapped through Jack's open window and hit him on the cheek. With terrified faces they watched as Juan calmly pulled the stalk to his nose, took a whiff and said, "I think my crop is nearly ready."

Joan believed in comic relief, but Juan was carrying things a bit too far. Maybe Jack was right. Maybe Juan was just flat crazy and they were not going to escape the policia. She knew she would have felt much better, both physically and mentally, if Jack were driving.

Like the horse it was named after, the Bronco came bucking out of the field, bombed its way over a hill, and then careened down a steep incline and tore along a long, narrow grade. Unbelievably, the jeeps were directly behind them.

As Jack began to realize that these were not ordinary regulation jeeps, he feared even more for their chances of escaping.

Juan opened the Bronco up and roared across a broad, parched flat. Unlike the humid, rain-soaked jungle, this area had not seen moisture in months. The Bronco's tires spun a rooster-tail of dust behind it as it streaked across the land.

Jack's eyes widened in horror as he stared at the river dead ahead.

"See that river?" Juan asked.

"The one without the bridge?"

"Two hundred and forty-five tributaries," Juan explained.

Joan looked at Jack. "What do you mean, 'the one without the bridge'?"

Juan continued his tour-guide rhetoric, unperturbed by the scream rising out of Joan's throat. "It feeds right into the Amazon."

Jack pointed straight ahead, clutched Joan's arm, and repeated his statement for her. "*The one without the bridge!"*

Juan accelerated the Bronco, giving it all the gas he could, and the engine screamed.

"This river is the main water supply for many villages," he continued.

The Bronco quickly neared the river's edge and Jack found he couldn't stand it anymore. "Juan! Where the hell ya going?"

"To Lupe's Escape. I've used it many times in the past."

Juan produced a small electronic box from under his seat. It looked almost like an electric garage-door opener and when he pointed it straight ahead and pressed the button, Jack wondered if Juan had completely flipped out.

Emerging from a camouflage of shrubbery, a narrow steel ramp rose out of the riverbank on giant hydraulic lifters that ground their gears in a loud screeching wail.

Juan gassed the Bronco again and Joan felt her heart lurch as they drew near the river. She could not see the ramp and was certain they were about to meet death. She clutched at Jack's arm, knowing that the last thing she would feel before she died was the press of her body against Jack's. Somehow, it was a small consolation.

At the last moment, the ramp appeared and the Bronco roared up onto it and then sped down its length, which crossed nearly three-quarters of the way across the river. With a final lunge on the gas pedal, the Bronco leaped across the remaining quarter of the river and landed on the opposite bank.

Juan stopped the Bronco to watch while the jeeps came roaring up to the riverbank. The first jeep driver downshifted his machine and yelled to his men, "Hang on!" Then he gave it all the gas he could.

At that moment Juan pulled out his electronic gadget, pointed it over his shoulder at the ramp behind him, and pressed the button. The end of the ramp closest to the riverbank flipped up like a lip. The jeep moving toward the ramp at full throttle did not have time to brake, and crashed into the metal wall. Four crisply uniformed members of Zolo's crack team went flying over the top of the ramp, then spiraled into precision-perfect freefalls into the river below.

Juan turned to Jack with a wide grin.

"Yeah, Lupe was one time with the Army Corps of Engineers. Some kinda guy."

Joan, relieved that she did not die in the river, exhilarated from the race, and still holding tight to Jack's arm, broke into raucous laughter. Impulsively, she turned to Jack, threw her arms around him, and kissed him. She had been laughing halfway through the kiss when suddenly she stopped and realized that she was doing precisely what she'd been thinking about for the better part of two days.

It hadn't been a conscious desire that she'd brooded about, but still it had been there. His lips were full and sensual and when he kissed her back, as he was doing now, she wondered what it was that made his kisses unique. No man had ever kissed her like this!

His arm stole around her shoulders and drew her to him. His chest pressed into hers and she felt the exact moment when his heartbeat quickened. He parted her lips with his tongue and outlined the edge of her lips, teasing her with promises of more to come. Joan was certain they had set off sparks, so electric was their reaction to each other. She knew he must be feeling the same things and when he reluctantly pulled away from her, kissing both her cheeks and then smiling at her, she could see that he did.

Zolo's jeep screeched to a halt at the river's edge. He stood in his seat, called for his binoculars, and peered at the far side of the river. The Bronco was speeding away from him. Once again the Americans had outwitted his special machinery, deadly guns, and most humiliating of all, his expertise. More than ever he vowed he would attain his revenge but instead of letting them die easily by a high-powered bullet, he would torture them slowly, just as they were torturing him now.

Chapter Seventeen

CRISTÓBAL COLÓN WAS the highest peak in the Sierra Nevada de Santa Marta mountain range, but Joan Wilder knew she was higher. Not even the night they had slept by the marijuana fire had she been this giddy, this exhilarated. They had nearly died back there at the river and now she felt as if she were ready to repeat the experience. If she hadn't been so carefree, so happy, she would have worried that she was either becoming immune to danger or had lost her mind.

She stooped down and picked a pink wild flower and sniffed it. It reminded her of jasmine and she giggled to herself. Wasn't that the wonderful part about life? One could be stranded in a foreign country, not knowing a soul, being chased by murderous men, and still there were pretty, fragrant flowers if you knew where to find them. She stood on the edge of the road, balancing herself lest she fall down the steep incline. She lifted her face to the wind and let it run cool fingers through her hair.

Joan had liked the thrill of the chase and the way

Juan had unnervingly bolted the Bronco over the land. He reminded her of an Arabian genie, living the way he did in modern splendor in the middle of no-man's land and making magical metal carpets appear out of nowhere.

She pressed her fingers to her lips, still feeling the tingle left by Jack. Jack's magical powers frightened her more because they were real. In a way, she did wish the chase could go on forever, and then she woudn't have to pay Jack his money and send him away. As it was now, she could pretend he wanted to be with her just for herself and not for the money . . . or the map. She knew he wanted to steal the map because she had seen him greedily eyeing her purse too many times. She was betting he couldn't do it. She hoped that he was not as mercenary as he would like her to believe and that his integrity would not allow him to breach their trust. That was putting a lot on a three-day-old relationship, but this time she was relying on her instincts, something she was discovering to be her best asset. Whether he was a thief or not, that had little to do with her feelings for him. At this juncture, Joan was ambivalent about everything.

She tried not to let herself get carried away since there was an even chance he could walk away from her tomorrow and she would never see him again. Perhaps she was more than cash in his back pocket, but that didn't mean they would have a future. Realistically, she was better off believing that Juan was an Arabian genie than she was to think that she and Jack would have anything more than these few days together.

She leaned her body against the wind. She would relish what time they had spent together and the few hours that were left.

Jack watched her as she walked along the road's edge like a gymnast mastering the balance beam. She was full of life, vital in a way that was foreign to him. He knew his way of life sounded exciting to her, and on the surface it would seem that of the two of them he was the one who had lived life and lusted after experiences; sometimes even dangerous ones.

He looked down at the book cover and then again at the woman dressed in torn clothes with her long hair flowing in the wind. Joan knew more about living than he ever would, because she was willing to risk her feelings. For years he had tried to deny—mostly to himself—that he had come to South America to escape the world.

He had used every psychological trick available on himself. He'd told himself that everything that passed before in his life was insignificant. He told himself he liked the danger of trapping wild birds, living off the land, and pitting himself against the jungle and mountains. In his melancholy moments he wondered if he weren't subconsciously suicidal.

He had yearned to return to the United States, telling himself it was the luxuries he missed. He'd even convinced himself that his dream boat would make all his wishes come true and solve all his problems. But if he would be honest with himself, every time he looked at the picture of his luxury yacht, he envisioned a woman, a faceless woman, who loved him. He was almost thirty-seven years old and he had no one to share his life, more important, he was not a part of someone else's life.

He couldn't go back to Wall Street, that was a jungle he found boring and filled with too many snakes. He wondered if Joan would stay with him in South America. No, he thought, she *did* have a life to return to: family, friends, her job. Still, she could write anywhere . . . it didn't have to be in New York.

He looked up in time to catch her glance at him over her shoulder and flash a seductive smile. Damn! He wondered if she had any idea what she did to him when she looked at him like that. It was not only unfair, but inhumane!

Joan Wilder was a special woman indeed. There were so many facets to her personality that he wondered if one lifetime would be enough to enjoy them all. And he wondered if he was the man for her. Even if he never saw her after tomorrow, he would count himself fortunate for having met her. He knew there would be times he would curse her name for showing him that there were people like Jeannine left in the world.

While Joan looked out at the mountains, Juan stood off to the side, explaining the countryside.

"Over that mountain the river becomes wild—*muy peligroso!* Waterfalls, rapids—Angelina country, right Joan?"

"Whatever happened to Lupe?" Joan asked as she teetered on the edge of the road.

"*Ai-yai-yai!* Terrible disappointment to family."

Jack held his breath while Joan regained her balance and began safely walking on the road again. He looked over to where Juan's voice was coming from and then noticed that Juan was standing behind a tree on the other side of the Bronco, relieving himself. Jack's eyes wandered up from the trunk of the dead tree to the three upper limbs that formed a tinelike fork.

Joan was still picking flowers and talking to Juan. "I can imagine . . ." she was saying.

Juan came walking back toward them, zipping up his pants. "He entered the priesthood."

Jack followed him toward the Bronco but couldn't tear his eyes off the tree. It was Satan's spear! The tree was the same as the one on Joan's map! He had found it! He'd actually located the treasure or at least he was close . . .

Juan was still babbling on. "I take over the business. Is for the best, I am not so reckless. He might have ended up hanging from Tenedor del Diablo," he said, indicating the dead tree with this thumb. "Like what used to happen to bandidos."

Jack quickly looked at Joan, who had walked over to him and was inspecting the tree Juan had mentioned.

"Ten-what?" she asked.

"Tenedor del Diablo."

Jack felt as if he would break out in a cold sweat any second.

"Oh," Joan said and turned away from the tree.

Jack let out a deep breath. She didn't make the

connection! If he could just find that treasure . . .

Juan startled Jack out of his thoughts when he reached over and grabbed Joan's book out of Jack's hand.

"Oh, Joan! I almost forgot . . ." He seemed suddenly shy. "Would you mind . . ."

Joan smiled at him, her genie, and took out a pen and autographed the book for him.

Jack began pacing while she wrote in the book. He looked at the tree once again and then at her purse. He had to get the map and make a copy of it. It was essential he know what those verses meant. He was positive they were directions of some sort. If he had that treasure . . .

Just then Juan grabbed Jack's arm and ushered him to the Bronco. "I'm sorry I cannot take you all the way to Cartagena. Beyond this town I am a wanted man."

"You've been fabulous. This is perfect, really," Joan said gratefully.

"But in the morning, there is always a bus. It will take you."

Jack was the last one in the Bronco and before he shut the door he took one last look at Tenedor del Diablo before following Joan's purse into the Bronco.

Chapter Eighteen

ELAINE'S SLIM WRISTS were handcuffed to the gilt arm of an antique Louis XVI chair. She was continually baffled by the incongruities of her kidnapper. She had been served some of the finest cuisine she'd had in her life—everything from tropical fruit compote, French croissants, and New Orleans coffee for breakfast, to roulade of flank steak and Spanish pilaf at supper, and yet Ira would not trust her out of his sight long enough to bathe. She'd played chess, backgammon, and gin rummy with him, but though there was an extensive library on board, he would not allow her to read a book. She speculated whether he was a split personality.

Most of the time, he treated her with the congenial attitude of a party host who is overly concerned with his guest's comfort. Other times, Ira would taunt her with frightening references to the crocodiles that slithered in the swamp just outside the freighter or he would wake her and remind her that if Joan did not turn over the map, he would instruct Ralph to kill her first and procure the map second.

From Ira, Elaine learned how her husband had become involved in smuggling.

Several years ago, Eduardo had gone bankrupt in his first business venture and owed a great deal of money. After months of being turned down by conventional bankers and loan companies, Eduardo went to Ira's uncle, Sol, who was a loan shark. Eduardo paid his debts, started the new bookstore, and was quite successful paying Sol back in installments. It was an arrangement amiable to both.

When the recession hit and book sales were down, Eduardo found he couldn't pay his debt. Sol "persuaded" Eduardo to become involved in the smuggling business, expressing concern for Elaine's safety, stating that she might meet with an "accident." Eduardo's only choice had been to cooperate with Sol.

Elaine thought Ira a disgusting, deranged, greedy man who thought he was being cruel by telling her these things about Eduardo but she was glad he had, for the truth didn't hurt half as much as her speculation.

Eduardo had loved her, he hadn't lied about that. But he'd made a very unwise decision the day he went to see Sol. She wondered if it had been pride that kept him from going to his family or if he had done just that and been refused. She wondered at the desperation he must have felt being forced to resort to criminals for help. She had always believed Eduardo was an honorable man; therefore, her shock upon discovering his involvement in smuggling had nearly destroyed her too.

The cruel mental games Ira played had backfired on him, for Elaine drew comfort knowing now that she had not misjudged Eduardo nor had he betrayed her. Eduardo had paid for his mistake with his life, but he had been unwilling to pay the even higher cost of Elaine's life.

The jangling of the ship-to-shore phone startled Elaine out of her reverie. Ira picked it up and though she strained to listen, Ira's voice was muffled. He paused for a long time and then began shouting.

"Ralph, of all the things you could say to me right now, 'I've lost her' is what's gonna get the most teeth broken in your mouth!"

Ralph stood in a red phone booth in Fiesta Town in dirty rumpled clothes. He was unshaven, exhausted, hungry, and furious with his cousin, who had no appreciation for what he'd been through.

"Lemme tell you something, Ira! I don't like you. I've never liked you. I don't like the way you think. I don't like the way you dress. I don't like the way you comb your hair either side of that silver-bullet head of yours . . . And one more thing, Ira . . ." Ralph paused as he looked up at the Grande Hotel across the street and saw Jack and Joan step out of the Bronco, shake hands with Juan, and wave as the Bronco laid rubber and sped away.

". . . you are the luckiest bastard that ever walked the face of the earth!"

Ira was incredulous at the other end of the phone. His smile was nearly as wide as his pudgy face. "She's there? She's right there? She probably wants to call me. Ask her if you can hold her handbag."

Ralph glanced back at Joan again and confirmed the fact that she still had her purse; therefore, she had not lost the map in the jungle. "She's with some guy."

"What guy?" Ira asked, now very concerned with any changes in plans.

"How the hell do I know? She likes guys, okay? So do you."

"All right, just knock off the pathetic attempts at humor, Ralph, and get me that map tonight. No more screw-ups. I don't care what you have to do, just get that map."

Elaine watched as her jailer slammed down the receiver, and she sighed with relief. Joan was still alive! They both still had a chance to escape this lunacy. Tonight . . . Perhaps she and Joan would be free tonight . . .

Chapter Nineteen

JOAN WALKED BESIDE Jack to the entrance of the Grande Hotel. In the ancient sleepy town, the six-story hotel made of limestone from nearby mines was a monument to the petroleum dollars that were bringing Colombia into the age of advanced technology. In the same block more than a half dozen boutiques, men's shops, and jewelry stores displaying Colombian emeralds had been built in the last few years. Their marble exteriors, track-lit window displays, awninged entries, and concrete sidewalks looked more like Worth Avenue in Palm Beach than the Spanish-influenced village she'd expected.

The hotel's ten-foot-high brass-and-lead-glass doors looked imposing as Joan stood outside them not knowing what to say to Jack. She looked down the street and saw the Bronco disappear around the curve. It was over, she thought, and a huge lump lodged in her throat. She felt the sting of tears in her eyes and immediately looked down at her feet, hoping Jack wouldn't notice how difficult this was for her.

Though she had told herself this moment would arrive, not once did she honestly believe it. In the last three days, she had lived more, done more, and felt more than she had in the sum of her whole life and now, here she was watching it all end. It wasn't the excitement, the thrill of the chase, or the danger they had faced both at the hands of the policia and the deadly jungle she would miss—it was Jack. She told herself not to overromanticize the situation and what they'd been to each other, but at that moment she realized she was in love with him. And it was too late.

They had not made a commitment to each other and Jack wasn't in love with her; in fact, she was not sure he even found her attractive, but she loved him all the same. She wished she had the guts just to blurt it out. She didn't care if he thought her silly, at least she would have told him. But in her heart she knew the one thing she dreamed of most, wanted most, was for him to feel the same. She said nothing and looked at the phone booth nearby.

Jack watched her as she eyed the phone booth and knew that she was probably trying to think of how to get rid of him now that she was close to freeing her sister. He didn't blame her; he would do the same thing if someone he cared about was in danger. He knew how he felt when he was protecting her and it was a feeling he preferred to this god-awful depression.

He wished it could all go on—not the part about being target practice for the policia—but the time they'd been together in the jungle. He glanced again at her purse. If only he could get that map . . .

"Guess I'll take my three seventy-five now."

Joan looked into his blue eyes, knowing she would never see him again. Quickly she opened her purse and searched for her traveler's checks before she started to cry.

"Three seventy-five . . ."

"That was the contract, right?"

"Oh, yeah," she replied, looking at the checks as if they were divorce papers. She couldn't let him walk out of her life just like that! She had to think of something.

"Look, why don't . . . why don't you just take me on to Cartagena?" Joan eyes were bright with hope as she looked at him.

"In what—my jeep?"

Joan thought the landslide she'd survived would have prepared her for the plummeting hopelessness she felt right now, but it hadn't.

"Oh, well—I—" There was nothing she could do but replace the checkbook in her purse and *try* not to get emotional. "I don't know what I'm saying. If the bus isn't until tomorrow morning . . ." She was beginning to falter and she choked back her sob. "I—I don't know what I'm going to do . . ."

"Why don't ya just make your call?"

"Yeah. Yeah. Okay."

"I'll try to get you a room to clean up in. It's fiesta night though. It might be too crowded."

Joan nodded and walked to the telephone booth that had just been vacated by a short man in rumpled clothes.

As Jack walked into the hotel lobby, he wanted to believe that Joan was not as anxious to be rid of him as he had thought. For a moment there he'd heard a catch in her voice, but then she had been so cool about handing over his pay that he must have been mistaken.

The hotel lobby was extensively floored, walled, and columned in expensive green marble. In the center of the immense area, Jack noticed sleek Italian sectionals and ultracontemporary slipper chairs upholstered in white satin which were grouped around brass-and-glass coffee tables. In the center of each table were black ceramic vases filled with every color of flower imaginable. The twenty-foot arched windows were draped in white silk banded in dark, forest-green satin. Three crystal chandeliers, each measuring more than six feet in width, were symmetrically positioned above him as he walked to the green marble reception desk.

Jack had seen the desk clerk inspect his ragged clothes, frown in disgust, and ignore him when he approached the desk. Impatiently Jack rang the brass bell. The clerk smiled indulgently.

"Buenas tardes, señor. Teine un cuarto para una noche—con baño?"

The clerk cleared his throat and replied in perfect English, "I have nothing but vacancies," and flipped the register open.

Jack leaned forward and whispered, "Ya got a Xerox machine in this town?"

The clerk pointed to a far corner near the elevators and gift shop. Jack smiled.

"Uh-huh," he said. It would do nicely.

Joan hung up the phone, walked out of the booth, and met Jack as he was coming out of the hotel. There were tears in her eyes when she looked at him.

"I spoke to Elaine and she's all right. They'll wait for me to take the bus tomorrow."

"Then slide, you're covered."

Jesus! he thought. Why did she have to look so forlorn? He had never learned the right things to say to women that made them feel better, and the task had never been so difficult as with Joan. He tucked a strand of her hair behind her ear, thinking of the night they slept together in his bedroll. He remembered waking up and watching her as she slept. That would be the way he would remember her most, with her hair curling around her face and the way she shivered and nuzzled up to him. He wanted to throw his arms around her right now and carry her back to the jungle like Tarzan and Jane. But he had nothing to offer her—no house, no luxuries, no future. Those were the things she would expect and he expected to provide them for her. If he played this right, there was still a chance to have it all.

"Guess this is it," Jack said, touching her cheek and letting his hand roam to the column of her throat.

"Look," Joan said, feeling sensual chills play across her body. "Let me at least buy you dinner."

Jack looked into her jade-green eyes, wondering who had fallen into whose trap. "Yeah. Okay . . . sure. You go on up, take a hot bath, and I'll go find us some clean rags." He pulled the key out of his pocket. "Here you go—number seven."

Joan's eyes were locked on his as he placed the key in the palm of her hand. "My lucky number."

"Mine too."

Ralph stood outside the hotel and watched as a patrolman walked by. He unwrapped a candy bar and munched on it as he watched the sun set. It wouldn't be long now . . .

Chapter Twenty

THE HOTEL ROOM was exquisite, she thought as she walked across the dark-stained plank flooring and onto the white wool rug. The textured walls were painted white and the ceiling was beamed in dark walnut to match the floor. Two double-wide arched windows were shuttered from floor to ceiling in walnut louvres. A fireplace with a raised hearth had been prepared with wood and kindling, should the night become chilly. Other than the bed, the only furniture in the room was a massive mahogany armoire, which upon further inspection she found was not a reproduction. She then turned her attention to the four-poster rice bed and discovered the same true of it. The bed was covered in a white lace comforter, French lace dust ruffle, and linen sheets with a five-inch lace border. All six pillows were down-filled and when she pressed on them, her hand completely disappeared. From the canopy above hung voluminous yards of white mosquito netting.

The bathroom was almost as large as the bedroom, and the floor and walls were covered in forest green tiles with tiny gold flecks. In one corner sat a mauve velvet chaise lounge and small smoking table furnished with gold-tipped cigarettes and gold lighter. Opposite it on the other wall was a three-way mirror, brass valet and French bombé chest for her toiletries.

On the far wall under a brass-and-crystal chandelier sat the largest, most ornate bathtub Joan had ever seen. Three green tiled steps led to a green marble, five-foot-wide tub fitted with gold-plated faucet and handles. On the corner ledge sat four glass bottles filled with bubble bath, oil, bath salts, and lotion.

Joan didn't waste a minute in stripping off her tattered clothes while the tub filled with steamy water. In the top drawer of the bombé chest she found towels, shampoo, rinse, a disposable razor, and a tiny sewing kit. There were advantages to civilization she conceded as she dumped half a bottle of exotically perfumed bath salts into the tub.

Joan spent forty-five minutes luxuriating in the water, soaping, rinsing, and shampooing, and when she emerged from the tub she felt like a new person.

As she towel-dried her hair, she glanced into the bedroom and saw two beribboned boxes on the bed. Wrapping the towel around her, she padded barefoot across the floor and sat on the edge of the bed. She tore into the boxes with little regard for the satin ribbons and expensive wrapping paper.

Inside the largest box was an Indian/Gypsy dress

like the one on the cover of her book, except that this one was updated and exquisitely made. The square-cut strapless bodice was made of lavender silk and the three tiered skirt was fashioned of row upon row of different bands of silk ranging in color from lavender to mauve to palest pink. A huge black chiffon rose with lavender and gold center was nestled at the waist. Joan would have guessed the dress to be a designer original, but there was no label.

In the next box was a pair of high-heeled, strappy, black sandals and . . . Lord in heaven! Pantyhose!

Joan picked up the dress, raced to the bathroom, wiped the steam away from the mirror, and held the dress next to her. The colors were ones she never would have chosen for herself, and she marveled that Jack's eye was better than hers, for the dress was perfect.

Joan took the dress as a sign that he wanted her, and the knowledge made her feel desirous, sensual . . . even beautiful. Never would she have believed it would happen! There had been times in the jungle when she thought he might have wanted her body, but at the same time, he'd treated her with an aloofness she'd never been able to penetrate. She was surprised at his allowing this much of his romantic side to surface and she had to confess to being unnerved by it.

All this time she had not allowed herself to hope that there could be more for them than three days in the jungle. But now he was telling her he cared about her. *He* saw her as Angelina even when *she* had not. Jack thought her special.

Joan wiped the mirror again and gazed at the dress, her wet, curling hair, and the spellbound smile on her lips. For the first time in her life she *was* special.

Jack sat up straight in the chair as the barber spun him around to face the mirror. It was amazing what a shave and haircut could do for a man, he thought as he stood, took off the towel and cape, and paid his bill. While he waited for his change, he helped himself to a bit more musk-scented cologne. He inspected his new white shoes and the cuffs on his white sharkskin pants he'd had the tailor let out a full two inches. He adjusted his blue-gray silk tie and buttoned the cuffs on his white cotton shirt. He placed a Panama hat on his head and giving it the slightest tilt, smiled at the reflection of a very sharp-looking guy. "Worth every penny," he said to himself as he tipped the barber and left.

Jack whistled to himself as he strolled up the avenue, the balmy night breezes ruffling the palm fronds overhead. He'd had a wonderful time spending his money for these clothes and the dress for Joan. He wished he could have bought more things for her. There had been a bathing suit—a dynamite black mesh thing that she would have been stunning in—and that nightgown, all pink and lacy and see-through. Perhaps it was just as well he hadn't bought them, for given half a chance he only would have ripped them off her body.

When he thought that he'd come all the way through the jungle with her, stood nude in the river with only inches of water between them, even slept beside her, and still had not so much as made a pass—he wondered if he hadn't turned into a eunuch.

Today when he'd bought that dress for her, he realized what he'd been trying to deny to himself for days now. He was in love with Joan Wilder. He'd played all those games with himself, pretending that he only wanted her body, thinking he would never see her again, telling himself all he wanted was the map. Well, he did want her body—badly. But he also wanted Joan and if he had the map and could find the treasure, then he would have the money for them to stay together. He pleaded guilty to the fact that he was a selfish bastard, but nothing was going to stop him from getting that treasure. Not even Joan.

The town square was decorated with lanterns, papier-mâché flowers, and colorful banners. Everywhere celebrators were shooting off Roman candles and sparklers. A group of children were lighting small fireworks that they had attached to the ends of sticks and when lit, they spun into the air, showering the sky with a waterfall of rainbow-colored lights. Beneath thickly branched laurel trees, Jack spied pairs of lovers who stole kisses and then ran laughing back to the park. Under a white-painted pavilion a large band played dreamy Latin music that sent the dancers dipping and swaying around the paved terrace dance floor.

Jack watched one particular couple whose bodies moved with a singular fluidity and grace. As they spun around, their bodies seemed to melt into one another. The crowd cheered and applauded them when the music stopped.

Jack had just turned to go when a small child walked up to him waving a handful of trinkets. Jack rubbed the boy's black curly head and started to walk away when the boy looked at him with soulful, dark eyes.

"Por favor, señor . . ."

Joan had called the desk clerk and asked him to inform her the moment Jack arrived back at the hotel. She knew he would take the elevator up to the room and that was the last thing she wanted.

A night like this was like something out of a novel and she planned to take full advantage of it. When they first arrived at the hotel she had noticed the fabulous brass-and-marble staircase that led to the second floor mezzanine and the hotel's dining room. Joan had dreamed of descending a staircase all her life and written about it in every one of her novels.

When the desk clerk called her, she rushed out of her room, took the elevator to the second floor, walked down the corridor, and came to the top of the stairs just in time to see Jack heading for the elevators. She watched as the desk clerk whispered something to Jack and he turned around.

Joan took the first three steps a bit too hurriedly, but slowed her descent, wet her lips, and watched

Jack walk toward her. When he reached the bottom of the stairs, he froze.

It was worth all Joan's maneuvering to see the open desire in his eyes, and she hoped he could tell how much she wanted him. He looked very handsome and now that his beard was gone, she was startled at the incredible blue of his eyes. They didn't look like bluebonnets! They were like the sky and the ocean; they were the world to her. She hoped her hair looked all right and that her mascara hadn't smudged. She hoped for so many things . . .

Jack was mesmerized by the vision coming toward him. He was glad she had let her hair curl naturally and fall around her shoulders the way he liked it. The light from the chandeliers danced in its softness so that when she stood next to him, he was compelled to reach out and fondle a long curl. He was not disappointed. Her jade-green eyes still held that touch of innocence he was unable to resist, and at the same time she did not disguise her desire for him. It was a deadly combination. He could tell that she was still a bit shy and a little self-conscious, for when she wet her lips, they were trembling.

They stood there, Joan on the step above him, at eye level, wanting to say so much and knowing that words were futile. Their eyes put meaning to the words and their smiles punctuated their thoughts. Joan wanted to tell him how handsome he looked but she only succeeded in nodding her approval.

Jack was so enraptured, he was unaware that other hotel guests were standing behind him. Finally, one man tapped Jack on the shoulder. Embarrassed and flustered, Jack excused hmself and offered Joan his arm.

"Joan Wilder? May I have the honor?"

Joan took his arm, and as they walked out of the hotel, she couldn't remember if her feet had taken the last step or not.

As Joan looked out at the dark purple and green hills and the star-studded sky above, Jack told her he had chosen this restaurant for the view from its terraced dining room, and she complimented him on his choice. The building was nestled on the side of a steep hill just outside town and all around them was the dense foliage she'd come to know well during her stay in Colombia. Tonight, the palms and night jasmine were an aphrodisiac. They sat across from each other at a round, linen-covered table for two. A single candle flickered while Jack took the pink orchid out of the vase and placed it in Joan's hair.

They were oblivious to the tourists and more well-to-do locals who were listening to a combo play light serenades to a party of twelve. Joan sipped chicha out of a thin crystal flute and gazed into Jack's eyes.

When the waiter came to clear their plates and asked if they wanted dessert or coffee, the man had to repeat himself twice before Jack responded.

Joan had never participated in a dating marathon during her life, but she hadn't lived in a convent, either. How was it, she wondered, considering the few dozen men with whom she'd had dinner, that not once had there ever been a night like this? Romance to Joan was a commercial property; a fantasy she wove stories around and sold to make a living. Her optimistic nature had always wanted to believe in romance and as Jack emblazoned himself on her soul, Joan finally had her proof.

Without checking in her compact mirror, she knew that her eyes had never been as bright, her skin as glowing, nor her smile as happy.

Redefining his goals had not been Jack's intention when he spent half his money on Joan's dress or chose this romantic restaurant, but as he lifted her fingers to his mouth and kissed the tip of each one, he found himself doing just that.

For years he had analyzed his feelings about Jeannine and wondered why he cared so much about a woman who was ninety-seven years old. At times he'd thought he was perverted and sometimes he told himself he had used Jeannine as an excuse for not going through with his marriage to Alecia. It wasn't until Joan stumbled into his life that he truly understood.

Jeannine had made Jack delve into himself, discover qualities he was unaware of, and then push himself to reach for his dreams. Joan's inner dignity and integrity stimulated Jack to stretch himself the same way Jeannine had done many years ago.

He'd been unwilling to admit that he was tired of running away from life but Joan had brought him face to face with it. The whole thing was amazing to him. He'd sat in the wilderness of New York for ten years and never met anyone like her, and then when he was stuck in the Colombian jungle with no plush apartment, no sports car, and no credit cards, his dream girl appeared out of nowhere! There was no justice!

He knew those things did not matter to Joan. When she looked at him the way she was now with her soul-piercing eyes, Jack felt a vital worthiness not only in her, but in himself. Without using words or actions, Joan had spawned a revolution within Jack. He'd forever disdained introspection and now it seemed he could do nothing else. Perhaps he'd always feared his discoveries; afraid he'd be even worse than he thought, but Joan gave him courage. Once he began rummaging around, he found he was a hell of a lot more decent fellow than he'd imagined.

He realized now that he wasn't a family disgrace for not becoming a doctor and that his parents continued to love him even through his cockatoo enterprise. And he probably hadn't really broken as many hearts as he'd thought. He was glad to discover he was not as callous as he'd pretended.

One thing he did know—what he felt for Miss Joan Wilder, alter-ego Angelina, was far more than lust.

The waiter placed steaming coffee and delicate pastries in front of them as Jack told Joan she was beautiful. The waiter smiled, thanked Jack, and left.

"Oh, come on, you don't mean that. You're embarrassing me."

"You're beautiful!" Jack kissed her hand again and held it to his cheek.

"Are you sure . . ."

"I got twenty-twenty vision."

Joan was blushing. "Because I never . . . thought so, really . . ."

"You got all kinds of beauty. And you got to me right . . ."

Jack's smile was a sexy, teasing one and he didn't have to say anymore to turn Joan's blush to scarlet. Jack searched around in his pockets.

"I got you a little something."

From his jacket pocket he withdrew a gold locket on a chain and explained that he'd bought it from a child at the fiesta. Joan took the chain and read the inscription.

"El Corazón? You're a softer touch than I thought."

Jack gazed into her eyes once more. "Sometimes even *I* get taken."

Joan knew he meant for her to read between the lines, but before she could respond, the band broke into a hot calypso and distracted them both. Jack pushed his chair back and took Joan's hand as he stood.

"Let's dance," he said, pulling on her arm.

"No, Jack, I can't—"

"No excuses."

Joan wanted to explain to Jack that she had been the only little girl in Akron, Ohio, to fail Martha Maye's Dancing School and that the only times anyone had asked her to dance were once at a college friend's wedding and once at a classmate's bar mitzvah when she was in junior high. Joan didn't dance.

Jack pulled her to the dance floor, put his arms around her, and pressed his body next to hers. With his hips he taught her the rhythmic movements of the calypso as his strong arms spun her away from him and then pulled her back. He held her closer and felt her long legs brush against his thighs and her arms tighten around his neck. When she buried her head in his shoulder and he smelled her floral perfume, he thought he never wanted the night to end.

Ralph stood just outside the doorway across the terrace, watching Joan and Jack as they danced. Joan's purse hung invitingly on the back of her chair. Between Ralph and the purse was a long row of linen-covered tables. He was proud of the fact that he did not need Ira to tell him how to steal the purse without being seen.

Ralph ducked behind a potted plant, waited until the couple seated nearest him left for the dance floor, and then slid underneath their table. On all fours, Ralph kept his eyes on Joan's purse at the far end of the linen-draped corridor.

When Ralph reached the second table, he watched as the man attached to the alligator shoes reached under the table and accepted a wad of bills from the woman who wore a black polyester skirt, plain black pumps, and stockings with a run.

At the next table, Ralph narrowly avoided brushing into a long, sleek, evenly tanned woman's leg. She wore an ankle bracelet with the name "Linda" engraved next to a small emerald. Ralph gasped and backed up as a salon-manicured hand reached under the table and began rubbing the man's leg next to her. Ralph was mesmerized, watching it move up and down his leg, and ever so slowly he felt his eyelids become heavy. When he heard the sound of the man's zipper coming apart, Ralph quickly crawled away.

Just as he reached the next table, a child's hand shot under the table and almost planted a wad of chewing gum in Ralph's hair. Instead, the gum was securely smushed on the table underside. Before he regained his equilibrium, a man kicked off his shoes and the odor nearly asphyxiated Ralph. He held his nose and scooted forward.

Ralph came to his first roadblock when he was confronted by a pair of size sixteen cowboy boots sitting across the table from another pair of equal or greater size. His progress at an impasse, Ralph's eyes grew wide as he watched a gnarly, callused hand reach under the table and pull a dagger half-way out of the boot. The boots on the other side of the table jolted and Ralph heard voices from above him. Then, slowly the dagger was eased back into the boot. Miraculously, the two pairs of boots walked away.

Ralph continued on, always keeping his eye on the purse, knowing he was only moments away from the prize—and a fortune.

Just then, a child's hand shot out in front of him

and unleashed a cargo of vegetables in Ralph's face!

Silently cursing the little monster, Ralph sat back on his heels and cleaned the debris off his jacket. Unbeknownst to Ralph, when he started on his way, the buckle of his shoe caught on the hem of a long dress; with every move he made, the fabric was pulled along with him.

After two dances Joan was beginning to gain enough confidence to try a few more steps. Jack was a wonderful teacher and he had a great deal of patience with her. She found she loved not only dancing but also the effect her swaying hips and undulating movements had on Jack. He was in the best of spirits, enticing her to try new steps and relishing her success when she mastered them.

The music downshifted to an exotically sensual melody and without coaxing, Joan placed both her arms around Jack's neck. Jack looked into her eyes and pulled her so close she felt as if they'd melted together. When his foot moved, her foot followed. When his hips dipped, so did Joan's and when he leaned her over almost in a backbend, his face was only inches from hers. The crowd applauded.

One of the band members tapped Jack on the shoulder and offered him a bottle. Jack chugged it and then offered it to Joan. She eyed it skeptically, then acquiesced to his and the band's urgings and gulped it down. Her eyes were watering and she dribbled the fiery liquor on her lips but she didn't care. Jack kissed her quickly on the mouth, tasting the liquor, and then held her arm up in the air. The crowd cheered again. Jack handed the bottle back to the guitar player and took Joan in his arms.

The rhythm picked up once again and more people moved onto the dance floor chanting along with the music and clapping their hands.

One by one, the diners' attention turned away from the dance floor and to the other side of the room.

The overweight, nearly bald man sitting at the table opposite Joan and Jack's was so astonished he spilled wine down the front of his new white silk shirt. The young woman dressed in the fuchsia, off-the-shoulder gown dropped her chocolate mousse in her coffee as she stared at the spectacle across the room.

At the end of a long table sat an extremely buxom senora, dark curls piled, teased, and sprayed on top of her head, wearing a strapless dress with gathered elastic bodice. The woman's heavily blue-shadowed eyes widened as little by little her dress was being pulled from beneath the table. The jersey fabric was being strained beyond its ability to endure and the woman's enormous breasts were in danger of being revealed to everyone present.

Underneath the tables, Ralph was completely unaware of the X-rated floor show he was producing topside. He inched his way toward Joan's purse, it beckoning to him like a lover. His shoe buckle strained at the senora's hem as he made one last lunge for the purse.

The man sitting next to the senora gaped and the

woman dressed in the flamingo pink sundress gasped, as the senora threw her hands over her nearly naked bosom and shrieked. The senora tugged on her bodice but found it would not give. Then she spied the strained fabric being pulled from under the table. Realizing that someone was trying to disrobe her, she shrieked again and yanked hard on the dress while her husband called for the maître d'.

Ralph's jaw hit the floor and he bit his tongue as his foot was pulled out from under him. Unceremoniously, he was dragged under the table, going back the way he'd come.

The senora pulled on her dress again, wondering what had weighted it down. She continued reeling in her dress and when a leg landed in her lap, she shrieked even louder and jumped up.

The senora was screaming as Ralph floundered like a fish out of water, trying to unhook his shoe from the woman's dress. Ralph knocked the table over, dishes went crashing, and everyone gaped in shock at the pervert flopping around inside the fat woman's skirts.

The maître d' finally arrived and forcefully ejected Ralph, swearing under his breath. Ralph, angry at himself for not getting the purse and livid at the fat woman for destroying a perfectly good game plan, pulled back and delivered a hefty underhanded punch into the maître d's stomach.

The young, three-time middle-weight contender for the Colombian boxing crown promptly picked Ralph up by the seat of his pants and with one hand carried him out the back door to the alley where he tossed Ralph on the ground. The maître d' waited until Ralph stood again before he proceeded to pound him senseless.

Chapter Twenty-One

JOAN WAS OBLIVIOUS to the disturbance in the dining area caused by some woman being disrobed in public. She heard nothing but hot music that was building to a crescendo. Arms over her head, fingers snapping and body gyrating, Joan danced as if possessed by a wild, untamed rhythm. Her hair flew out in a long veil as she spun around. Jack's hands circled her waist and slid down the side of her hips and onto her thighs, and then he spun around, clapping his hands and stamping his feet. They laughed and shouted along with the music as it grew louder and quicker.

Suddenly the music ended with a wild, final blast and, as if on cue, the sky burst into a shower of a hundred multicolored fireworks. Jack put his arm around Joan's waist while they watched the flaming displays explode around them. Thundering booms, loud-pitched whistles, and the little cracking of penny firecrackers filled the air.

Not a moment after the last firework disappeared from the sky, the heavens turned on a shower of their own and drenched the diners and dancers on the terrace overlooking the Colombian jungle.

Joan looked at Jack, who smiled, took her in his arms, and continued dancing while the calypso band played on. One by one the dancers left the terrace for the shelter inside and Joan and Jack found themselves alone.

Standing in the middle of a warm rain shower with dreamy music wafting around them, Jack cupped Joan's face in his hands and drew her to him. His lips were soft and cool and precious, she thought, as he placed three tiny kisses on her lips. For a brief moment he gazed deeply into her eyes as if looking for an answer to a question she didn't understand. When he closed his eyes and parted her lips with his tongue, she felt as if she were lost in a vortex. She could feel the rain washing down her cheeks, cooling the fiery seal he had made on her mouth with his lips.

With deliberate slowness, he teased and tasted her lips and tongue. Like an equatorial heat wave, Jack's kiss blazed through her body, wilting her reserve and charring her resistance.

She arched her body into his, feeling the crunch of his shirt buttons against the thin silk of her bodice. She lifted her arms and put them around his neck, her mouth, torso, arms, and legs sinking irrevocably into him like a dying moth that for a split second had realized the flame had always offered but one consequence.

His torrid kiss invaded the secret recesses of her mind, unleashing all the passion she had stored away. With a wild desire and wantonness she hadn't believed possible, Joan kissed him back, hungering for every second that his lips covered hers. He was her savior and she clung to him, telling him with her mouth and tongue and body that she wanted him as equally as he wanted her.

She felt the press of his hips against her and when his hands grasped her derriere and pulled her even closer, she knew she would have him.

Jack's kiss consumed her totally, shredding the last of her self-control and savagely severing the reins she'd so often held on herself. The world had turned completely around for Joan and when Jack lifted his head and peered at her with his intense blue eyes, she knew they were about to embark on a journey that could be more perilous and exciting than the sum of all they'd experienced in the jungle.

They walked in the rain across the plaza, through the brick-paved streets, and down the sidewalk, back to the hotel. Joan became chilled and shivered. Jack stopped under a streetlamp, took off his jacket, and placed it around her shoulders. He leaned down and kissed her long and hard once again. As they walked out of the circle of lamplight, Joan was reminded of the young lovers she'd seen from the window in her apartment.

When they arrived at the hotel, Jack drew a hot bath for Joan, insisting that a South American chill could be quite dangerous. After all the hardship she had been through, he said, peeling the rain-soaked dress off her body—grateful now he hadn't had enough money for underwear—she could never be too careful about things like that.

Jack's breath caught in his throat as he looked at her standing nude in front of him. She was a *goddess!* He'd seen her about as close to unclad as possible and yet it still had not prepared him for such beauty. She wore her body like tailor-made clothes. He was awestruck and could only gape at her.

Suddenly Joan's arms crossed over her breasts and tears sprang to her eyes. "Please, don't look at me like that!"

"You got it wrong!" he said instantly, taking her in his arms and kissing her again. "You're just so beautiful."

He looked into her eyes and knew she didn't believe him, but he also knew, given enough time, he would convince her. He kissed her eyes and tasted her salty tears, kissed her cheeks and ears and nose. He whispered soothing words as her tears abated.

Jack peeled off his clothes as well and lifted Joan into his arms. He carried her up to the bathtub and gently placed her inside. He stepped in and sat opposite her.

Joan handed him the sponge but he dropped it carelessly on the floor. When she reached for the soap, he grabbed her arm and pulled her toward him until her breasts touched his chest.

"This is what I should have done in the jungle."

Jack bent his head and when their lips met, he devoured her with a ferocity that turned Joan's spine to liquid. She felt a ball of heat catapult from one end of her body to the other, igniting her nerve endings. Every inch of her skin was eager for his touch.

His hand slowly slid from her neck to the base of her throat with such agonizing languor that before his hand came to rest on her breast, she thought she would go insane with the wait. Momentarily, his hand stopped; Jack held his breath and then he moaned when he kissed her again. She understood now the wait had been even more torturous for Jack.

His hands slid over the silky terrain of Joan's hips, thighs, and legs as his kisses became more ardent. When he massaged her breast again, his hands were trembling.

Suddenly he stood up, scooped her into his arms and carried her soaking wet into the bedroom. He felt like an outlaw who had run with the loot for weeks and now was only inches from crossing the border. A sense of freedom, power, and courage filled him, for he held the greatest treasure he would ever find. He gazed down into the satin-soft lights in her green eyes and knew that she was bound to him. She buried her face in the crook of his neck, her tiny kisses feeling like a shower of flower petals against his wet skin.

When he placed her on the bed and lay down beside her, he was astonished to find that the urgency that had compelled him to want to take her even on the dance floor had vanished. He put his arm under her head and gathered her close to him. It seemed endless, time-out-of-time moments as they listened to each other's heartbeat, the sound of one another's breathing, feeling the warmth of their bodies mingle.

Jack placed his hand on her rib cage and watched it rise and fall as she breathed, then he took her hand and laced his fingers with hers. Without speaking a word, a clamoring communication was taking place and it seemed the room was full of words. They were important words to Jack and yet he dared not speak them, for there was something sacred about this moment. His whole being cried out for her and yet he did not move toward her.

He felt vulnerable, but rather than feeling afraid, he immersed himself in an awareness of their shared emotions. When he looked into her eyes, she seemed to descend into his soul, taking up residence and claiming him in a spiritual intercourse so wondrous he shivered. She pulled him closer, circling her arms around to his back and gently stroking him.

From the innocent play of her fingertips on his back, Jack felt his passion ignite once more. He nuzzled his face in the crook of her neck where a soft patch of white skin gently curved and offered itself to him. Her damp, curling hair smelled of gardenias and night jasmine as he traced a line of warm kisses around her neck and down the narrow valley between her breasts. With his tongue he teased and pulled at her nipples until they were hard and he heard her gasp with pleasure. Never had a woman's body thrilled him like Joan's and never had he expected she would be as thrilled with him.

Her hands rested on his head as if she were protecting him, securing him, lest he go away. She did not push him or guide him, but seemed to derive pleasure simply from touching him.

Every pore in his body drank her in as he reverently explored her body. Fulfilling his fantasies of the past four days, he lingered long over her inner thighs, rewarded with the pliant, inviting flesh beneath his lips. He tickled the backs of her knees with his tongue and wreathed her ankles in chains of tiny, urgent kisses.

When he moved over her, he sought the comfort of her breast once again and rested his head close to her heart, assuring himself that this was not a dream. He gazed into her eyes, her infinite trust urging him to take her.

She was so wet in her desire for him that he entered her effortlessly, and a slow, slick stroking began. With each of his penetrations, she lifted her hips to meet him and every time he withdrew, she placed her hands on his buttocks as if to assure herself he would not leave her. Together their ecstasy grew like rising mist, nearly overpowering them in its intensity. Wanting and craving more from her, Jack quickened his pace and carried her to dizzying heights until ultimately her moans scurried into a climactic cry.

Joan quivered beneath Jack, her sweat-soaked

body ignited by her desire for him. He pulled at her breast, teasing and nibbling so exquisitely, she thought she would scream from the pleasure he gave her.

Still hard and inside her, Jack rolled onto his back taking Joan with him. She liked the possessive way he held her, keeping her meshed to him. He traced the outline of her cheekbone with a tentative finger, started to say something, stopped, and pulled her head into his shoulder, and hugged her fiercely. Never had Joan felt such joy and fulfillment.

A cornucopia of dreams, desires, and emotions flooded her, combining with the physical exhaustion of their lovemaking, as Joan fell asleep in Jack's protective arms.

Joan awoke to find it still the middle of the night. At some point in time, Jack had arisen, started a fire, and draped their clothes on the valet and placed them next to the fireplace to dry. A bottle of wine was chilling in a bucket of ice next to him on the floor and the diaphanous mosquito netting had been lowered, sealing out the rest of the world.

Joan smiled at him as Jack leaned on his elbow and with his other hand traced his name across her naked breasts. She touched his cheek and ran her fingers through his rumpled hair. He bent his head and kissed her nipple, then teased her as it grew hard.

"Do you know what I think you are?" he asked with an amused grin as he traced the curve of her breast from her arm to the side of her ribs.

"No, what?"

"You are smooth . . . sleek and graceful . . . just like my lady."

"Your . . . your lady?"

"Course, she's a bit faster than you are and sleeps more." His smile grew mischievous and he laughed as he pressed lightly on her belly. "You only sleep one."

Seeing the worried look in her eyes, Jack reached down to the side of the bed, took the picture of his dream boat from his pocket, and unfolded it. He showed the picture to her, noting her sigh of relief.

"Someday . . . if I had the money." He looked yearningly at the picture.

Joan rolled onto Jack, who wrapped his legs around her and placed both hands securely on her buttocks. He grinned at her as he felt himself getting hard.

Joan's mind was racing ahead of her. "Jack, maybe this is someday. I wanna do it. I wanna go for the heart."

Jack, taken aback by her off-the-wall comment, wondered if she was trying to let him go the easy way. Suddenly, he was uncertain about everything.

"Uh . . ."

"Listen," she said, "you said it—if I just waltz into Cartagena and hand over the map, are they going to let it go at that?"

"I don't know. You know—"

"It's been bothering me. He allowed me to stay here tonight."

"Who?"

"The man on the phone! The one who's got Elaine. He sounded so secure."

"Sure—you're bringing him the map. It's what he wants."

"I don't *want* him to be secure. I want the next play to be in *my* court."

Finally, Jack thought, she was making some sense as he moved his hips beneath her. He cupped her breast. "Who says it isn't?" he said, teasing her nipple with his tongue.

"You. If I had more than just the map—if I had the treasure."

"Ah, you don't know if it's treasure or what." Jack continued playing her body, eliciting responses that made him smile seductively at her.

Her voice was low and breathy when she said, "I thought that's what all old maps lead to."

Joan bent her head and kissed him lightly and started to pull away when Jack held her face next to his, shook his head and kissed her deeply. Once again, she felt electric shocks shoot through her veins.

When Jack released her, she folded her arms across his chest and rested her chin on her hands. She looked at him, as if waiting for an answer to her question. Jack could tell she was not going to give up the idea—yet.

"What do you want me to say?"

"Jack, we're *close*, you know we are."

"It's a big province."

"The *tree!* You know the one, Devil's Fork. That's where we stopped with Juan today. I didn't make the connection at first, but it was right there."

"Where?"

"Where we were! And on the *map!*"

"Nah," Jack said, wishing she would get her mind back to what was important.

"Yes, it was—look—"

Joan started to reach out of the mosquito netting for her purse when Jack grabbed her arm and stroked it. His eyes were smoldering again when she looked at him.

"Maybe you're right," he said. "We'll get up early. Maybe it's not such a reach—not for an arm like this." He kissed her arm and took each one of her fingers into his mouth and kissed her palm.

Joan's skin tingled as if being teased by the fluttering of bees' wings. She didn't understand a thing Jack was saying, and at this moment cared very little about maps. "Boy," she said, catching her breath when he kissed that very sensitive and vulnerable spot at the base of her throat, "you get silly with your clothes off."

"That's not all I get," Jack said, pulling her toward him again. There was no mistaking the urgency in his kiss, Joan thought as she slipped her arms beneath his head.

Jack caressed Joan's hip with one hand while the other stole beside the bed, pulled the map out of his shirt pocket, and placed it back in Joan's purse.

He rolled her onto her back, stroking her with torturously slow movements. He felt her tremble beneath his hands and twice as he passed over the soft skin of her inner thighs, he heard a tiny gasp and he smiled to himself.

"I met a reformed cannibal one time," he said, lowering his head to her breast, "and he told me what part of the human body was the tastiest." His head moved to her belly.

Joan was moaning softly as her hips undulated, nudging him toward them.

"What part?"

Chapter Twenty-Two

DAWN BURST OVER the mountains, painting the sky bright colors of pink, red, and gold. Tangible memories of the fiesta littered the brick-paved streets as the vegetable and fruit vendors opened their stalls. An early cleanup crew, bleary-eyed from the revelry the night before, swept the town plaza, discarding broken bottles, wilted flowers and wet confetti and streamers. Banners that ran across the width of main street were taken down, carefully folded, and stored until next year.

Ralph staggered down the sidewalk, still stunned at what had happened to him the night before. After two hours at the emergency clinic and five stitches in his cheek, all he could think about was rest. He touched his swollen eye, winced at the pain, and remembered that the doctor told him he would need surgery on his broken nose. If he'd had the energy, he would have killed Ira. Instead, he decided he needed Ira to pay for the surgery. If only they had Blue Cross . . . but Ira never listened.

Ralph stumbled and almost didn't make the last block to the hotel where he'd parked his Renault. When he reached the car, he opened the back door, spread the blanket and fell asleep before his body made contact with the backseat.

The specially equipped jeeps of Zolo's death squad roared into town. Zolo's eyes were cold as he observed a drunken man draped over a tree limb, a discarded party dress lying on the sidewalk, and seemingly endless yards of empty liquor and wine bottles.

Zolo revealed none of the weariness his men displayed. He sat ramrod-straight, black-gloved hands clenched in his lap, and eyes trained for any sign of the Americans. Two of his crack team kept nodding off in the backseat, but Zolo was unaware of them as he instructed the driver to head for the Grande Hotel.

Zolo's adrenaline surged through his veins, knowing that he was very close to the Americans. He could feel their presence in this town.

"It's time to bring in all the reserves. They will not escape this province."

He had promised his men a few hours sleep and a solid meal before they began their search again. Though he could go for days without a break, they were not as driven as he. More important, he needed them. The Americans had proven more elusive than he had thought, and until now he had enjoyed the sport they had provided him. Unfortunately for them, he was weary of the game.

The jeeps screeched to a halt in front of the

Grande Hotel. As Zolo's men dragged themselves inside, Zolo took one last look around the town. It was possible the Americans were right across the street.

Since the hotel was still mostly vacant, Zolo and his men were given rooms on the first floor. Zolo gave his men brief orders before they retired to their rooms. Zolo walked down the hall, came to two adjacent doors and stopped at number seven. He took out his key, started to insert the key in number seven, and then rechecked the number on the key. He took a sidestep, inserted his key in number six, and unlocked the door.

Zolo lit a cigarillo, kicked off his boots, and collapsed on the bed. He puffed lazily and listened to the early morning sounds of the town awakening. He stubbed out the cigarillo and closed his eyes.

Just as he was about to fall asleep, he heard bedsprings squeaking in the room next to his.

Jack was exhausted and Joan was wide awake, tickling him. She was bouncing around on the bed, laughing and giggling, and Jack didn't have the heart to stop her—until she found his weak spot on the back side of his ribs just under his arm. In two seconds he grabbed her arms, hoisted them over her head, rolled on top of her and pinned her to the bed.

"Do you know what happens to little girls who don't behave themselves?"

"No. But can I guess?"

"No nookie for a week."

She twisted her arms free, grabbed his buttocks, and pushed him to her. "Hmmmm. Can you last a week, Jack?"

"No."

Jack rolled her on top of him again and as he did, there was a pounding on the wall from the room next to them.

Jack yelled back in Spanish and the pounding stopped.

"Finish what you started, little girl," Jack said as he pushed her head down his stomach.

This time when the squeaking started, Zolo jumped up and pounded on the wall four times, very emphatically making his point. He was answered with a long stream of muffled Spanish obscenities and insults. The last word came through the paper-thin walls in clear, unmistakable English.

"Americano," Zolo said to himself and stealthily pulled out his gun, checked the ammunition, and slid on his boots.

He slipped into the empty hallway, placed an ear to the door of number seven and listened. With one sleek movement he raised his foot and kicked the door open. Zolo charged in and found the mosquito netting neatly hung around an empty bed.

He turned to the bathroom door, slammed his back against the wall, cocked the gun and turned the doorknob. The door eased open and Zolo leaped into the doorway to find that the bathroom too was empty. He rushed to the small terrace, opened the doors, and walked out onto the balcony.

Down the street, Jack and Joan were racing toward a parked Renault, still putting clothes on as they ran. Once they reached the car, Jack threw his backpack and the rest of their clothes in the backseat.

Zolo smashed his fist down on the railing and swore. Zolo lost no time in arousing his men.

Ralph was awakened by a backpack being thrown in his face. Then he heard a woman say, "I'll never forget that cough."

Ralph slowly eased his head up enough to see Jack sitting in the driver's seat with Joan next to him. Quickly he ducked back under the covers, knowing he was in the best place to be.

Jack was pulling out wires, trying to jimmyrig the car but he was all thumbs. Finally Joan, who had been watching the hotel for any sign of Zolo or his men, turned around and saw him fumbling underneath the dash. She bent over and turned the key that was left in the ignition. With a sputter and cough, the Renault started and Jack peeled out of town.

Zolo roused his best marksmen, who joined him on the terraced balcony with a high-powered rifle. But just as the man aimed it at the departing Renault, Zolo pushed the barrel down and ordered the man not to shoot.

It was all too easy and now that the game was over, he wanted the Americans to sweat just a bit longer. He lifted his walkie-talkie and barked orders to the man at the other end. He gazed at the Renault, which was almost to the edge of main street.

"East road, stay with them, but don't show yourself. Let them think they're safe."

Chapter Twenty-Three

JACK FOUND THAT by pumping the gas three times and then pressing the accelerator to the floorboard, he could make the little Renault really move. Besides new shocks, a tune-up and probably a new carburetor, the Renault was in relatively good shape. Jack only wished it had been a high-performance Porsche 928-S as he glanced in the rear view mirror. This time he was quite unsure about their chances of escape.

Joan sat next to Jack, studying the map. She turned it around and tried to locate their present position according to the old roads indicated on the map.

"Anything?" Jack asked.

"I don't know. Look! There's some stuff on the back, too."

"Does it mean anything?"

"Maybe it's supposed to be folded." Joan folded it several times, following old creases and making new ones, but nothing seemed to work. "No, I guess not."

"The hell with it. We'll take one landmark at a time. Anyone after us?"

Joan turned back. "No, we must be okay."

Ralph kept to his hiding place as Joan looked right over him. What luck! Not only did he have Joan and the map, but they were going to drive him right to the treasure. He would be able to go back to Ira with the map and the treasure. Ralph nestled further down into the seat, wondering just what would happen if he didn't tell Ira anything at all. Perhaps all the dreams he'd ever had, especially freedom from Ira, might very well come true.

Jack followed the directions Joan gave him and after several hours they found themselves on a primitive country road. Joan scanned the countryside, looking for a roadside shrine. She kept one eye on the road behind them, wondering why she hadn't seen the charcoal jeeps. At top speed Jack had only been able to get the Renault up to seventy miles an hour and she knew the jeeps could do that in seconds. She also knew Jack was more nervous than she about the jeeps, for his eyes seemed glued to the rearview mirror.

Joan was more convinced than ever that her decision had been the right one. With the treasure in her possession, Elaine's chances of survival increased greatly.

They turned a corner and Joan spied the roadside shrine. She pointed to it and Jack skidded to a stop.

"There it is! The shrine!"

"That asthmatic of yours must be right behind us. Are you sure you want to take the time?"

"Risky, huh?"

"Damn right."

"We'll take the risk. Let's go," she said.

Jack shook his head and put the car into gear. She was a hell of a woman, he thought, and wondered what it would take to stop her once she had set her mind to something.

Beneath a clump of mahogany trees on a low hill sat a soldier on horseback. With his binoculars he peered a hundred yards down the road, making certain it was a man and a woman in the car. He raised a walkie-talkie to his mouth and spoke in Spanish.

"They've turned into the road of the Virgin. They won't get far." He smiled maliciously as he replaced the walkie-talkie and picked up the binoculars again.

The Renault bumped along the rutted jungle road, swerving right and left to avoid fallen tree limbs and large rocks. Joan hung on to the door handle, her eyes scanning the terrain for anything that remotely resembled the markings on the map. She was growing worried, for they had driven over forty minutes and had found nothing but increasingly dense vegetation. She glanced at Jack and knew that he was worried about the policia finding them.

Suddenly Joan's heart plunged hopelessly to the pit of her stomach. The jungle road dead-ended at a tremendous wall of vegetation that bordered a river.

Jack stopped the car, put on the emergency brake, and got out. Joan stood next to him, staring at the end of the road as it dropped off into nothing.

"We must be close."

"It's a bust," Jack said.

"The eternal optimist."

Jack shook his head. He had looked at the map enough times to know that there was nothing on it about a dead end. Something was wrong. "The map didn't say anything about this."

"Jack . . ." Joan cocked her head and listened to the sound of tumbling water. "You hear that?"

"It's a waterfall. So?"

Joan took the map and fumbled with it again, playing the parts like a Rubik's Cube. But this time when she finished and showed him the back of the map, a picture of a waterfall was created.

Jack was astounded. "Where'd you get this thing? Out of *MAD* magazine?"

When Jack went back to the car to get his backpack, Ralph had been watching them discuss something at the edge of the deadend road. He couldn't hear what they were saying, but he intended to find out. Just as Jack got to the car, Ralph ducked out of sight once again, felt the backpack being lifted out and then heard the door slam. He would wait until it was safe to come out.

Jack took Joan's hand as they descended the incline by the river and then used his machete to break through the wall of vegetation. They made their way down the river's side, walking toward the sound of the waterfall. Jack held his backpack over his head as they waded further out into the water while Joan read the Spanish inscriptions on the map aloud to Jack. Together they tried to decipher the meaning and directions.

As they turned a corner in the river, they came to a magnificent waterfall high above them. It had two breakpoints before the water hit the pool in which they were standing. The bouncing water mixed with the afternoon sun, creating colorful rainbows around them. Joan stood in wonder, thinking this was the kind of place she would describe for two lovers to meet in secret. She looked over at Jack. He was watching her and smiled. With his head, Jack indicated the mouth of the cave that was nearly hidden by the curtain of water and together they entered the cave by using a break in the falls nearest the cliff wall.

Jack took out two flashlights and shined them on the map.

"'Leche de Madre'?" he said as they inched their way down the narrow dark tunnel. Joan kept her flashlight focused on the cave floor while Jack aimed his straight ahead. It was cool and wet inside the cave and Joan's bare feet kept slipping out from under her. It was like walking on ice, she thought as she held on to Jack's arm.

"What does that mean—'Leche de Madre'?" she asked.

"Mother's milk. The heart is warmed by mother's milk," Jack said just as they turned a corner.

Jack stopped dead in his tracks. "I'll be damned."

They stood at the entrance to a naturally formed cavern easily the size of the lobby at the Plaza, Joan thought as she aimed her flashlight up the walls. Near the ceiling a row of stalactites dripped water onto a sloping rock where the water droplets ran together forming little rivulets that cascaded down into a smaller version of the waterfall outside and into a shallow pool. Over to the left, Joan shined her light on rows of stalactites which had, over the centuries, dripped enough calcite to form matching rows of stalagmites that rose up to meet them. The end result was a stunning curtain of pink, blue, peach, and pastel green rock that looked like a pipe organ. A deep pool beneath the "pipe organ" was ringed in green and yellow lichen, and velvety moss cascaded down the rock walls to form a hidden glen inside the earth.

Joan focused her beam on the walls surrounding her, awestruck by the natural beauty of the cave, while Jack poked around behind her.

Jack had found a formation of rock that looked like a Chinese temple and just in front of it hung a very colorful row of stalactites. His flashlight focused on one especially large and bright stalactite that dripped calcite deposits into a pool of white liquid directly beneath it.

Joan turned just in time to see it and when she focused her flashlight on the stalactite, the water was nearly fluorescent, it was so white!

Jack tore into his backpack, pulled out his fold-out field shovel, and started digging in the slime. Joan searched around and found a stick and began poking and stirring in the white water.

"Mother's milk," she mumbled to herself as she pushed her hair out of her face with her forearm. She smiled happily at Jack. They were going to find the treasure! Elaine was going to be free, Jack would get his dream boat, and she and Jack . . .

"I can't believe I'm doing this," she said, looking over at him as he hacked away at the rock, mud, and slime.

"What?"

"Digging for treasure . . . with you."

Jack stopped for a moment and looked at her and smiled. He was glad she was here with him, too.

"Jack, last night . . ." She paused, not knowing how to say what should have been so easy for her, especially now. Last night words would have broken the magic they were weaving, but now she wanted him to know that she loved him. She supposed that when you had never told anyone you loved them, the first time could be difficult and she hoped that was why he hadn't said anything to her. She hoped. She practiced saying it in her mind . . . I love you, Jack . . .

"You're the best time in my life," she said aloud. It didn't have the same ring to it.

"I am? I've never been that to anybody before."

Jack was having the same problem as Joan, but he knew why he couldn't say it—he was too damned scared. He was hoping he wouldn't have to say it first, because he wanted to be sure of her feelings for him.

Before he had a chance to think about it another second, his shovel struck something hard and odd-sounding. Jack froze. That was no rock! He flung his shovel on the ground and on his knees he tore at the earth with his hands.

He felt through the slime and finally located a long, solid object. He tried to get a handhold on it, but he kept losing his grip due to the lime and calcite deposits. He cleared away more of the rock around it and finally got a good grip on the object and pulled. Just as he felt it move out of the rock it was embedded in, he lost his grip and went tumbling backward. This time he dug in his heels as he locked his hands around the object. With one long straining movement, Jack pulled the treasure out from under the rock and held it up to Joan.

She was thunderstruck when she stared at the statue.

"Jack, look . . . a priceless statue!"

"Priceless, hell. It's a clay mold. My birdseed is worth more."

Joan couldn't believe it! They had risked their lives for days, fought their way through the jungle, and eluded the policia—not to mention her sister who had been kidnapped, and Eduardo, who had died—for a piece of trash? It was ludicrous. And as she looked at the statue more carefully, it was also impossible.

"In *Treasures of Lust,* my first book, they hid the

treasure inside the statue."

Jack's face lit up with wide grin as he grabbed the statue away from Joan, and cracked it open with the head of his flashlight.

Like green fireflies, streaks of light darted around the cavern and bounced against the walls as the statue shattered into hundreds of pieces. Jack held a huge heart-shaped emerald in his hand, knowing this *was* worth a fortune!

Joan grabbed her flashlight and shined her light on the jewel. It shimmered with a forest-green iridescence, its glow intensifying as Jack held it up. The cavern was filled with green illumination as they gaped at the treasure.

Jack was spellbound. "Jesus Christ . . . we could get in trouble for this."

"My God!" Joan gasped. "What is it?"

"An emerald," a voice from behind them said.

Ralph walked in and pointed a pistol at Jack's head. When he cocked the gun, the sound echoed through the cave, sounding like a firing squad.

Chapter Twenty-Four

BATHED IN GREEN light, the cavern resembled the Emerald City and Ralph looked like one of the Munchkins, Joan thought as she stared at the rumpled little man who appeared out of thin air.

Ralph glared at her and tossed a Pan Am flight bag at her. She caught it just before it hit her in the face.

"Put it in there, Ms. Wilder—I hated your book."

Joan looked at Jack, who was obviously just as puzzled as she.

"Who's he?" he asked her.

"I never saw him before."

Ralph stamped his foot like a temperamental two-year-old. "*I'm* talkin' here!" he yelled.

Joan leaned closer to Jack. "Sounds like he's from New York."

"Is there *anybody* who isn't following you?"

Ralph was nearly sputtering, he was so angry. He was holding a loaded pistol at their heads and still they gave him no respect. They were treating him the same as Ira did. Ralph couldn't stand it much more. If he'd had a machine gun he wondered if they would accept his authority any more.

"I haven't seen New York in three years! Y'got that? I haven't tasted a blintz since I was thirty-eight! Now, gimme the bag. You leave your crap where it is, and *move it.*" He waved the gun at them, once again punctuating his instructions the best he knew how. "I get nervous when I'm more than eight thousand miles from a Hilton."

Jack was dumbfounded. He still thought he should know who this character was and how he had followed them into the middle of nowhere.

"Who is this creep?" Jack asked Joan again, knowing certainly she could provide an answer—*just this once.*

"Shut up! Shut up! See this? I got firepower here— You people put me through *hell!* Look at ya—you're too clean!"

Ralph bent down, picked up a handful of slime, and threw it at Jack. His rage at years of abuse at Ira's hands unleashed itself as he scooped another handful of mud and slung it at Joan. Again and again he threw mud at Jack, splattering the white sharkskin pants with brown-green ooze. He pulled out Joan's book and brandished it in the air.

"You call this a book?" he screamed at her, and then threw the book on the ground and jumped up and down on it.

"I'm gonna kill you! I'm gonna kill that asshole Ira! I'm gonna kill anything that makes a move in the next seconds!"

This time Jack and Joan said nothing. A maniac like this guy could easily do as he threatened. Jack put the emerald in the flight bag as he was ordered and handed the bag to the short, highly excitable man.

With Jack leading the way, Joan directly behind, and Ralph at the rear carrying both treasure and weapon, the trio made their way out of the cave and into the water. Trekking through the shallow river, Joan wondered if the lunatic behind her was going to shoot her in the back or drown her in the river. He had no reason to keep either of them alive now that he had the treasure.

They made their way to the riverbank and up the rocky path to where they had parked the car. Ralph stopped Jack and made him stand at the wall of foliage that blocked the view of the river. He motioned for Joan to get into the driver's seat.

"Time *I* had a chauffeur."

"Would you give us a moment—to say good-bye?"

"What am I, Miss Lonely Hearts? This ain't the climax of one of your potboilers. Get your butt behind the wheel."

As Joan gazed at Jack, she was afraid this *was* the climax. Suddenly she felt as if her world were being ripped apart and something told her she would never see Jack again. If she hadn't been so frightened, she would have cried. She could tell that he wanted desperately to say something to her, but she couldn't read his lips.

Ralph poked the gun in her ribs and Joan slid

behind the steering wheel and shut the door. She kept staring at Jack, who paid no attention to the gun that was pointed at him. He started to take a step toward her, but Ralph cocked the gun again and Jack stepped back. Ralph slid into the passenger's seat and ordered Joan to start the engine.

Jack's eyes were glued to Joan, who knew now she *was* going to cry.

"I'll see you again," Jack said to her with a smile that was meant to give hope.

Ralph leveled the gun at Jack once more.

"In your dreams, buddy! See how you like being stuck in South America!"

Joan gunned the motor just in case this creep had any ideas about shooting Jack; at least he would only wing him. Joan kept her foot to the floor and watched out of the rearview mirror as Jack grew smaller.

As Jack watched her disappear he thought he'd never been so impotent in his life. There was nothing he could do to save her and suddenly the brilliant emerald didn't have much appeal for him. Why didn't he tell that creep to take the emerald and leave Joan with him? Why hadn't he tried to wrestle the gun away from him and leave him in the jungle to rot? Why hadn't he told Joan he loved her?

Jack started toward the road thinking he'd never despised a place as much as he did South America.

Chapter Twenty-Five

JOAN PITCHED BACK and forth as the Renault maneuvered around deep ruts and holes in the jungle road. Out of the corner of her eye, Joan saw Ralph snuggle down in the seat and clutch the Pan Am bag like a child. Joan bit her lip to keep her emotions under control. She wished there were a way to get the gun from him, but he kept it trained on her, even when he watched the road ahead. For the first time in her life, she truly felt capable of murder. Not only was she in danger, but so were Jack and Elaine, and all because of this little twerp's interference.

Joan pressed the accelerator to the floorboard as they streaked through the tall grass and shot around clumps of trees. Joan pushed the Renault to its limits, doing a slalom around rocks, trees, and impenetrable thickets. With sadistic satisfaction she watched her captor's face turn ashen when she zoomed the car across an incline, sending the Renault airborne for a long, glorious moment. Joan jerked the wheel to the right when they landed and avoided missing a cliff's edge by a fraction of an inch.

Ralph thought he was going to vomit and was unable to shout orders to his prisoner. He wondered for a moment who wielded the power; he with his gun, or she with the steering wheel. It was a moot point.

Joan rammed the accelerator once again as they approached a tall hill, where, on the other side, they would find the main road and the shrine to the Virgin.

Just as they crested the hill, Joan's face turned white and Ralph tasted bile in his throat, for on the road was an awesome roadblock consisting of sixteen charcoal-and-black jeeps! Joan slammed on the brakes with all her might and stopped the Renault before it was too late.

In the foremost jeep stood Zolo, his high-powered binoculars focused directly on Joan's face. She could feel the chill of his deadly smile reach up the hill and clutch at her stomach.

In horror, Joan watched as the crisply uniformed death squad aimed their expensive rifles with telescopic sights directly at her. She jerked the car into reverse and smashed her foot against the accelerator just as Zolo gave the signal. Gunfire filled the Colombian air as bullets zinged off rocks and embedded into trees. Not a single crack shot came close to hitting Joan.

Joan drove the car in a zigzag back down the jungle road, trying to miss the ruts and not succeeding. It was her first experience at driving in reverse for more than the length of a driveway. Understandably, she was nervous.

Jack was slow-jogging down the jungle road when he heard a growing noise like rolling thunder moving toward him. Then he heard distant gunshots, which could only mean the policia were back. Jack looked up just in time to see the Renault coming around the bend at breakneck speed—in reverse!

Jack stared in astonishment as an endless string of Zolo's jeeps bombed around the same bend, guns blazing.

Once the road widened, Joan jerked the wheel, fishtailing the Renault, and succeeded in heading the car in the right direction.

Jack's eyes darted around him, searching for cover in an area that offered little. For days he had struggled against oceans of vegetation and now, when he needed it, there was nothing. Jack turned on his heel and raced down the jungle road the way he'd come.

Joan glanced out of the rearview mirror and saw Zolo's jeeps gaining on her. Ralph was petrified, being tossed around in the car with the police firing at him. He jammed the flight bag in the console between him and Joan and then braced himself against the dashboard with both hands.

Joan was wild-eyed as she watched Jack running away from her, yet she couldn't slow down for fear she would be shot.

Jack glanced back over his shoulder, trying to

gauge the distance between himself and disaster. When he turned around, Jack stopped in a mid-stride freeze.

In the distance, directly in front of him, was a mounted posse of twelve horsemen thundering down the jungle road! The riders all wore the charcoal-and-black uniforms that Jack found very familiar. He also spotted their high-powered rifles, heavily loaded ammunition belts, and sheathed machetes.

Joan stared at Jack standing in the middle of the road as if he'd been turned into a pillar of salt. She strained her eyes through the windshield and when she saw the posse, she screamed. Ralph's hands flew to his mouth as he turned a bilious green.

Jack was caught in the middle of the posse and jeep cross fire and hadn't the slightest notion of how he was going to survive this one. Just then, he turned and saw the Renault bearing down on him.

Joan cranked the wheel to miss him and sent the car spinning around itself three times. The passenger door flew open on the third spin, ejecting Ralph, who went sailing into the road, huge mushroom clouds of dust emerging in his wake.

Jack watched as the Pan Am bag tumbled out of the car and rolled down the road. Before the bag bounced on the ground the third time, Jack was barreling after it. He scooped up the bag with the agility of an L.A. Rams lineman going for the fumble play of his career. With the bag tucked securely under his arm, Jack sprinted for the Renault. He took long strides, paced his breathing, and pushed himself even more but found he still could not catch up to Joan. Finally, with a burst of adrenaline, Jack ran even harder, until he was alongside the Renault. He looked at Joan and realized that she was driving like hell and had no intention of slowing down for him!

"*Slow down!*" He yelled at her.

"*They're gaining on us!!!!*"

Joan leaned over and flung the door open so that Jack was able to jump into the car Pony-Express style.

Jack didn't have time to question her reasoning, for they were bearing down on Zolo and his jeeps! Jack's eyes were bulging as he braced himself for the inevitable crash.

Hearing brakes screech and gravel crunch, Ralph picked himself up from the dust in time to see the Renault spin in a U turn and head back toward him. Directly behind the approaching Renault was Zolo and his deadly jeep squad. Quickly, he glanced in the opposite direction and saw the posse thundering toward him. It didn't take much intelligence to determine that he, Ralph, was the point of impact.

Suddenly the air was raining bullets, and in self-defense Ralph dropped to the ground in the nuclear-bomb-defense-position he'd learned in grade school. With head down and arms curled close to his body, Ralph could hear the bullets as they zinged off the Renault and pelted the road around him. He could feel the earth vibrating beneath him as the horses galloped toward him. In minutes he would be crushed into a matzo ball!

Spying Ralph in the middle of the road, Joan expertly cut the car to the right and drove off the road. One by one, the jeeps swerved away from Ralph and raced after Joan. Just as the last jeep left the road, the posse came charging through.

Ralph kept his head down, afraid to look death in the face. Gone were the roaring motors, galloping horses, and bursting gunfire. He was surprised at how painless death was, for he'd braced himself for horrible agony. Quickly he said a prayer and thanked God for making it easy on him. Cautiously he peeked over his arm, but could see nothing but dust, or perhaps it was a cloud . . .

A gust of wind whisked the dust away and as Ralph's vision cleared, he found he was looking at a wall of horses' legs. Miraculously, he had been saved! But as he looked up into the vacant eyes of the mounted riders, he reburied his head in his arms and wished he *had* died.

Remembering much of this terrain she had just covered with Ralph, Joan dodged ruts and foliage and for a time was eluding the policia. But as they drew closer to the river, the wheezing Renault was no match for the jeeps with their high-powered motors. Though the windows had been shot through with holes, Joan had avoided the majority of the gunfire. She counted herself lucky that none of the bullets had hit her or Jack.

Joan glanced back in the rearview mirror.

"They're gaining!"

"Fast!" Jack affirmed as he double-checked.

Jack knew this time there was no escape for them. There was no jungle cover, no vines to swing across the river, no hydraulic bridges, and no hope. He and Joan had led them a merry chase and had continued on when even he had doubted their chances. Jack watched solemnly as the impassable vegetation near the river's edge loomed in front of them. Never in his life would he have thought death would sound like the engine roar of a jeep.

Joan gunned the Renault at the precise moment Jack had expected her to brake, causing him to brace himself. A break in the wall of vegetation appeared only feet away from them.

"Joan! Where are you going?"

"Where am I going?"

Joan jammed the accelerator to the floorboard and blasted through the foliage, streaked down the embankment, and raced straight into the river.

"Lupe's escape!" she cried as she threw her hands up, a look of wild triumph on her face.

Tiny spouts of water rushed in through the bulletholes in the doors and windows. In moments the car was partially submerged. Before the Renault could touch river bottom, a fierce current grabbed the car and dragged it downstream. As they picked up momentum, Joan could see tree limbs and rocks in their path and to avoid them, she frantically began steering the car.

Jack burst into raucous laughter watching her. Joan was wild-eyed as they darted around the rapids, twisting the wheel first to the right and then to the left. She had to be doing some good for they had missed two deadly boulders, she thought.

Jack hugged the Pan Am flight bag to his chest and patted it. He was overjoyed at the fact that he was still alive and for good measure, he had the treasure *and* Joan.

The jeeps slammed to a perfectly precisioned halt, forming an orderly straight line at the wall of vegetation. Zolo stood in the lead jeep shouting orders. Scrambling from their jeeps, the first squad of soldiers raced to the embankment and began firing on the floating Renault while a second team worked their way to the river's edge.

Zolo aimed his high-powered rifle at the Americans, but only managed to hit the side mirror. As the Renault was swept around a bend and out of range, Zolo succumbed to his inner rage and threw his rifle on the ground, swearing revenge. Joan, he decided, would be the first to die and it would be a very slow death.

Chapter Twenty-Six

JACK PEERED OVER his shoulder and watched the soldiers disappear from view as they rounded the bend. He shared a triumphant smile with Joan and, still holding the flight bag in a tight grip, he put his arm around her shoulder, leaned over, and kissed her.

It was an unusual boat ride to be sure, but Joan thought it romantic as Jack kissed her. If she lived to be a hundred she knew she would never tire of the thrill of his kisses. As he parted her lips with his tongue and probed her mouth, Joan's pulse quickened and everything around her was blocked out except for the distant roaring noise in her ears.

Jack pulled her next to him and caressed her breast, causing her heart to pound fiercely against her ribs. The roar in her ears grew in direct proportion to the intensity of Jack's kiss. Joan felt as if she were flying through the heavens with nothing beneath her. She was giddy with joy, knowing they had outsmarted the policia, found the treasure, and rid themselves of the little creep who had tried to steal it from them. As Jack's hand reached inside her dress and teased her nipple, the roar in Joan's ears was nearly deafening.

Simultaneously, they both opened their eyes, realizing their kiss was not *this* earth-moving. Turning their heads to the front, they stared in horror as they approached their doom!

Dead ahead of them the river dropped completely out of sight; the gargantuan roar they'd heard was due to the murderous plunge of a thirty-foot waterfall!

Panic-stricken, Joan pointed at the falls and screamed at Jack. "What are we going to do?"

Jack clutched the Pan Am bag, thought for a split second, and yelled back, "Jump!"

Gaining speed, the rapids pitched the Renault around as if it were a child's bathtub toy. On Jack's instruction, Joan immediately pushed against her door, trying to get out, but the rushing current pressed against the outside of the door. When the Renault tossed onto its left side, Jack used the moment to open his door and jump free of the car.

Joan continued fighting with her door but it was no use; she was a prisoner. The waterfall loomed in front of her, its monstrous roar engulfing her. She tried to roll the window down but it was stuck. For an instant, Joan nearly resigned herself to remaining inside the car when she took the falls, but then a rush of water flung Jack's door open. Joan scrambled across the seat and jumped into the river.

The Renault was swept along the river at an

alarming rate of speed and then plunged over the falls. Joan tried to scream for Jack but every time she did, water gushed into her mouth. She vainly tried swimming against the rapids, her arms flailing about, but she was no match for the powerful current. Water was everywhere, in her ears, eyes, and mouth as she searched for Jack. Only a few yards from the deadly falls, Joan continued fighting against the mighty river. With eyes filled with horror, Joan realized she had lost as a last rush of river current pushed her, and the falls reached out and pulled her, to her death.

Plummeting downward and skimming the wall of water, Jack was guzzled up by a mountain of white water. For a fatally long period of time, Jack pitched and rolled beneath the water, fighting his way to the surface. Finally he swam away from the foot of the falls and when he surfaced, the river carried him downstream.

Exhausted but still struggling for shore, Jack worked his way to the left bank. For long moments he clutched at reeds and grasses so as not to be swept away again. He coughed up and vomited what he thought was at least half the river's water. Still clutching the flight bag, he hoisted himself onto shore. He rolled onto his stomach as he spit out more water and frantically tried to breathe normally.

Realizing he was going to live, he inched himself onto his knees, smiled at the flight bag, and looked for Joan. Then it hit him. She was not beside him where she should have been!

On trembling legs, Jack stood and scanned the river just in time to see the Renault go pitching over the falls and disappear into the water below. Seconds later he spied Joan, screaming what sounded like his name, as she was hurtled over the waterfall.

Desperately he searched the raging white water for any sign of Joan. Tons of water poured over the falls, hit bottom, and rose phoenixlike in soaring crystal fountains. Joan did not emerge.

The churning water vented its anger on Joan as she felt herself being thrashed about. Her lungs were burning and she thought her head would split in two. Terrified, she could not locate the surface. For an eternity she struggled upward, only to discover she had been turned around and was headed for river bottom!

She struck her arm on a rock, which sent sharp pains through her whole body. She felt as if she were being assailed from all sides and feared she would not survive.

Jack dropped the flight bag, the pleasure gone from everything. Frantically he scanned the river one last time before diving in to find Joan. He had just taken a step toward the edge of the bank when a smile lit his face.

Twenty yards downriver he saw Joan's head pop up from the water. Choking and coughing up river water, Joan crawled onto the opposite bank.

On all fours with her purse still strapped across her shoulder, Joan struggled to catch her breath.

"Hey!" Jack yelled downriver. "Hey, Joan Wilder!"

At the sound of his voice, Joan looked up to see Jack triumphantly holding up the Pan Am flight bag.

Jack was ecstatic that she was alive. "What a comeback!" he yelled over the noise of the rushing river.

"Yeah." Joan was half-dead and wondered how he could be so cheerful and full of energy.

"I thought you drowned, man!"

"I did!" Joan yelled as she tried to stand, found the effort too much for her, and fell. On the second try, she succeeded. She stood on the opposite bank glaring at him.

"You're okay, then!"

"I'm great! I'm super! *Only you're on that side!*"

Jack's shoulders slumped in defeat as he gazed down at the stormy river. Hoping that he could find a break to cross the water, he soon discovered there was none.

Joan was pacing up and down, her anger at both Jack and the river boiling inside her. No wonder he looked so happy just then! He had the treasure and now that she was stuck over here, she was afraid he would leave her just as he'd tried to do in the jungle many times before.

"There's no way to cross this sucker!" he yelled.

"*Try!*"

"*You* try!"

"Are you always gonna stay with what's safe?!" she screamed.

"You bet!"

"What about me?"

"I love you!"

His words rang in the air, drowning out the sound of the river, reverberating in Joan's head. She had wanted so desperately to hear those words when he made love to her, but now she wondered if he truly meant them.

"Then *come* to me," she pleaded. Please, Jack, don't be lying to me, she thought.

"I'll come to you in Cartagena. Hotel Emporio, right? You just keep walking toward the sunset, you'll get there—and I'll meet you there."

Joan was furious as she walked downstream. Just what was Jack Colton's game? If she could get across this river, she would throttle him within an inch of his life. Like hell he would meet her in Cartagena!

"You expect me to believe that? You, with El Corazón in your pocket! What about my sister?"

"They don't have to know any better. You got the map!"

"You got the stone!"

Before Joan could say any more, several rifle shots sounded in the distance. Jack and Joan both dived for cover in the thick undergrowth.

Zolo and his death squad reached the top of the falls just in time to see Joan scrambling onto the riverbank. From this vantage point, Zolo was unaware of Jack on the opposite bank and assumed that he had drowned.

The specter of a malicious smile wavered momentarily on Zolo's lips as he issued terse instructions to his men. Slinging their grappling hooks into the rocky cliffs, Zolo's men shimmied down long ropes like black widow spiders stalking their webs. Zolo observed the descent of his first squad through his ever-present binoculars. Satisfied that his men had safely reached the bottom of the falls, he ordered the second squad to reload their rifles. On his command they stood poised and ready to shoot.

Stealthily, the first squad worked their way down to the river's edge, keeping to the cover of the underbrush. Zolo observed every move his men made with a tactical eye, never losing sight of Joan's position.

When she had emerged spitting and coughing from the torturous falls, Zolo had been stunned to find that he applauded her victory over death. Moreover, he *respected* her; and for Zolo, that was as close to emotion as he was capable. Joan Wilder was an extraordinary woman. Though he never doubted his ability to ultimately defeat her, he appreciated her courage as an epicurean appreciates artistically displayed cuisine. As the high-powered rifles behind him cocked, he almost wished she could hear them, too. Almost. But the element of surprise was his forte.

Instead, he picked up the walkie-talkie and ordered the first squad to move in closer.

The first lieutenant informed Zolo that Jack was still alive and was in their range on the opposite bank. Zolo kept his fury in check and ordered his men to shoot to kill.

Jack stood on the riverbank, a victim of Joan's laser look. Her jade-green eyes shot across the distance, pleading with him and pulling him to her. She was magnificent, he thought, standing there, feet spread apart and hands on her hips. Her wet clothes clung to her body and even at this distance, he could see the outline of her fabulous long legs. An unexperienced rush of emotion flooded him. At this moment, he wanted to tell her everything about himself—about Jeannine and Billy, about his old job in New York; he wanted to take her to Malibu to meet his parents. He wanted to tell her that he would always be there for her when she needed him; he wanted to hold her, protect her, and comfort her. And it was impossible.

By virtue of its deadly power and great breadth, the river denied Jack the luxury of choice. He and Joan were being forced to find separate ways to reach Cartagena. She was still glaring at him and he knew there wasn't a chance in hell that she would believe him.

"Trust me!" he yelled across the river and blew her a kiss.

He looked at her one last time. She was a resourceful lady, but even he knew she never would have made it through the jungle alone. As she scowled at him across the raging waters, Jack thought that if nothing else, Joan's anger at him would give her the strength she needed to reach

Cartagena. He forced himself to believe she would make it, but his doubts swooped inside him like nervous bats.

Just as he lifted his arm to wave to her, a round of bullets zinged the ground near Jack's feet. Quickly, he ducked into the forest, leaving Joan to glare after him and then she too disappeared into the trees.

Darwinism states that survival belongs to the fittest. As Joan charged through the tropical forest, she prayed for a chink in the theory. Without Jack she was more frightened than ever and realized now just how greatly she had depended on him. In her favor was the fact that the undergrowth was light and she didn't need a machete. It was difficult enough just pacing herself to reserve her energy. Her thighs ached from climbing the hilly terrain and the soles of her feet were masses of scratches and cuts, for she had long ago discarded her dressy sandals. Though she might not be the most fit, she was the most determined and she counted on that to save her.

Joan used every trick Jack had taught her. She listened for the enemy but she could not hear rifle shots, machetes being slung, or the sound of jeeps or footsteps. But Jack had taught her well, for she *felt* their presence. She knew they were behind her just far enough away that she could not hear them. She had a good start on them but if she faltered too long or stumbled one too many times, they would overtake her.

With every passing minute, Joan's senses grew more heightened, and for the first time she was aware of the direction of the wind, the texture of the ground, and the growth patterns of the tree roots that seemed to reach out and clutch at her ankles. During the first hour of her trek, she had been the victim of tree branches and limbs that had scratched her face and arms and tore at her dress. Now that late afternoon was approaching, she found she anticipated minor collisions and successfully dodged most impediments to her progress. When the wind shifted, Joan altered her direction slightly and avoided low-swaying limbs that were wont to whip her face.

She avoided the rocky side of the hills and stayed to the northerly grassy, wooded slopes. When she reached the top of a hill, she would fix her eyes on a point on the next hill and set that as her goal. By doing this she found she did not become discouraged and kept a steady pace.

The climate in the hills was not as hot or humid as the jungle and Joan found her energy level still high as the sun began to set. Her "survival training" had stood her in good stead, for as she paused to catch her breath, she was quite proud of the extensive area she had covered.

She now stood on the top of the third and highest hill. From her vantage point she could see the river in the far distance. She scanned the hills for any sign of the jeeps and finally discerned that if she were being followed, Zolo and his men were on foot.

As the sun quickly disappeared, Joan watched the green hills turn a deep purplish blue as the sky became streaked with banners of pink and mauve and lavender. It reminded her of the sunset in the jungle by the river and of the dress she wore that Jack had bought for her. She looked down at the tattered silk and felt the prick of tears in her eyes.

Refusing to give way to emotion when her very life was at stake, she judged she could make a distant clump of thick-growing trees on the opposite slope before nightfall.

Joan carefully worked her way down the incline, which proved to be more steep than she had imagined. By clutching at tree limbs to maintain her balance, she covered the distance in less than fifteen minutes. When she reached the clump of cinchona trees, the massive limbs had cut off the last of the sun's evening rays and the opaque veil of night blanketed the forest.

Joan remembered what Jack had told her about ground cover, and she collapsed into the hollow of a fallen tree. Already the forest was growing cold and she pulled her knees up to her chest and stretched her skirt down to cover her ankles. She let her chin rest on her knees as she listened intently to the forest sounds.

This time she was educated in the strange sounds she heard. She knew the distinction between a cockatoo and a cock of the rock. There were no lions, no laughing hyenas, and, mercifully, no humans. For a while she was safe.

She should have been exhausted enough to fall

right to sleep, but all she could think of was Jack. Her instincts and senses had been so alert all afternoon, guiding her, helping her to survive; and when those same instincts told her that she would never see Jack again, she acquiesced to the tears that filled her eyes.

She chastised herself for being a victim of romance, which was only scene-setting and make-believe. She, better than anyone, knew that, for she made her living weaving fairy tales. It was her own fault she had allowed Jack to take advantage of her vulnerability.

From the night he had watched her stand naked in the river, Jack had begun his pursuit of her map, using Joan's attraction to him as his wedge. Hadn't she arisen in the morning to find him studying the map? It seemed that every time she looked up and caught him off guard, he was forever staring longingly at her purse. Now that she looked back on it, all the puzzle pieces seemed to fit.

Where once she had been blinded by her attraction for him and ambivalent about his feelings for her, she now knew the truth.

Jack Colton was a mercenary, just as she had originally deduced. Whether the fault lay in the sultry, exotic jungle or her own sexual desire, Joan Wilder had made a fool of herself.

Not only had she lost her heart to a rogue, but she was risking her sister's life because Jack possessed the emerald. If she did not play her role coolly and expertly when she met the kidnappers, Elaine would pay for Joan's incompetence with her life. Joan could never let that happen and she resolved to do everything she could to make the kidnappers believe the map was genuine and still valid.

A strong gust of wind whipped through the trees and Joan hugged her knees even tighter to stay warm. She listened again for sounds of her trackers. The birds had gone to sleep and only the chirping of cicadas broke the stillness. She leaned her head back, relieved she was not in immediate danger.

She wondered if the policia had gone after Jack, somehow sensing he had the treasure. Perhaps they had caught him already; knowing the extent of their technological advantages, it was plausible. Were her instincts trying to tell her that she would never see Jack again because he was already dead? Had the policia killed him with one of their high-powered bullets or had they caught him and then slowly severed his head from his body?

Joan's stomach lurched and the chill that coursed through her body came from fear and not the cold. She wouldn't believe that! Jack had to be alive! He couldn't leave her now, not when she was this angry with him! Not when she still loved him!

Tears were running in hot streams down her cheeks as she remembered him standing on the opposite side of the river, yelling that he loved her. He *had* said that! She had barely paid attention at the time, she was so incensed over his *obvious* delight in still possessing the emerald. But he had said it, hadn't he?

It was a simple thing to say, and yet Jack had found the courage to say it when she had failed. She remembered when they had made love; she had tried to tell him then, but found herself talking about the stupid map instead. And then in the cave, she almost blurted it out.

She smiled through her tears. Jack loved her! How could she have been so blind as to miss him saying something that important? Where were *her* priorities?

Joan's guilt hammered at her. "Mega-creep, that's what I am!"

Never had she felt this desolate. It was an even chance that Jack was dead and if he was still alive, he must think her a coldhearted bitch, or worse—a stone, like he had called her before. Just this once she wished she *were* a stone; then she wouldn't hurt this much. Jack loved her and here she sat, tearing him and his love for her apart. She was still angry at him for planting doubts in her heart when they should be trusting each other.

Again Joan was stabbed with a pang of guilt. He had asked her to trust him! God! Why was this so difficult? Loving and trusting had always sounded so simple, like child's play. Why were they almost impossible for her? She had hacked her way through an impenetrable jungle, dodged bullets and murderers, and driven at breakneck speed around mountain cliffs, and yet she could not trust the man she had lost her heart to!

Joan tried to still her sobs and failed. "Jack Colton . . . damn it," she moaned as her eyes closed involuntarily.

Zolo glanced over his shoulder at the setting sun and cursed. Without light it was useless to continue their search for Joan Wilder. Regardless of the fact that she had a considerable head start, she had left an easily detectable trail through the forest.

Though he had been detained at the waterfall deploying his men to the far side of the river to continue their pursuit of Jack, Zolo was not concerned about the inevitable outcome of his mission.

Because he admired her tenacity and, more important, because she still carried the map, Zolo chose to lead this squad. Of the two Americans, he believed that Joan Wilder would lead the more interesting of the chases. Besides, Zolo was planning a special celebration for himself and Joan once he caught her. It would be a private affair for the two of them and it would end in her death.

Chapter Twenty-Seven

By DEFINITION, A nightmare is a frightening dream accompanied by a sense of oppression that awakens the sleeper. It can also be an experience that produces a feeling of terror. For Joan Wilder, huddled inside a tree trunk in the middle of the Colombian forest, her nocturnal dreams of being tortured to death by vacant-eyed uniformed soldiers were only slightly less terrifying than the ominous reality of her situation.

Anesthetized by exhaustion and fear, Joan found it difficult to distinguish between the screeches, whines, and howls of the forest animals and those in her nightmare. The air around her seemed alive with sound, beckoning to her. Initially frightened by the unfamiliar noises, Joan curled into a tighter ball, but soon their intensity grew.

In her dream, her torturers cursed at her through clenched teeth, then laughed and howled in graveled voices when she screamed from the pain they inflicted. She moaned in her sleep and begged the evil men for mercy. They taunted her with promises of freedom if she would awaken. Petrified of the punishments reality held for her, she chose to remain asleep and let them continue their deadly games.

They whipped her with a cat-o'-nine-tails until Joan could stand the pain no longer. As she fell into unconsciousness, Joan saw a bright light. One of the torturers whispered in her ear that the light meant death. Joan didn't care if she died. She looked for the light and listened to the rumbling that accompanied it, which she knew was thunder. With it and the light she would meet death.

Joan was numb to the sting of the whip and deaf to the soldiers' taunts in her dreams, but she continued to listen to the thunder. She crawled out of the hollow tree and stumbled toward the light. It grew brighter as she advanced toward it and she smiled, knowing her escape from the soldiers was imminent.

The thunder roared in her ears and the light nearly blinded her but Joan ran faster. An evenly timed clicking began and Joan's smile grew wide as her eyes focused clearly and she came fully awake.

One by one, empty wooden boxcars of a night freight train rolled past Joan. She ran faster alongside the train and reached out for a side bar. She missed the first car and drew back momentarily to gain her bearings. The second time she stretched her arm a bit farther and this time she made contact and pulled herself up. In three quick movements she was inside the boxcar, exultant arms raised over her head, bidding farewell to the tropical forest.

At 12:35 in the afternoon, the lobby of the Hotel Emporio in Cartagena was filled with earnest businessmen and women shoppers who were dressed in expensive silk and handcrafted leather shoes. The garden restaurant with its white wicker furniture, pink linens, and potted plants were overrun with patrons inbibing rum-based cocktails and conversing over seafood salads.

For decades the Hotel Emporio had been committed to a policy of excellence and decorum. Every aspect of the decor, from the Chinese rugs and brocade upholstered Hepplewhite furniture to the French baroque chandeliers, announced—in subdued tones—that this hotel existed as a monument to refinement.

When the hotel director, himself a standard by which all hotel employees modeled themselves, looked up from his leather note pad to see a disheveled and dazed woman, her hair wild and tangled with dried leaves and twigs, his dignified jaw dropped to the tip of his conservative white collar.

Joan leaned on the gold-veined, white marble reception desk, peered at the man through swollen, bloodshot eyes and said in a slightly punch-drunk voice:

"I'm Joan Wilder. I have a reservation. I'd like the largest suite you have, with the biggest possible bathtub. Send up a bottle of red wine. I'll be ordering dinner to go with it and let me know the minute a Jack Colton checks in."

The hotel director spun instantly on the heel of his alligator shoe, produced a key to one of his finest suites, and ordered a bellboy to escort the woman upstairs as quickly as possible. As Joan proceeded to the elevators, the hotel director surreptitiously scanned the lobby for any signs of disruption. Seeing relatively few, he breathed a sigh of relief and went back to his notepad.

Once the bellboy opened the drapes, adjusted the air conditioning, and pointed out the closets, bath, and light switches, Joan dismissed him, forgetting his tip. She locked the door behind him and went directly to the telephone. She dialed the number the kidnappers had given her. Once the connection was made, it was picked up immediately.

Ira was delighted to hear from her and it showed in his voice. "So you made it, finally. Got the map?"

"Yes, I've got it. Can I talk to Elaine?"

"After I get the map," he said tersely. "Now here's what you do. See the fort across the bay? The tower?"

Joan walked across the room, opened the glass door, and walked out onto the terrace. "Yes," she said, peering out over the bay. There in a direct line from her room was a tall, ramshackle structure that had once been a battlement.

"You take the water taxi, right outside your hotel. You meet me there at nine o'clock tonight. All by yourself. Okay?"

"The tower, yes, okay. But—"

Before she could say anything else, the kidnapper hung up and dashed her hopes of speaking to Elaine. For a moment, panic gripped her when she doubted Elaine's safety, but she pushed the feeling aside. She had come too far and fought too hard to have it all end in ashes. Elaine was safe, she told herself.

Joan replaced the receiver and caught a glimpse of herself in the mirror for the first time. She looked half-dead! Her eyes were swollen and her cheeks gaunt. Every inch of her skin seemed to be scratched, cut, or bruised. Her beautiful dress had been reduced to a rag and it would take days of combing just to untangle her hair.

Joan picked up the phone again and rang for room service. She ordered a thick steak, baked potato with the works, a tossed salad, extra rolls and butter, and two pieces of cheesecake for dessert. She needed strength, both physical and mental, for the ordeal tonight and she intended to get it any way she could.

She phoned the gift shop in the lobby and had a comb, brush, shampoo, and toiletries charged to her room and sent up. She inquired about the hours in the boutique next door and discovered they took American Express traveler's checks.

Simultaneously, her meal, wine, and toiletries arrived. It took her less than twenty minutes to consume the dinner and while she ran a tub of hot water, she ate every bit of the first piece of cheesecake.

After four washings, the last of the forest leaves and grasses swirled down the drain. An hour's soak in the tub took most of the sting out of her scratches and cuts, and the wine numbed the pain of her bruises. An eyewash cleared the red out of her eyes and an ice pack reduced the swelling. By three o'clock she looked almost human again.

She called the front desk. "Has a Jack Colton checked in?"

The hotel director informed her in courteous tones that Mr. Colton had not.

Joan replaced the receiver more disappointed than she cared to admit. Even though she had found the train to Cartagena, she still believed Jack should have made it to the city by now. She convinced herself that there was still a two-hour play she could allow him before panic was necessary.

In the meantime, she could not wait around Cartagena in a torn dress with her breasts half-exposed. She checked her purse, satisfied she had enough money for shoes, underwear, and a dress. She left the room and headed for the boutique.

Shopping was more Elaine's forte than Joan's and with her anxieties over her sister and Jack, it was little wonder she could not decide between the imported Gianfranco Ferrè oversized asymmetric blouse and slim black leather skirt or the Perry Ellis shapely linen jacket and narrow cocoa skirt to match. She chose the Ferrè, wondering if the designer from Milan would mind that she wore it to a ransoming. With sheer black stockings, black high-heeled shoes, and a new shoulder-strap purse, she left the boutique.

Joan returned to her room, placed a call to the airline, and booked a flight for herself and Elaine bound for New York that night at fifteen after midnight. Joan intended to lose no time chatting with Elaine's kidnappers. Another phone call confirmed that a taxi would await her outside the hotel to take them to the airport.

At 5:15 Joan had finished the second piece of cheesecake and the last of the wine. When Joan rang the front desk, her hands were trembling.

"Has Jack Colton checked in yet?"

This time the hotel director was more curt than polite and his answer did little to settle Joan's growing fears. The nightmares she had in the forest came back to her, but this time the screams she heard were not hers, but Jack's.

Chapter Twenty-Eight

THREE HOURS WAS not a long time and yet within those one hundred eighty minutes, Joan's nerves had been peeled raw. She phoned the desk a minimum of once a minute. It was nearly time for her to meet the kidnappers and still there was no sign of Jack.

When she exited the elevator and headed toward the front desk, it was the wild, haunting look in her eyes that drew the attention of the other guests. She was oblivious to their stares as she fought to control her anxiety over Jack's fate. Always the optimist, she put her hopes on the hotel director's answer this one last time.

He cringed when he saw her approach him, but smiled wanly, noting the obsequious gazes the patrons gave him.

"Has Jack Colton checked in yet?"

He turned and glanced at the lobby clock. It was precisely 8:30. He produced a weary sigh.

"In the last two minutes, no."

Joan bit her lip to prevent an outburst of tears

she felt entitled to, turned away from the hotel director, and rushed through the front doors.

A thick coastal fog rolled into the principal seaport of Colombia, obliterating Joan's view of anything beyond two feet. As she looked around, she was unaware of the long black Lincoln with smoked glass windows that sat across the street from the hotel.

Joan crossed the street and walked down the sidewalk until she came to the wharf. She passed by fishing boats moored in neat rows, their repairs and peeling paint hidden by the dense fog. She could hear the water lapping against the wooden dock supports and boat bottoms as she neared the end of the dock where she hoped to find the water taxi.

At the very end of the pier sat an old man dressed in a pair of faded blue jeans and a short-sleeved knit shirt that exposed his numerous tattoos. He wore a billed cap over his bald head and his smile was toothless when he greeted her. He spoke just enough English to convey to Joan the price of the trip to the tower. With his steady arm he helped Joan onto the boat and then he started the engine. As they pulled away from the dock, Joan was unaware of anything but her sister's rescue.

A 1976 Ford LTD with no air conditioning or radio and recently painted the electric blue of the Cartagena Cab Company pulled up in front of the Hotel Emporio. Jack Colton stepped out of the cab, paid the driver with the last of his pesos, and rushed inside the hotel.

The hotel director dropped his jaw for the second time that day when the scruffy-looking American carrying a Pan Am flight bag walked up to his desk and announced that he was Jack Colton. When the hotel director informed the American that Joan Wilder had left the hotel only moments prior, Jack startled the hotel director by cursing aloud in English and then bolting through the lobby and out the front doors.

The hotel director succumbed to an attack of nerves brought on by gasps of outrage from several of his more conservative guests and by the fact that the hotel vice-president stood behind him and ordered him to the executive office.

Jack raced across the street and down the dock. He too failed to notice the black Lincoln. Jack pounded down the wharf and reached the end of the pier in time to see the water taxi pulling out of sight!

"Joan!" he bellowed into the fog. "Joan!"

The sound of the boat motor disappeared and he knew she was too far away to hear him. Before Jack had a moment to think—*click!!*

A gun cocked at his temple.

The smell of hundreds of years' decay assaulted Joan's nostrils when the water taxi deposited her at the small wooden bridge that led to the Spanish fort. Joan leaned over the railing and looked down into the foreboding water beneath the decking, thinking it looked incapable of supporting life. Suddenly she was very unsure of everything, especially herself. She must not allow fear to overtake her. Elaine was here, she just had to be, Joan told herself. The boards creaked and moved under her feet, negating her positive thinking with every step she took.

Inches-thick mildew clung to the limestone squares that formed the battlements and walls. Joan entered the compound, her eyes inspecting every darkened corner and doorway. Ground mist swirled around her feet and eerie shadows produced menaces where there were none; she could feel death hanging in the air. Had she been writing a gothic novel, she could not have chosen a more appropriate setting.

The Spanish began construction on the fort in 1578 to protect the seaport city from attack by pirates and from invasion by the English, with whom they were at war. The Chibcha Indians, now submissive to the Spaniards, quarried the limestone rock out of the nearby mountains and hauled the block by horse- and mule-drawn wooden carts to the site. It took over ten years to complete the rambling structure with its many wings.

At sea level there was now a stone wharf area where small boats could dock. An iron staircase led up from the wharf to the main level where Joan now stood. Four wings, which at one time had held officers quarters, dormitories, kitchen, and dining rooms, extended from the main building like points on a compass. The main building was three stories high and in its center a forty-foot tower shot into the sky for the purpose of housing the lookout. From that vantage point a trained man could spot an approaching ship for miles.

Surrounding the entire area and encompassing the structure was a six-foot-high battlement wall which contained nearly a hundred cannon portals, all symmetrically spaced. Should an attack occur, this wall and the artillery it housed were the only protection the soldiers had. Most of the cannons were missing, leaving cavities that created the frightening sensation of deadly eyes watching her.

Joan looked up at the iron bars in the windows above her and wondered how many people had been unjustly imprisoned behind them. She had once read an article in the *National Geographic* on haunted buildings, which stated that this fort was haunted. Two psychics and a parapsychologist had investigated the area, and they produced photographs showing blurry hazes that were thought to be poltergeists. Joan hadn't taken the article seriously at the time, but as she peered more closely into the windows, she thought she saw a green glow coming from the fourth window on the left.

Joan shuddered and hugged herself tightly but the light seemed to glow brighter. She forced herself to look away but only succeeded in blinking her eyes. She looked back again and the glow was gone. Whether it was her imagination or a real ghost, Joan had no intention of sticking around to find out. Quickly, she moved along the wall.

A freighter moored nearby cast pools of light

through its many windows as she crossed a swampy expanse. She passed beneath a barren flagpole and still she saw no one. Frightened that the kidnappers had discovered the truth about the treasure and that Elaine might be in mortal danger, Joan choked back the lump in her throat and continued on. Cautiously she made her way to the tower.

"Hello? Anyone here?" she called out, and even she was surprised at the temerity in her voice.

Not far from her she heard water swish for a moment and stop. Then, an odd sounding flapping noise from across the swamp reached out at her. She froze, listening to the silence, and something told her the noises were not human.

Joan inched her way along a low stone wall, passed under a palm tree, and peered through the rising mist. She could see less now than when she had arrived. From somewhere in the gloomy fog a disembodied voice called out to her.

"Stop right there!"

Joan halted mid-stride, afraid to breathe.

"Let me see the map," the voice said.

"Where are you?" Joan asked as she fumbled in her purse and squinted into the distance.

"Let me see the map," the voice said sternly.

"Let me see Elaine."

Just then, Elaine, hands bound behind her back, was thrust into view, the light from the freighter illuminating her frightened face. Joan could not see who was holding her from behind but it was evident he would not release her until they had been satisfied about the map.

Elaine gasped at the woman in front of her, wondering who she was. She sounded like Joan, but through the mist she was unable to tell. Joan never wore clothes like that and this woman's hair was thick, curled, and somewhat lighter, she thought. If something had happened to Joan, she would never forgive herself.

"Joan?" Elaine called. The woman cocked her head to the side and smiled, and Elaine sighed with relief. "Joan."

The voice called out again. "Drop the map and back off."

Joan did as she was instructed and watched as Elaine's kidnapper stepped from the shadows. He was short, bald, and tacky-looking, but Joan didn't miss the cold gleam in his eyes. He didn't look like the sinister man she had envisioned in her mind, but she was wise enough not to underestimate him either. He still had the power to control both her and Elaine's life. As he passed by her, Joan glanced at him with all the pent-up anger and frustration she'd felt since the moment she'd received Elaine's phone call in New York. How she wished she had a gun! She could easily pull the trigger and feel no remorse at all.

Ira shot Joan an equally dark look.

"If this isn't genuine, if you've pulled a fast one . . ." he said as he walked toward the map and retrieved it. From his shirt pocket he withdrew a penlight and focused it on the map.

Joan scanned his face, weighing his reactions.

He was not happy. His eyes narrowed as his eyebrows shot upward in a menacing look. Joan noted the tight line to his lips and the tense set of his jaw. As he inspected the map further, a nervous tick settled at his right temple.

Joan braced and Elaine shriveled.

Ira pulled out his jeweler's loupe and scrutinized the map even closer. The moments passed in an agonizingly deadly silence. Finally Ira looked up at Joan and scowled. His eyes were icy pools and Joan knew then, if pushed too far, he was capable of murder.

"Joan Wilder . . . you and your sister . . ." His voice was threatening and Joan felt her muscles tense.

". . . can go." Ira finished his statement simply and without fanfare, even laughing at his little joke.

Two huge men dressed like longshoremen stepped into the light. Joan took special notice of their rifles, which one of them shoved into Elaine's back. It was a scare tactic used to let the women know who had the power over life and death. Joan refused to be intimidated by the oily-looking little man or his hired bullies.

Elaine jumped and embraced her sister. "Joanie . . ."

"It's okay, Elaine. We're going home."

Joan tossed Ira a parting glance and ushered Elaine toward the low wall. Joan had taken but two steps when sudden machine-gun fire shattered the night air, exploding a line of bullets across Joan's path, only inches from her toes.

Two men in black-and-charcoal uniforms sprang out of the shadows and thrust the butts of their rifles into the heads of the two longshoremen. Simultaneously, the two heavyset men dropped their guns and crumpled to the ground.

From behind a palm tree a dark figure emerged, only his shiny black boots and gleaming gun visible in the obscure light. Ira felt the cold steel of a gun muzzle rammed into the back of his head before he saw the soldier who carried it. Ira held his breath and raised his hands to the sky.

As if by magic, Jack suddenly appeared in the brightest pool of light. Joan instantly smiled and started toward him before she realized there was a gun pointed in his back. She froze as three more soldiers emerged from the darkness, surrounding both her and Elaine. She felt Elaine's grip tighten on her arm and they both stared in horror at the half dozen high-powered rifles aimed directly at them.

As Joan looked into Jack's eyes, she knew he'd come back for her. He had told her to trust him and she hadn't, not really. True, she had prayed for his safety and *hoped* he would return to her, but trust was something he had to earn. As he stood before her, Joan knew she could always trust Jack.

Jack wished like hell Joan wouldn't look at him like he was her savior. He was grateful she had survived the forest but he saw no way out of their dilemma this time. A lot of good he'd been, practically leading this maniac right to her! He had no weapons to defend her and no jungle or forest in which to hide. He would have to rely on his wit and with a gun barrel stuck in his backside, he didn't feel very witty.

Just then, off to Jack's left, a lighter flared in the darkness, illuminating Zolo's face. In his moment of triumph, his sinister lips parted in a smirk. Lighting his Colombian cigarillo, he sauntered into the light like a theatrical producer about to give direction. It was the end of the play and the curtain was about to come down on Joan and Jack.

Chapter Twenty-Nine

LUST GREW LIKE a sty in Zolo's eyes as Joan watched him leering at her. The color of black pitch, they slid over her body, lingering too long over her legs and breasts. There were times in the jungle when she had felt his lecherous eyes raping her through his binoculars. She had dismissed the notion as another product of her overactive imagination, but one thing Colombia had taught her was that fact could be more incredible than fiction.

Joan stood stock-still, her eyes defiant, her nerves frayed and screaming from tension. As she watched him she knew then he was more interested in her than in the map. He was a sadist and if she survived long enough, she swore she would not make it easy for him. Her fingers flexed as she itched to wrap them around his throat and tear at his jugular. Her fury grew when she heard him laugh and then blithely toss his cigarillo aside as he turned from her. This was part of the torture, she thought, for she was certain he would come back to her.

Zolo walked over to Ira and calmly held out his hand. Ira stared at his captor momentarily and then painfully surrendered the map. Zolo stared at it, flipped it over, and observed the foldings that revealed the waterfall. Then he flicked his lighter and set Ira's precious map aflame.

Ira gasped and looked first at Zolo and then at the map.

Zolo sneered at Ira and then dropped the flaming map to the ground. Horrified, Ira pounced on the map, hoping to stamp out the fire before too much damage was inflicted.

Zolo looked down at the pathetic sight at his feet. "That map is worthless."

At that moment, Ralph was shoved into the light by the two remaining soldiers.

Zolo nodded to his lieutenant, who held Ralph in an iron grip. "They already have the stone," Zolo said.

Ira was dumbfounded and glared at Ralph, who smiled sheepishly at his cousin.

"I had it, Ira, in my hands. Magnificent! You should have—"

Zolo grabbed Ralph's arm as casually as if it were a chicken bone and flung the rumpled little man against the stone wall. With the wind knocked out of him, Ralph fell to the ground, coughing and wheezing.

Zolo took out another cigarillo and lit it, glaring momentarily at each of his captives. Methodically, he paced around as he planned his strategy. He passed a rotten wooden gate in the low brick wall and peered over it. He leaned down a bit further, paused, and then took the cigarillo from his mouth and tossed it over the wall.

With lightning-quick speed an enormous crocodile with rare yellow markings snatched the cigarillo in midair. In moments, the king crocodile was joined by several more crocodiles and together they moved into the light.

When Zolo looked up from the marshy swamp and moved toward her, Joan thought she had never seen such evil in a human's face. She hated him with every fiber of her being and he knew it. It was the magnitude of her anger that spurred him on. She tried to control her emotions but found she'd created an internal war that could destroy her. When she glared at him, a malevolent smile settled on his lips. Her jaw tightened in fear and she thought every muscle in her body had turned to stone. She could hear her heart thundering at her temples.

Elaine cowered behind Joan as Zolo drew near, not understanding anything about who these men were and how Joan seemed to know them.

With his face only inches from Joan's, Zolo's deadly black eyes bore into her.

"Where is it?" he demanded, his breath cold as ice.

"I don't know!"

"Where is the stone?"

"I don't . . ." Joan was faltering as she watched his eyes grow more menacing. She sensed the movement of his arm as he reached for his gun.

"We dug, there was nothing there."

Zolo didn't buy it and she knew it.

Zolo pointed to Ralph. "He saw it."

"He's a liar! He lies!"

Zolo straightened and barked some orders in Spanish to two of his soldiers. They grabbed Joan under the armpits and dragged her to the wall. For a moment she struggled and tried to wrest herself from their grip, but one of them hit her in the ribs just hard enough to thwart any further attempts at resistance.

Jack instantly started toward her, but the soldier behind him jammed a gun into his back and cocked it. Jack scanned the area looking for a means of escape but found none. He felt utterly helpless.

Zolo advanced toward Joan with reptilian movements, much like the crocodiles that slithered in the putrid swamp behind her. She gasped as Zolo reached for her hand. With the grace of a dandy he raised her hand to his lips as if he were going to kiss it.

His touch was cold and damp, and just imagining how his hands would feel sliding across the smooth skin of her stomach and breasts was nearly enough to make her faint. She doubted there was blood in his veins, for there was no warmth to him at all. She found it impossible to imagine his ever having had a mother, for something like Zolo rose out of the depths of hell.

He forced her to look at him when he spoke.

"Crocodiles shed tears while they are eating their prey. You have heard of these tears, I am sure. But have you seen them?"

In one quick movement, Zolo whipped out his stiletto, its blade flashing silver in the light as Joan watched it descend and slash a deep razor cut in her hand. She wanted to scream from the pain but bit her tongue instead.

Jack tried to wrest away from his captor. "Stop!" he yelled, panic filling his voice. The soldier jammed a rifle into Jack's stomach and he doubled over in pain. His vision blurred as he struggled to stand. A band of pain seemed to twist around his midsection like a lasso and then jerk at his insides, making him want to scream. He blinked again, clearing the mist in his eyes. His eyes held on Joan and he mouthed the words "I love you."

Joan's eyes locked on Jack, knowing if she thought about something else, she would not feel pain or fear. She put all her hope and trust in Jack. He would think of something—he would save her.

One of the soldiers tightened his grip on Joan and she felt a sharp pain shoot down her arm. She winced again. Zolo forced her arm over the low gate and with sadistic pleasure slowly lowered Joan's arm almost within reach of the crocodiles.

Joan could feel rivulets of blood running down her fingers and dripping into the slimy water. Zolo's face was very near hers and she could feel his cold breath against her cheek once again.

He leaned his body into hers, pressing harder on her arm. He was deriving sexual pleasure from his torture and Joan was more disgusted than ever. He was not human at all.

Joan was losing what little hope she had been clinging to. She had no more defenses against Zolo. She heard water slosh as the crocodiles moved toward her hand. The sound grew louder as they slithered by her, charting the territory. She felt scaly skin brush her fingertips and she tried to jump away but only succeeded in moving closer to Zolo. His smile was evil and lustful as he gazed down at her face and then down further to her breasts. She was unsure which was less dangerous, the crocodiles or Zolo.

She continued to stare at Jack with pleading eyes. She kept trusting in him, but he was making it very difficult! Just how much longer was she going to suffer before he spoke up? Was he going to wait until her hand—and then her arm—became an evening meal for that yellow-striped crocodile down there? Tears were brimming in her eyes, but she fought them back, her anger overcoming her fear.

"You can forego this agony. Simply tell me; Where is El Corazón? Where is the heart?"

"All right! All right!" Jack bellowed at Zolo. "You want it? I'll tell you where it is."

Zolo smirked at Joan but eased off her arm and nodded to his soldiers, who relinquished their painful grip. Joan's eyes smiled gratefully at Jack.

Jack was hesitant. "It's, ah . . . there's a bar on the way into town. I think it's called Lupe's. I met a woman there. She took that stone with a straight flush. Damn, you should of seen it."

Joan winced at the pitiful lie. She hoped he knew

what he was doing. It was obvious he was stalling for time, but she was afraid that she would be the biggest loser, should the ploy not work.

Zolo spun around and faced Joan once again, dismissing Jack with a grunt.

"I hope he was a better lover than he is a liar."

Jack saw the desperation in Joan's eyes. She was depending on him to save them all and he had no trump cards left. Even if he gave them the emerald, he seriously doubted their chances to escape. He could tell it was a thought that had *not* occurred to Joan. Zolo was a desperate man who had killed at least once for the emerald, and a few more bodies tossed in the swamp would not matter.

Zolo clenched Joan's arm and once again forced her hand over the wall, enticing the crocodiles.

Joan didn't think she could stand it much longer. The crocodiles were snapping their jaws as her hand inched closer to their mouths. She knew she was going to scream, for she could hear it mounting inside her chest and rolling into the tunnel in her throat. She fought to control herself and wanted to look at Jack but for the first time she was afraid he was going to let her down. She had wanted to believe they could escape but all their chances were gone. She had tried to make Jack into a god and he was just a man. He couldn't save her any more than she could save herself. As she peered into the murky water, she saw a particularly vicious-looking crocodile only seconds from tearing off her hand!

"Okay, okay. Let me try again . . ." Jack started, when a soldier shoved his rifle butt into Jack's groin. On impact, a peculiar clinkish sound filled the air. The soldier froze and Zolo eyed Jack with suspicious interest.

Jack cried out in pain and doubled over. His arms crossed and hugged around himself, and then he slowly straightened up. All eyes were on him.

Joan saw the pain in his eyes as he looked at her, but there was something else there . . . defeat? Suddenly Jack's face contorted into a thousand emotions and he looked as if he'd gone crazy. He reached around behind his back, his arm going up over his head and back down again. His leg shook nervously as if he were convulsing. He turned, twisted, and gyrated into several positions, none of them normal. For an instant, Joan wondered if he were having some type of seizure. His eyes darted from face to face, settling nowhere.

Joan saw the murderous look on Zolo's face as he continued to hold her arm over the wall and watch the crocodiles move in closer. She knew Jack couldn't stall any longer. Elaine was plastered against a stone wall, her eyes giant with horror, and Joan thought she could almost hear her sister's heart pounding.

The two kidnappers were as spellbound as everyone else by Jack's strange dance. His leg jerked out one last time and then, suddenly, Jack stopped and smiled charmingly at Zolo.

"The heart? It's where you find it."

The huge green jewel dropped out of Jack's pant leg and onto his scruffy boot.

Joan snatched her arm away from Zolo and glared at Jack. "Just how long would you have waited?"

Jack returned her smile and kicked the stone into the air. The fabled El Corazón arced high in the air, refracting sparkling emerald shafts of light. Joan was mesmerized by the sight of the priceless jewel as it created a cometlike tail in its upward spin. She thought of how her life and that of Jack and her sister had depended on that stone. El Corazón had caused murders to be committed, lives to be ruined, and—for one of them yet to be seen—a fortune to be made.

All eyes were focused skyward as they watched the green treasure tumble through the air. When it reached the apex of its flight, the emerald seemed suspended momentarily before it hit a palm frond and then dropped completely out of sight.

Joan felt hopeless, thinking the emerald could have brought their freedom. Long moments passed before the emerald reappeared, rolled down one palm frond, and then cascaded onto another. As if being passed from hand to hand, the jewel slid from leaf to leaf, moving ever downward.

It seemed an eternity to Joan as she watched her only chance of escape sparkle like a giant dewdrop on the end of a tropical leaf.

When El Corazón reached the last frond, a hand reached out to retrieve it. Ever so gently, it dropped into Zolo's right hand. Possessively, Zolo's fingers wrapped around the enormous emerald as he looked over at Jack with lethal eyes.

"Thank you," Zolo said.

At that moment Jack knew Zolo would order their deaths.

Zolo raised his arm and opened his mouth to give the order and . . . *crash!!!*

The gate on the low stone wall shattered into a hundred pieces of rotted wood as the yellow-striped king crocodile smashed through the flimsy barrier and sank his razor teeth into Zolo's arm. With one mighty twist of his head, the crocodile divested Zolo of his hand and El Corazón.

Zolo's screams splintered the foggy night as he instantly sank to his knees, dropping his stiletto on the way down. He grasped the bloody stump with his good hand and stared disbelievingly at his mangled arm. His face, contorted with pain and hatred, looked like a medieval gargoyle.

Seizing his only advantage, Jack drew back and rammed his fist into his guard's face. The man was well trained and faltered for only a split second before delivering a punch to Jack's stomach. Whether due to adrenaline or sheer guts, Jack was unruffled and smashed his fist into the man's face again and again, pelting him with a series of rapid blows that in less than fifteen seconds rendered the man unconscious. Before anyone realized what Jack was doing, in the midst of the confusion and Zolo's screams, Jack had possession of a machine gun and instantly began spraying the unsuspecting soldiers with a round of bullets.

While the uniformed soldiers and kidnappers dived for cover, Joan snatched up Zolo's stiletto and yanked Elaine behind a cargo crate.

Joan watched with a victorious smile as Jack's bullets zinged off the limestone fort walls and splintered the wood planking. One of the soldiers who had been slow to react fell to the ground clutching his leg where one of Jack's bullets had found its mark.

Jack twisted around and sprayed the ground once again, catching another soldier who had tried to sprint for cover behind a stack of hemp rope. He screamed and fell, and then crawled behind the rope, still grasping his wounded arm.

Zolo, still in agony, staggered behind a stack of old wooden crates. His stump was bleeding profusely so he used his necktie as a tourniquet and then wrapped his jacket around the entire arm. Satisfied that he had done all he could for his injury, he leaned back and took stock of the situation. With a trembling left hand, he reached into his pocket, withdrew a cigarillo and lit it. He inhaled deeply, savoring the smoke in his lungs. Vengeance boiled in his blood, giving him the energy to attack once again. Zolo ripped a board from a crate, intending to use the protruding, rusty nails as his weapon. He would use it on Joan Wilder first. There was a glint in his eye when he thought how loudly she would scream when he raked it across her face.

Ralph raced past Zolo and down the walkway, trying to avoid Jack's bullets and the snapping crocodile at his heels. He looked back over his shoulder and saw nothing but glistening sharp teeth and scaly skin. Again he cursed Ira for the entire misadventure and swore vengeance of his own. Suddenly Ralph stopped. He had run into a blind alley and had nowhere to go—but up.

Ralph flung himself against an old rickety flag-pole and quickly shinnied to the top. The old pole groaned and swayed under his weight, but Ralph held on for dear life. Beneath him the crocodile snapped his jaws and waited.

With remarkable agility, King Croc moved along the battlement wall.

Jack spied the emerald-carrying reptile, tossed the machine gun on the ground, and lunged for the crocodile. His first attempt was lousy as he mis-judged the swift-moving tail. On the second try, Jack made contact but was unprepared for the crocodile's slick skin and slid off when King Croc flipped his tail to the right, tossing Jack against the wall. Momentarily stunned, Jack was not about to give up. Catching his breath and sizing his prey more accurately, this time Jack succeeded in grasp-ing onto the crocodile.

"Gotcha! You yellow-bellied lizard!"

Jack was busy taming the crocodile and did not see Ira zigzagging across an open space and squeezing off shots at Zolo's men. Ira turned to the left and hid behind the battlement wall.

Ira waited while Jack moved closer to him. King Croc couldn't have been more cooperative if Ira had trained the animal himself, for he was moving directly toward Ira.

Twice, ricocheting bullets nearly struck him, but

Jack refused to relinquish his hold on King Croc. Jack was unaware of who was firing at whom, all he cared about was getting the emerald. His hands were bloody masses as he tried to strengthen his grasp, but the crocodile's scales were sharp and the tighter Jack made his hold, the more his skin was cut. When the crocodile flipped his mighty tail and sent Jack against the battlement wall for the second time, Jack nearly passed out. He saw flashing lights and his eyes refused to focus. Gasping and wheezing, he fought for his breath but his lungs failed. Jack's hearing faded and he was completey disoriented.

It was when King Croc's tail hit the wall again causing a sudden vibration that jolted Jack's head, that Jack began to regain his bearings. He could hear people scurrying about and guns being fired. A long moment passed before he remembered where he was.

Finally, when Jack looked up his eyes were clear and he spied King Croc heading for an empty cannon portal. Though still unsteady, Jack scrambled to his feet.

Suddenly, Ira jumped from out of the shadows and slammed the revolver into Jack's chest.

"End of the line, pal," Ira leered.

Irate that anyone would dare interfere in his pursuit of the crocodile, Jack balled his fist and simply knocked the gun out of Ira's hand. The gun went spinning across the battlement wall and stopped near the portal. To Jack, Ira was more an insult than a real threat and so, with both hands on Ira's collar, Jack picked him up as if he had no weight and tossed him over the wall and into the swamp.

Jack turned back to the cannon portal just in time to see King Croc slide through the opening. Jack dived after him before he disappeared from sight and caught the mighty King Croc by the end of his tail. Jack struggled to retain a firm hold as the crocodile flipped him effortlessly back and forth. This time Jack knew he would not lose his hold on the crocodile for he had assessed his prey and he was convinced of a final victory—provided nothing else interfered with him again.

The sound of sirens in the distance wrested Joan's attention away from Jack's struggle with the crocodile. Quickly she grabbed Elaine's arm and inched her way along a stone wall, knowing that she had to escape now.

Elaine clutched her sister's hand so tightly, Joan thought her circulation would be cut off. It was the first real indication Joan had of how frightened her sister had been. Elaine had barely said a word and Joan had attributed her silence to Elaine's good sense and self-control. Now she realized that her sister was in a state of shock and probably was not fully aware of the danger they were in. Elaine's eyes were a bit too glassy to be normal and now Joan worried about her all the more. As they stealthily made their way along the stone wall, Joan was careful to keep to the shadows while Elaine said nothing and allowed her sister to guide her. Joan prayed the soldiers were more intent on the sirens and the last of the longshoremen who were returning their fire. One final look told her that if she moved quickly, her last sprint across the open ground to the fort staircase would go undetected.

Suddenly, chills raced down Joan's spine when she heard a familiar rasping cough behind her. She spun around to see Zolo less than eight feet from her! His arm was wrapped in a jacket, blood oozing through the fabric and he carried a nail-studded board in the other hand. He glared at her with murderous eyes as he moved toward her. He drew heavily on the cigarillo that dangled from his lips and then slowly blew out the smoke as he started to speak.

"How will you die, Joan Wilder? Slow like the pace of the turtle, or fast like the shooting star?"

Joan frowned at him, thinking she had written dialogue better than that! She laughed nervously to herself thinking what strange and inconsequential things one thinks of when faced with certain death. She regretted she would never finish her book or go to Paris in the autumn after the summer tourists had left. She would never learn to ice skate or perfect her backhand, or try the cheesecake at Miss Grimble's on the Upper West Side. She needed to clean out her refrigerator, own a kitten, and make love to Jack again. She really didn't want to die.

Joan shielded Elaine with her body as she moved slowly backward. Elaine was bug-eyed, clutching at her sister's shoulder and staring at the monster that loomed before them. It was Elaine who felt the wall first and whispered to her sister that they were at a dead end.

Joan watched as the mutilated dark figure was silhouetted from behind by a frightening diffused light. Joan was glad, for she didn't think she could survive looking into his hellish eyes another time. He advanced slowly, using the endless moments as mental torture.

Feeling Elaine's body behind her, Joan wished she were made of an impenetrable material so Elaine could be saved. But all she could offer was flesh and blood, and that wasn't much. She had to think of something! It wasn't just her life at stake. Just then she remembered it! It was her only chance and it was an odds-on good one, too.

Behind her back Joan clicked open Zolo's stiletto and patiently waited for him to take one more step . . .

He had just lifted his foot when she quickly slung the stiletto into the air and it flipped end over end—and dangerously off-target as well.

In a lightning move, Zolo dropped the nail-studded board, shot his arm upward, and snatched the stiletto out of midair by the handle.

Joan choked down the lump in her throat, knowing she was out of tricks. Why had she done that? At what point had fantasy overtaken her mind and become her reality? Had she really thought a stunt she'd contrived in one of Angelina's stories could have stopped this fiend?

The sight of Zolo in possession of the knife once again caused Elaine to faint and slide down the battlement wall behind Joan.

Zolo's eyes gleamed brighter than the stiletto

blade as he took another stop toward Joan. Fear turned Joan's blood to ice as she opened her mouth to scream.

"Jack!"

Still holding his own with King Croc, Jack glanced over in time to see Zolo stalking Joan across the way. He was caught off guard for a moment, realizing all this time he'd thought Zolo out of commission, having his arm chewed off by his scaly skinned friend here. He scanned the area between them and spied Ira's gun, but it was out of reach.

Tasting Joan's death with his every pore, Zolo lunged for her. Self-preservation caused Joan to twist her new shoulder bag and shove it in front of her face. With the purse as a shield, Joan was able to kick Zolo once in the knee and scratch at his eye deeply enough to draw blood. She was frightened more by the satisfaction she felt, than by the resolute sneer that seemed embedded on his face. She wanted to hurt him, destroy him before he could kill anyone else.

When Zolo pulled back for another stab at her, she lunged at him and gouged the other eye. This time he overpowered her with his physical strength, and with one arm, he slammed her against the wall. She felt as if every rib in her back had cracked.

"Jack!" She managed to scream again.

Jack refused to let go of the crocodile and strained his foot toward the gun. If he could just snag it with his toe and move it closer, he could shoot Zolo and save Joan and not risk losing the treasure. He groaned as he tried to stretch his leg even farther, but the gun was still too far away.

King Croc must have sensed Jack's dilemma for he flipped his tail with a greater force, but Jack was equal to the struggle. The muscles in Jack's arms seemed locked in place, they were so tense from the strain.

Jack glanced at Joan, then at the crocodile, and then at the gun again. He was torn with indecision. Finally, he compromised and let go of the crocodile with one hand and reached for the gun, but it still eluded him. Jack was caught in a web of divergent desires. If he let the crocodile get away, then he and Joan couldn't be together. However, if he didn't save Joan there was no sense having the money anyway. He wanted it both ways and knew he couldn't have it. God! How stinking reality was!

"Jack!" Joan screamed at him.

"Sonuvabitch!"

Jack released the crocodile's tail and without any regard, King Crocodile quickly belly-flopped into the water, escaping his would-be tamer with the fabled El Corazón securely stowed in his stomach.

Jack dived for the gun, aimed it at Zolo and fired. *Click, click, click.* The gun was empty!

"Sonuvabitch!" He pitched the gun into the water and took off running toward Joan.

Zolo held Joan to the wall with his knee and shoulder as he inched the stiletto toward her face. His eyes were white-hot with rage and they frightened Joan more than the knife. Joan clutched at his wrist, holding his arm at bay, but her strength was being sapped. Her muscles trembled visibly but she continued to stave Zolo off. She focused all her concentration on her arm, willing it to hold the stiletto in check.

Her legs were giving out on her and though she and Zolo were stalemated, she knew she wouldn't be able to hold out much longer. She was counting on Jack! Jack would save her, she told herself as she stared at the razor-sharp edge that had so easily slit her other wrist. She felt her thighs cramp and buckle as Zolo pressed his body into hers and pushed her down against the stone wall to the ground.

Out of the corner of her eyes, Joan spied the nail-studded board only inches from her free hand. If she could hold Zolo off just a moment longer . . .

Jack thought he had been running all his life and still he was over a hundred years away. A raging fire was burning inside his lungs as he gasped for air. This must have been one of those nightmares he used to have when he lived in New York, for he felt as if he were on a treadmill and no matter how fast he ran, he would never gain any ground.

He could see the stiletto was only inches from Joan's face. He pushed himself more, but when he opened his mouth to yell at Zolo—anything to divert the maniac from killing Joan—nothing came out.

Jack did not see Ralph above him still riding the flagpole high in the air. Ralph strained to one side while watching Jack and shifted his body one time too many. The crumbling brick base finally gave way under the pressure of Ralph's weight and snapped free. Ralph screamed as he rode the flagpole astride like a horse. He sailed through the air looking like the climax scene in a cartoon.

Jack glanced up in time to see Ralph aiming his body directly for him, but was unable to make a counter manuever. Ralph fell directly on Jack and together they tumbled to the ground. Jack shoved Ralph off him and struggled to his feet. Then Ralph stood, grasped Jack's hand and shook it.

"Thank you, thank you. You broke my fall. You saved my life! If you hadn't been there . . ."

Jack growled at the frumpy man who had almost cost him his life and Joan's. Jack grabbed him by the arm and tossed Ralph against the wall and finally rid himself of the pest.

Joan had deadlocked the stiletto less than two inches from her right eye. Zolo glared at her, the cigarillo still burning between his lips. He had one foot on her arm keeping her from the nail-studded board. Joan tried to wrench her arm free but only succeeded in cutting her wrist on the heel of his boot.

Weary of toying with his victim, Zolo pressed in for the kill and took a long puff of his cigarillo. Zolo coughed.

Thinking fast, Joan switched handholds on Zolo's wrist and grabbed the cigarillo from his lips. She smashed the burning hot embers into his hand, enjoyed the sound of his sizzling flesh. Zolo screamed and instantly dropped the stiletto. Joan took her chance.

Joan smashed her fist into his face feeling the small bones in his nose crunch under her fingers. It was more satisfying than gouging his eyes and this time she didn't feel guilty at all. If she'd had knuckles she would have delighted in breaking his jaw.

Zolo grabbed his face and reeled away from her.

Joan leaped to her feet and grabbed the nail-studded board as she rose. Zolo struggled to his feet and reached for her, but Joan turned, and using both hands to clutch the board, she batted it across the side of his face and knocked him backwards over the wall. In a final graceful movement, Colonel Zolo, deputy commander of the Secret Police, plunged to his death.

Joan raced to the wall in time to see him land in the dark swamp where he was joined only seconds later by four vicious-looking crocodiles.

At that moment Jack came rushing up and peered over the wall. It was gruesome to watch a human being being devoured by reptiles, he thought.

He looked at Joan, perspiration glowing on her skin, her eyes wide and gleaming with her victory. She had eliminated Zolo single-handedly, something he wondered if he would have been able to do. She was more beautiful now than she'd ever been—wild, confident, and brave. He would never find anyone like her again, for she was every inch his equal. Jack nodded his approval.

Finally catching his breath, Joan smiled back at

him. There was great satisfaction in knowing she was her own heroine.

"Helluva windup you got there, Joan Wilder."

At that moment the bay was filled with a multitude of police boat lights. Sirens from the Cartagena police cars pierced the air and suddenly Joan was awash with a relief she'd never thought possible again. This time is was truly over and they could all live again without the threat of death hanging over them. She beamed at Jack, but he was backing away from her.

"Get to the American Consulate. Just explain what happened . . ."

Joan was incredulous. "Where are you going?"

"They might just believe you. But don't mention my name," he said as he noticed the horde of policemen streaming up the stairs beneath him. "Cartagena cops and I go way back."

"You're leaving? You're leaving me!" She screamed at him.

This wasn't happening to her! After all she'd been through, she was supposed to win the hero! What happened to happy endings? Didn't he know she wouldn't have written the story like this? How could he leave her here when she was in love with him?!!!

Jack was almost out of sight. "You'll be all right, Joan Wilder," he said as he darted into the shadows. "You'll be just fine."

Joan could only see his smile and then it too faded away.

"You always were . . ."

He was gone, as if he'd never existed. Joan was stunned.

"Jack Colton . . . I love you."

Chapter Thirty

SPRING HAD LINGERED in the wings that April, reluctant to make its debut as Joan walked up the path in Central Park. She pulled her knit scarf tighter around her throat to cut the blustery wind and shoved her bare hands into her jacket pockets. Daffodils and crocuses poked their heads through patches of snow while only the uppermost tree branches had begun to bud.

It was exactly three months to the day that she had left Colombia. Her first days back in New York had been difficult since she was still in shock over Jack's apparent abandonment of her. But Elaine needed her then for strength and comfort while she dealt with her grief over Eduardo's death.

During her explanations to the Colombian authorities, Joan had little respect for Eduardo until she and Elaine returned home and his will was read. Two days before his marriage to Elaine, Eduardo had taken out an insurance policy for half a million dollars! Elaine paid off the mortgage on her brownstone and invested the capital needed to give the bookstore a new image.

Elaine quit her job at Hewitt Corporation and assumed the management of the bookstore. Just last evening when she and Joan had dinner together at Erminia's on the Upper East Side, where the pasta was beyond sublime, Elaine stated she was seriously considering opening a second store in Soho.

Joan was happy for Elaine, who was beginning to put her life back together, and she was proud of herself for doing the same.

Joan no longer avoided book-signings, radio shows, or interviews arranged for her by Avon, but viewed them as an opportunity to know her audience. When she sat down to the typewriter, her characters had more depth and her stories possessed a purposefulness they had lacked before. Joan was proud of her work and it showed in every line she wrote.

When Elaine began housecleaning and donated Eduardo's things to charity, Joan decided it was a good time for her to do some sprucing up of her own. Joan had never decorated a room in her life, having always relied on her mother's furnishings and Elaine's taste to accomplish the task for her.

Since her bedroom was the most neglected room, she began there. She kept the two-tiered bachelor's chest that had belonged to her parents but that was all. She stripped the walls of their French blue floral wallpaper and painted them with a textured white paint to cover the cracks and pits in the plaster. She stained the wood trim, molding, and doors a dark walnut and installed a dark, planked floor. She had the one large window louvered in wooden slats and bought a fake electric fireplace. She ordered a reproduction mahogany rice bed with canopy and bought twenty-seven yards of mosquito netting from Pier One.

At night after she finished a day wrestling with Angelina and her tempestuous exploits, Joan bathed in floral-scented water, turned the electric fireplace up full blast, and then would lie inside the mosquito netting thinking about Jack.

Being the romantic she was, not once in the ninety-one days since she last saw him did she ever give up hope. She loved him and trusted him. It was as simple as that. She knew there was a very real possibility that she would never see him again but it wouldn't be because he didn't love her. If he was wanted by the Cartagena police it might be impossible for him to get out of South America, but something told her that escaping the country would be a simple matter for Jack Colton.

Joan did not allow her love for Jack to keep her from living, either. She and Elaine went out more now than she ever had before and Carolyn had introduced her to several eligible men. Even Andrew, the stockbroker, let it be known he was available. Though she enjoyed the company of other men, she still loved Jack. If it was to be her fate to forever love a man she had known for only four days, then so be it. She didn't care.

At first she had expected opposition from Elaine, but found none. Elaine told her she only worried that Joan would closet herself away as she had done in the past. Once Elaine's fears had been resolved, she joined Joan in hoping that she would find Jack again.

As Joan emerged from the park that day, there was a new spring to her walk and an assurance in her smile.

Just as she passed the Museum of Natural History, she heard the sound of tinkling bells similar to those she'd heard when she and Jack met Juan, the bellmaker. She turned the corner and found a Puerto Rican vendor's display cart of countless lockets hanging from a bar. Hearts of gold, jade, crystal and tourmaline were interspersed with tiny bell-laden wind chimes.

Joan touched the locket Jack gave her, which she still wore, then smiled at the vendor and walked away.

On a bench just ahead she saw a group of tough-looking punks who were sitting with legs outstretched as they hassled the girls who passed by.

One rough-looking boy with a vivid scar on his cheek reached out and pulled on a pretty girl's skirt. Joan paused for a moment, then straightened her back and continued on the way she had intended. Not long ago, their kind had intimidated her, but that was before she had met men far more dangerous than these boys and she, Joan Wilder, had bested them.

When the punks spotted her, they jumped to their feet, surrounded her and then made lewd comments about her good looks. Joan kept her head high, stared them down, and walked away, her hair flowing proudly in the wind.

When Joan reached her building she heard a strong honking noise unlike any car horn she'd ever heard. She looked up the street and saw nothing unusual, but when she turned around to look the other way, she nearly jumped with surprise.

Driving down the middle of her street was a monster luxury boat. It was easily two stories high and virtually blocked out the sun. It had teak decks, brass railings, and three tall masts. Joan inspected it further and realized that it was not driving itself but was being towed . . . by Jack!

As the boat stopped alongside her, Jack smiled his little-boy smile and tossed her a thick envelope.

"Your half . . ."

Joan picked it up and eyed it. "Half! Who said you could have half?"

"That's what equal partners take," he said, and planting a foot on the side of the boat, he leaned over and grinned at her.

Joan took one look at the unique leather and said, "I like the crocodile boots."

"Yeah, that poor old yellow-striped guy developed fatal indigestion and died in my arms."

Joan's eyes smoldered when she gazed up at him. "Can't blame him. If I were going to die, that'd be the place I'd pick."

Jack tore his eyes away from her for a moment and looked around. "How about *you* taking *me* on a tour for a change?"

"Okay."

Jack reached down and pulled her up to join him.

"Then we'll come back here and you can pack."

"Pack?" she asked as his arms went around her waist and he pulled her into him. His blue eyes blazed with passion as he looked down at her and she put her arms around his neck.

His voice was low as his face moved closer to hers. "Isn't it time we got out of the jungle?"

Standing on the deck of El Corazón, Joan and Jack were unaware of the neighbors that stared at them through their apartment windows. All they knew, when their lips met, was that their adventure was just beginning.

The publishers hope that this Large Print Book has brought you pleasurable reading. Each title is designed to make the text as easy to see as possible. G. K. Hall Large Print Books are available from your library and your local bookstore. Or you can receive information on upcoming and current Large Print Books by mail and order directly from the publisher. Just send your name and address to:

G. K. Hall & Co.
70 Lincoln Street
Boston, Mass. 02111

or call, toll-free:

1-800-343-2806

A note on the text
Large print edition designed by
Lyda Kuth
Composed in 16 pt Times Roman
on a Mergenthaler 202
by Compset Inc., Beverly MA